TO CATCH THEM UNAWARES

By
K.N. Brown

*Note: Anna's family is a noble English family. She is the daughter of an earl, and so she has the title of lady. Her father is the Earl of Wincherton, so he goes by the title Lord Wincherton. Her mother is a countess, so she goes by Countess or Lady Wincherton. Anna is the one who uses their real last name, so she is called Lady Anna Lovelace.

To anyone who wants to be a writer

CONTENTS

Part III

Part IV

PROLOGUE

Tuesday, March 19, 1889

As printed in the Lancaster New Era

Dear Townspeople,

Your fear amuses and strengthens me. I can feel it in the streets, hovering around our fair city like a fog. It emboldens me to go forth and continue my duty, my sacred calling, for which I experience the highest of pleasures. You will never know where I will strike next and cut, cut, cut. My knife guides my path. Not even I know of my victims before I spy them among you, like hams laid out on a platter.

You ask why women are the target. Why? Because they are the most beautiful victims, their skin gleaming with death once I am finished with them. A man does not die with nearly enough grace to tempt me. Besides, do not women hold all the power in their hands? The power to hurt us so deeply, the power to capture hearts. So, I will take their hearts with me. Yes, yes, it is too amusing. You may have been wondering where the hearts have gone from your beautiful ladies? They are with me, all with me. I am looking at them now in my glass jars as you read this. I can send you one if you like? But only one, for they are my sweet, little treasures, and I would hate to be parted from them.

Women are heartless and heartless they shall remain as they enter death. I care not for class or race. There is no one who is above or below my blade. So, you ladies in your fancy homes full of lace and teacups, you must also be wary. My eyes are watching you, and my knife is waiting.

No one can stop me now for I am but a shadow, a mist, floating through the city ready to catch them unawares. Call me Jack if you like, but I have my own name and wish to create my own reputation.

Always fear the darkness, for the darkness is where I tread.

X.

PART I

CHAPTER

1

A fly buzzed between the china cup and saucer laying on a lace-laden table in a grand garden. Lady Anna Lovelace watched the fly idly, as it licked up the drop of milk that had spilled there. She sighed, albeit too loudly, and thought, *if this is not boredom, then I know not what is.*

She caught a glare from her mother and smiled tightly, straightening up. Anna, an English lady, and her mother, the Countess Regina, wife of the Earl of Wincherton, were listening to the positively ancient Lady Croft drone on about the Season back in London and how well each of her granddaughters had done.

Lady Croft sat in all her taffeta glory, sitting upon a plush cushioned chair, her mittened hands clutching her beautifully designed teacup. Anna watched the wizened face of the boring woman, her white hair still long and placed up under a lace cap.

She must have been something in her time and now must fill her old age with gossip and scandal.

"My eldest granddaughter, Henrietta, why, she is the real beauty of the lot. She did excellently well, snagging a duke for herself!" Lady Croft chuckled heartily. "I always knew she would make such a lovely match! The rest of my granddaughters also did well for themselves, getting husbands of respectability and moderate wealth. My duty as a grandmother is now complete."

Her mother smiled, taking another sip of tea with grace and decorum. "My hearty congratulations to you, Lady Croft. I only hope that my Anna will have just as much luck in this Season, despite us living in America now."

Anna's eyes snapped to her mother, jolted out of the daydream that was slowly taking over her mind with each newly uttered word from the elderly woman. Lady Croft leaned towards Anna, looking through her pince-nez, scrutinizing the girl's face. Anna wished she could be anywhere else just then, her eyes moving about around the garden, not wishing to stare into the milky depths of Lady Croft's gaze.

With a pinched nose, Lady Croft paused for a moment taking young Anna in, and Regina bit her lip. Anna knew her mother was worried about how her daughter would fare against the woman who held one of the highest places in London society before she moved to Pennsylvania. But Anna didn't care a whit. Despite the Croft's slight change in circumstances, the woman still held a high position.

"England is going to the dogs, you know," Lady Croft had mentioned over and over throughout their teatime.

Anna felt like an eternity had passed before Lady Croft spoke again, returning her pince-nez to the lacy tablecloth.

"An earl's daughter should do very well for herself here in America. She will be a sort of exotic thing, Lady Regina. These wealthy Americans are all hungry for such a match. Your daughter is quite lovely to be sure. The figure is very good but perhaps too sensually curved. Enchanting green eyes, well-colored flaxen hair, good teeth, pink lips, and her complexion is perfect."

Anna blushed under such a close analysis of her features, discussed as if she was a dog, coming to showcase the good points of its breed. Her fingers began anxiously twisting together under the table.

"But I cannot say the same for her manners, I'm afraid." The old woman slowly placed her fan on Anna's twisting hands and gave her a look of warning.

Her mother spoke again. "Yes, I do believe you are right. I have taken great pains to improve them for social outings, but she will not always adhere to my instruction."

Her mother looked at her with a raised eyebrow. Anna heard the pleading note in her mother's voice. She felt rather like she should be sprawled out on an examination table, ready to be picked apart. She did not know what to say in reply.

So, this is why Mother insisted I accompany her to visit Lady Croft this afternoon. If only I wasn't discovered in the library, I could have freely read all day and avoided this torturous interaction.

Lady Croft squinted her eyes at Anna once more and spoke directly to her. "Young lady, do you not wish to make a good match?" Her fan came out again and rapped Anna on the arm making her jump. "A man will not want a woman to maintain his household who has naught to provide in the way of manners and social graces. Does it not matter to you that you do well this Season? It may be your last. We have all been forced from our own country and come to flounder here. Think of your mother and father, young woman."

Anna watched as Lady Croft's expression matched the vehemence of her words, and she presented to Anna the image of a puffed-up bird, ready to peck at its young chicks for misbehaving. Anna had the greatest urge to laugh, but she held back, tightening her lips, knowing that would only embarrass her mother further. She decided as she lifted her chin to give her strength, that the best course of action would be words. Words impressed and words were powerful. Surely, Lady Croft could respect such a strong woman, when she was one herself? Anna took a deep breath and plunged into her impassioned speech.

"Lady Croft, surely you can understand my feelings. I truly have no interest in marriage and children, at least not at this time, when there is so much to do. If it happens, then so be it, but it has never been my end goal. I think of Mary Wollstonecraft when she wrote, 'Men, indeed, appear to me to act in a very unphilosophical manner when they try to secure the good conduct of women by attempting to keep them always in a state of childhood." Anna did not notice the angry color that was spreading over Lady Croft's face as she spoke.

She continued on. "My end goal is to live a life I am proud of, having followed my own mind and my own pursuits, not remaining subject to and victim to the constraints of a society I cannot fully respect. Women should not have to endure their lives. We should enjoy them! Surely a woman as strong as you, Lady Croft, could understand such a feeling. And besides, we are no longer in London. America has its own way of doing things. It not the same as a London Season here. How refreshing a fact!"

Anna smiled widely, armored and energized with her speech but saw that her mother paled and looked on the verge of tears. Anna turned back to Lady Croft, whose bird-like appearance had become wolf-like if it was possible for an elegant lady to become so. Her teeth were slightly bared, and she hovered on the edge between reason and outright violence.

"Pray, young woman, do not pretend to have such a familiarity with me who is your elder and your better. Do not presume to know what I may or may not understand or commiserate with. I confess, that in this case, I most certainly do not. A woman's role has been written down in the Bible. It is up to us to fulfill our great purpose, as Christians, and live accordingly. To do otherwise is heathenish and disgraceful. Your dear mother ought to be ashamed of you, young lady. I know that no man will select you for his partner if you choose to engage in the Season with such an attitude. You will be left to a life of loneliness, despair, and social isolation. And above all, to quote to me the words of a revolutionary and a bluestocking! For shame!"

Lady Croft sat back in a huff, her skirt rustling as she moved, exhaling sharply after her lengthy tirade. She waved the fan in front of her face and called for a servant.

"Please do ready the Countess' and Lady Anna's things. They will be leaving shortly."

Anna felt a little anger tingle in her belly, but she kept her mouth shut, feeling her body tense. Her mother colored deeply and stood, curtseying.

"Lady Croft, do forgive my daughter for her impertinence. Thank you for your time and trouble."

She glanced at Anna once more before moving toward the house to collect her gloves and hat. Anna stood and curtseyed hastily, knowing that the afternoon was entirely ruined. There would be no library for her any longer. Only a swift rebuking.

"Good day to you, Lady Croft."

The old woman nodded and waved her away. Anna was still a little in shock at the turn of events. Shocked and frustrated.

How could society possibly move forward with such people hostile to refreshing, powerful ideas?

At the doorway, Anna opened her mouth to speak.

"Quiet!", her mother replied with a hand held aloft, and Anna closed her mouth again.

They left the steps of the Croft mansion on Orange Street, her mother hurrying on ahead, avoiding Anna's gaze. Anna watched as her mother quickly and roughly pulled her gloves on, not looking back. The Lovelace family lived close by to the Crofts, and the weather was fine, so they walked home instead of taking the carriage. Anna trailed behind, inwardly bemoaning her brash words. Not for the content but simply because they had embarrassed her mother, who had been embarrassed enough already in the last few years.

Countess Wincherton was not used to this new life they led in America, yet Anna loved it for its newness and slightly reduced restrictions. They walked by the churchyard of St. James Church, and Anna whispered to the gravestones, "You are lucky to be dead and done with it all! The marriage mart is madness!"

A few minutes later, a servant opened the door to a harried Anna and her mother. Anna had her eyes cast downward, and as she handed away her gloves and hat, her mother called for sherry and pointed wordlessly to a chair in the sitting room. Anna did as she was told and sat down, bracing herself against her mother's next attack. She knew she had spoken unwisely, and yet, it was still the truth. How long could she fight the truth? She waited and waited for her mother's outburst to begin. Pacing in front of the fireplace, her mother had her hands on her hips, awaiting the arrival of her glass of sherry. It came, and once the servant curtsied and left, she drank the whole crystal glass in one swig.

She crossed her arms. "Anna Margaret Lovelace, you are the only daughter of an earl. It is no matter that we live outside of London and all its connections now," her mother said bitterly. "You must conduct yourself accordingly. Whether you agree with Lady Croft's opinion or not, she holds the highest place in Lancaster society. If she is displeased, your chances are ruined. We are all ruined. You know the state which we are in." Her mother began to pace again, flailing her arms about, empty glass in hand.

"After all the embarrassment I have suffered in having to leave my beloved country and home in London, you would deign to embarrass me in such an open and public manner? My own daughter?" Her mother's blue eyes were misty as she stared down at Anna.

Anna spoke slowly. "I am sorry, Mother. It was not my intention to embarrass you; you can be certain of that. I just thought…"

"Thought what? What could you have been thinking, Anna?"

"I had hoped that now that we were not in London, you would not push me so into finding a husband at each of the balls they put on here in the city. I had thought that I would be free to pursue my interests and pastimes in peace."

Her mother looked as though she might fly into a fit of rage once more. But instead, she took a breath and sat down in the chair next to her daughter. She took Anna's hands in hers. Anna was reminded just how beautiful her mother was with her narrow face and still golden hair.

"My dear, you know that you are your father's only hope. The mill is going well, but it may not be for long. We have spent almost all we had left to move to this new land to try once more. You must make an advantageous marriage. It is not for our sakes. It is for yours. Your father worries for your comfort and welfare. He wants you to be well-provided for if something may happen to us."

"But Mother, if I was allowed to work, there would be no need. I could take care of myself and my needs, so that you, Father, or a husband would not have to be burdened with me. It is this frustrating world that won't allow me that small independence. Instead, I must wait upon a man! The injustice! Do you not see it? Can't you understand my anger?" Anna's green eyes flashed with righteous indignation, and her cheeks colored at the unfairness of it all.

Her mother smiled and placed a hand on her daughter's cheek. "You are a changeling, darling. The fairies must surely have switched you in the night, for I know not where you get your ideas from."

Anna sighed. Her mother would never or could never understand. She was from a different world, an old world while Anna now resigned in a new world and perhaps had the chance at a brighter future.

"I will think of something, Mother, so that you and Father will be well-provided for. But to do penance for my behavior to Lady Croft," Anna hesitated, dreading her next words. "I will attend a few of the balls that we have received invitations for."

Her mother stood and clapped. "Excellent! And do penance you shall! To the dressmakers, we must go!" She rushed out of the room, and Anna sank back in her chair.

Oh, to have been born a man.

CHAPTER

2

A few days later

An invitation was put before me at the breakfast table this morning. It is a ball, taking place tonight, reminding me of my obligations to society. Ah, yes, I had forgotten I had received it a few days before, but it was such a meaningless thing; it passed from my mind easily. Oh, these blasted constraints. If only these people knew how much I loathed them all, with their tightened waistcoats straining to cover too-large bellies. But freedom from all constraints comes with death, does it not? I smile to myself, fingering the invitation in my hands.

"'Lord and Lady Croft to host a ball on the corner of Duke and Orange at the newly built Hamilton House'."

Yes, I have seen the mansion. Tall and imposing, built mainly for the old English and elite citizens of the city to have gatherings. More importantly, there sits a graveyard just across. Peaceful, quiet with high grasses, full of shadows. A good place to hide. A good place for a lover's tryst. A good place for much darker deeds. Perhaps the evening will not be such a waste after all. It may be time for my plan to finally come to fulfillment.

My steward has come to bother me once more with discussions about the business. I need to cut my breakfast short for such a useless aim. What good is business when sacred callings await and primitive urges tickle under the skin? But I suppose my money is my protection. No one knows about me, for there is not one person as clever as I.

Business is endless. I can never be free of it, thanks to my father. My stupid, idiotic father who had not the head for anything else except money and cigars. Nor had he any sort of strength. I am so unlike him with my head full of destiny and the beauty of action. And then there was my mother.

The bitch of a woman, always complaining, always begging, always asking for things she did not need. Always controlling her weak husband. Never noticing me, her own son, as someone worthy. The beatings, the starving, the awful pain. No matter. She's gone now. They both are. And not even at my own hand! Although I admit it did cross my mind. He should have died for his weakness, and she for her heartlessness.

I do not even know what my steward is saying anymore. He drones on and on about worker's payments and striking. I do not want to think about the plight of peasants. I want to think about the ball. I want to think about the shadows in the graveyard and how to get a woman out there. One woman in particular that has drawn my gaze time and time again. There was merely one obstacle in my way. But that should take care of itself.

Stupid women. They always think my secret lures are for a kiss or a caress, but it is more, so much more. I make them look more beautiful than they ever have. Why do they not understand? They always cling to me in the end, fighting, but if only they could know that it is I am the one who sets them free! Free from the desires that hold them back from such beautiful escape!

He calls my attention again. "There is a problem down at the factory, sir. You should come and see for yourself. The workers are asking for you," he says.

I sigh loudly. So draining, so pointless. These mere workers should be beneath my notice. But it is not their class that I despise. It is their lack of thought, of intelligence, of perspective. They have nothing better to do with their lives than grub for their next meal and argue with others. However, I must agree to assist if to only to quell their rebellion so that I may continue in peace.

"Fine then, Mr. Parker. I will be at the factory directly."

Finally, Parker is appeased and is gone, and I can sit in the parlor with my cup of tea for a few moments longer, reading my newspaper. Will I feature today? It only takes me a few moments to find the article. There I am! My handiwork, displayed for all the world to see.

'Another Female Found Slain on the Streets of Lancaster. Keep

Watch Over Your Wives, Daughters, and Sisters'

Sipping at my tea, I frown at the journalists' lack of creativity. Surely, they could come up with a better title than that. Keep watch over your wives, daughters, and sisters? A fair warning, but who wants to read such a boring title over breakfast? It was more, so much more than that. Yes, she was female, but she was not found on the streets. She was found in the flower beds in Penn Square, the center of town. I thought it to be one of my finest works. They do not even mention how she was displayed. Laid perfectly, like a queen. She was beautiful in death. No more screams of terror or tears of begging for her life. No more connection to the darkness or the lowliness that plagues womenkind. My mind swirls with Tennyson's poetry at the memory:

'A pearl garland winds her head:
She leaneth on a velvet bed,
Full royally apparelled,
The Lady of Shalott.'

Her heart is now gone and in my possession. Ah yes, my glass jars. My dearies locked away downstairs. But such a short blurb in the paper for me! Surely there is more here - ah, yes! How delightful!

'Police are Baffled by Multiple Murders'

That's a little better. Baffled is a good word. Yes, they are. They shall never catch me, the dolts. The idiots! They never think to look beyond their own noses. They will never find me here! Safely tucked away. Hmm...perhaps I could endeavor to help these poor, sweet, policemen. They are struggling to make a living after all. Their intention is to help make the Lancaster streets safe for women.

Ha! When it is these women who are in the wrong and deserving of their fates. Their overwhelming cravings and desires trap them and make them easy prey, whether it is the sweet elixir that draws them or the simple desire to hear the compliments of a man. It disgusts and repels me. Such earthliness. Such useless violence. Her own desires degrade her and send her sullied back into the world. I set her free. Yes, yes, I do!

It is time for my new murder and my new victim. I have waited long enough. No, I shall not use that word, 'murder.' It lowers what I do to base wrongdoing. Let me call it 'vindication'. My fingers are already itching again. The thirst is becoming more difficult to slake. But I must be careful. Hmm...before I go to the factory, I shall entertain myself here in the parlor with my tea. I must call the maid for more. The ball will be the perfect place to pursue my next beauty.

***

Senior Officer George Ford sat with his legs up on an oaken desk in the Lancaster City Police Department. It was a slow day, and he was impertinently lounging, having only recently moved up in the ranks from officer to senior officer. Reading the newspaper and pulling on a cigarette, he was searching for articles about the only exciting thing that was going on in this old, historic town. Lancaster was a strange mix of green fields and red brick, and there was hardly anything thrilling that ever happened.

But there it was, glinting like a beautiful gem: a feature article on the recent murders that have been occurring as well as the body his colleagues had found just last night. Everyone was buzzing about it. Nothing of this magnitude had happened before in Lancaster. At least not to his knowledge. The closest thing that he'd heard of were the horrific Ripper murders in White Chapel, London. The detectives and policeman in his unit were excited to finally have something to do besides taking in the town drunkard or sorting out mobs at the cotton mill and cigar factory.

George felt occasionally guilty for his thoughts, but he remembered how his blood had pumped heartily through his veins after hearing about the murdered victim laid out in Penn Square. Or rather each time a victim had been found. It was a new piece of the puzzle to be put into place. What excited him even more was the letters from the killer to the newspapers, which scorned, shamed, and taunted the town and the police. The one the killer had sent just a few days ago was its most taunting, thrilling George down to his core. *'The darkness is where I tread,'* the killer had written, and it had made George all the more determined to be the one who caught him.

Twenty-five-year-old George Ford had always wanted to be a policeman, ever since he could remember. It was his way of finding a better path than his father had done who had remained in the same police position for his whole life. George's dream was to rise in the ranks to become a detective, solving the grisliest of cases. This one intrigued him, and he wished he could work on it as lead of the case. Perhaps that would make his Jenny look at him proudly. For once.

He sat back thoughtfully, leaning his head up so that the cigarette smoke trailed towards the ceiling. He had seen a few of the six victims, who were all female, of varying races and classes. All of their throats cut, hearts gone, expertly removed from their chests. That was the only thing that was the same between the women. That and they were all around the same age, and they were all beautiful, stunningly beautiful, even though some of them looked slightly malnourished, dirty, or sick. Diphtheria was still raging around the streets, and the delights of the night were all too tempting for those who had nothing real to live for. After viewing their bodies, whether in the lantern light, morning light, or moonlight, the thing that had stuck with George was the graceful way they had been laid out, as if tenderly cared for.

He thought it strange. There was a sort of gentleness to this case that differed from other murders he'd seen or heard about. The ones which frequented the streets of his fair city occurred amongst the poor or desperate, in protests, or in domestic situations. They were brutal but done on the whim of a moment and thus sloppy. In contrast, these recent murders were so intriguing because of the care that was taken. It was as if the killer wanted the women to be somehow respected after the fact. It was both confounding and fascinating.

After the Ripper murders last fall, George had read as much as he could about them, consuming nearly ever article he could get his hands on. When they stopped occurring after a few months, police in both countries suspected that the murderer might have moved to a new location. With the upsurge of similar murders in Lancaster, many thought perhaps he had made his home here.

The problem was, they weren't prostitutes this time at the end of this killer's blade. It was anyone and everyone. Just as the killer's most recent letter had shown, no one was safe. George shuddered to think of lovely and innocent Jenny, his fiancée, being victim to such an act. Newspapers warned that women should keep indoors and protect themselves as best they could.

But that wasn't always possible, was it? Especially for working women. And even so, this murderer seems to find a way to slink through the cracks and find even the most unattainable woman.

George tapped a finger on the desk. The door to the office slammed open and George nearly fell off his chair in surprise. His cigarette tumbled from his mouth, and he winced as it landed on his arm.

"Damn it."

"Ford. There's a disturbance up at the cigar factory. We've been called in to assist." His Sergeant, Sergeant Donaldson stood tall and impassive before him, hand on the door lifting a chastising eyebrow in his direction. "Get your men and go."

"Yes, sir."

George nodded, placing a hand over his burned arm, trying to not let his superior see his pained face. He stamped the cigarette out in the ashtray as his superior left his office, coloring a little that he'd been caught in thought and not doing any proper work.

Another disturbance at the factory, is it? What else is new? When will there be another murder?

CHAPTER

3

Anna sat at the breakfast table the next morning, a piece of her father's newspaper spread out before her. Her mother ate wordlessly, to silently rebel against her daughter being allowed to fill her mind with such things. However, Anna's father, Edward Lovelace, the Earl of Wincherton, was kind and indulgent in matters of learning. He did not seem to remember the societal restrictions on Anna's gender as much as her mother did.

This served her purposes well. She glanced at her mother, but quickly turned away when her mother looked back at her. Anna spread her hands across the page, smoothing it down against the table.

It smells so worldly.

Ink and paper. Touched by the highest of lords to the lowest of factory workers, if they could read, of course. It made each man's hand dirty after reading. It was their equalizer.

Anna often entertained herself with her little philosophical rebellions. She enjoyed breaking things down and putting them back together again in a new way that defied tradition. She entertained herself further with the realization that safely ensconced in the realm of her imagination, Lady Croft would never be able to chastise her. Anna enjoyed all puzzles, and to her mother's potential dismay if she ever learned of it, crime and murder were her favorite puzzles to solve.

She had been enthralled with the recent murders in the city and was eternally grateful to her father for allowing her to read the morning newspaper with him before her mother took over her life for the rest of the day. Murder was the ultimate puzzle because it was so stark, so undeniably wrong, that it fascinated her. It continually shocked her that people would commit such a crime. She had seen so little of the world and its people that it seemed so separate from her. And when someone murdered with such a flair as this new Lancaster "Ripper", it fascinated her all the more.

She was lucky to have found the article in the paper this morning about police confusion with the murders. She sighed quietly to herself as she read.

If only I was able to join them in their investigation and didn't have to fill my days with such nonsense. She smirked. *Then, they might actually achieve some progress. The solving of murders needs a woman's touch. Men are too blundering, too prideful, and too blind to see what is right in front of them. They must be missing something.*

Could it really be Jack the Ripper returned to action after a time away from England? She didn't think so, although the murders had somewhat eerie connections. From what Anna could tell, the killer stood to gain nothing from the murders. Nothing of value was ever removed from the victims, if they were of a wealthy background. It appeared that he did it simply for his own pleasure, she supposed, although that was a horrid thought to have. His letter to the newspaper had spoken of his 'sacred calling'.

Suddenly, her mother's cheery voice filled the room. "Anna, we must visit your cousin today. We will be discussing our outfits for the ball tonight! We should have gone earlier, but my dear sister was not well enough to receive us then. And there wasn't enough…time for us to get a new dress made for you. But we shall find something at your cousin's house, I am sure of it."

Her mother then bustled away, and Anna sighed. Her father looked at her apologetically.

He shook out the folds in his newspaper and smiled, lines crinkling in the corners. "Make her happy, Anna. Soon enough you will be able to do anything and everything you want to do."

"Oh? And why's that, Father?" Anna was intrigued.

"Because ever since we've moved here, you have had a look in your eye. A look that tells me you have plans of your own. Your mother told me what happened with Lady Croft. She would not approve of my approval, dear girl, but approve I shall. You will find your own way." He winked.

Anna beamed, then quipped, "Oh Father, before I go stunting my mental growth by discussing ball gowns," Her father chuckled. "Who do you think this murderer is?" She gestured to the paper, her heart beating excitedly.

"Hmm...I think it's someone we all least expect. It always is, is it not?" He returned to reading the paper, and Anna left the room, that thought in her mind.

Someone we all least expect. Who is 'we all'? What identity would surprise us all? A policeman? A woman? A minister?

She contemplated the options.

Surprising. Unexpected.

She paused in the hallway, and looked down at her hands, covered in ink from the paper.

The great equalizer. From the richest of men to the poorest of factory workers.

Absorbed in her thoughts, Anna followed her mother out of the door.

***

Ophelia Marshall, Anna's first-generation American cousin, resided in a beautiful sprawling mansion on the edge of the city. Her great wealth, connections, social status, and tragically beautiful name were enough to make her exceedingly vapid and dull. To the contrary, Ophelia was vivacious, interesting, and kind. Anna loved her cousin, and they had been inseparable since Anna's arrival two years before. Ophelia had made Anna's quick departure from England bearable. She had that distinct "Americanness" about here, not so stuck-up as the ladies from England with a very natural inclination to laugh.

Anna and her mother rode down the narrow Lancaster streets towards the Marshall mansion. Her mother was quiet, and Anna wondered if she was feeling a little downtrodden that they had to borrow a dress instead of having one made new. Anna's eyes and focus, however, were soon turned to the scenes that passed by.

Lancaster is no London, but it has its fine moments.

The taller brick and stone buildings gave a stately air to the otherwise working-class town. It was a great step down for the Lovelace family, but for Anna, it had been somewhat of a relief. Her family had been quite wealthy and prestigious in London society for many years. Her father owned both a London house as well as a sprawling country estate. Anna knew her mother had been planning the most advantageous marriage for her in order that Anna could carry on their long tradition.

Lady Wincherton's sights had been set on some duke or other while they still remained in England. She didn't remember his title, nor did she care, but before her mother could seal her fate, her father's fortunes changed. With the growth of the middle class, and the lessening power of the aristocracy, Ophelia's father, Lady Wincherton's brother-in-law, had invited them all to live in America, and her uncle had given Lord Wincherton a silent partnership in the mill. To everyone's surprise, he took to his new duties with alacrity.

With Anna's removal from London society and arrival onto American soil, she felt like she could breathe for the first time. The pressures of her station were gone, and she would not have to work as hard to gain her mother's approval or even society's. Her mother would have to be satisfied with what they could get, and Anna had hoped that would mean she would allow her a little more freedom. However, it hadn't really turned out that way.

Anna's thoughts were interrupted by her arrival to her cousin's home. As Anna emerged from the carriage, she was reminded of how much she loved the view of the Marshall's beautiful estate. The Marshalls were distantly related to Supreme Court Justice John Marshall, whose name was on the college just nearby. Therefore, in Lancaster, they enjoyed one of the highest statuses, underneath Lady Croft, of course. She was old money, and they were new.

"Industry," Anna's Uncle Jack could often be heard saying. "That is the way of things now. There is much money to be made."

With a squeal of delight, red-haired Ophelia ran towards Anna, arms wide, a vision in lavender and lace rushing from a grand doorway. The slightly shorter woman threw her arms about Anna and squeezed.

"My goodness, it feels as though it's been forever, even though I know how close you are. But ever since you arrived, I am afraid you'll go away again. What was my life before you, dear cousin?"

Anna laughed at this intimacy. Her cousin was wonderful, but always one for the dramatic. "I could not have borne my move to America without you, Ophelia. Now, I hear I am to be instructed in the art of fashion by you and your mother today." Anna lifted her eyebrows jokingly.

"But of course!" Ophelia held onto Anna's hand and pulled her toward the house, leaving her mother and her sister Louisa to greet each other warmly. Ophelia said, "You have never been one to care about such things. That's why you have me! We have some excellent dresses that I have picked out just for you, and..." lowering her voice she added, "I have so much to tell you!" Ophelia winked and hurried ahead, Anna following behind reluctantly.

Not only was she dreading the onslaught of criticisms and scrutinizing glances from her mother as she tried on each dress, but she was also a little nervous about what Ophelia's news could be. Her cousin was quite headstrong, despite the restrictions of her status, and Anna had been surprised many times in the last few years by the things she would say and do. It was not that Anna did not admire her, but unlike Anna, Ophelia would do things on the whim of a moment, without any sort of planning or thought. There never seemed to be any sort of logic. Passion ruled her mind and heart while logic filled Anna's mind.

What could she want to share with me that I don't already know?

Despite the worried thoughts that whizzed through her mind, she was soon trudging up the stairs after her excited cousin, heading to her dressing room in order to find something appropriate for Lady Croft's ball that very evening.

They spent what seemed like hours, sorting through gowns of all shapes and sizes. Her mother was tight-lipped, but she nodded at a few gowns that she deemed acceptable, and Ophelia's lady's maid aided Anna in trying them on for everyone. After a couple of hours, Anna was beginning to fade, and she wished for anything that she would be allowed to leave or at least to stop parading around in front of her judging family members. A cup of tea would do her nicely and perhaps something sweet to go with it.

Finally, and to Anna's relief, a dress was found that both her mother and Aunt Louisa found stood above the rest. It was pale blue with creamy white ribbons and a low neckline. Buttons fell down the back and connected with a large skirt, falling in folds as it cascaded from the large bustle to the floor. Anna's waist was slim, and so the large size of the skirt was even more pronounced. Long white gloves completed the look.

Anna's mother clapped her hands together, her face brightening for the first time since they'd arrived. "You are a vision, my dear. Certainly, you will put yourself back in Lady Croft's good graces. With the proper coiffure, you shall be the lady of the evening."

Anna sighed. It was the last thing she cared about doing. Instead, she wished she could have another look at all the newspaper columns she had accrued in recent weeks. She would have to be satisfied with her mother's rare compliment, though. Lady Regina Wincherton was a very beautiful woman, and according to her Aunt Louisa, had been quite the debutante in her day back in the London Season. Anna knew that her mother wished that her daughter could live up to what she herself had become, but it was too much.

While many would also say that Anna Lovelace was a very attractive woman, Anna knew that she could never be what her mother wanted. But as her father had advised her, she needed to make her mother happy, at least for a time, until she could forge her own path. It did comfort her that the dress looked rather pretty on her.

Her mother and aunt called for tea, and Ophelia asked for her own tea set to be brought to her personal parlor, so that she and Anna could be alone. Once Anna was dressed in her own comfortable day dress again and the door closed against her mother and aunt, she breathed a sigh of relief. Ophelia, smiling, poured them each a cup of tea.

"You were lovely, Anna. You are going to catch someone's eye at this ball, for certain."

Anna lifted the cup from the saucer. "Ophelia, you know that I care naught for such things. Where are the lectures? The academic events? The other somethings that a woman could attend which have nothing to do with the way she looks or what she wears? I want to go to one of those instead of wasting my time with such drudgery."

Anna's eyes brightened and her voice grew more animated. "The recent murders have me absolutely mesmerized. I wish I could be the one to help the police in solving the case."

Ophelia placed a hand atop Anna's. "Perhaps one day you will. You never know. I always say that a woman should be allowed to do as she pleases." Her eyes were wide and cheeks flushed as she said, "In that vein, I should tell you, Anna. I have met someone."

Anna was struck dumb for a moment. "Why, Ophelia, that's excellent news! I am happy for you. Where? When? How?" She ignored the little pang of disappointment that her cousin might leave her soon.

Ophelia stood up, clearly too excited to stay put. She began to pace, and Anna could smell the comforting scent of rose oil that Ophelia always wore. Anna could see a slight hesitation in her cousin's face.

Ophelia said slowly, "It has been going on for some time. A few weeks in fact."

"I see." Anna felt a prickle of anxiety, but she didn't let it flourish just yet. "Where did you meet? Why didn't you tell me?" Anna was hurt at her cousin's lack of intimacy.

"I'm sorry, but I couldn't tell you yet. I have a feeling he shall ask me to marry him soon. Don't worry about anything. D said it will be fine, and it all will be! We will have to elope, of course, but I would do anything for love! Anna, he is a most excellent man. Well-mannered, intelligent, kind. Ever since we met for the first time, we have written scores of letters. I have kept every single one from him. They are not much, only about where to meet next, but they are a reminder of our future. I met him by chance, when I was returning with a few books from Mr. Hanley's store, and I tripped over a loose stone in the road. The books went everywhere, and D was there to help me. We walked for a time afterward." Ophelia sighed, a dreamy look coming into her gaze.

Anna frowned. "D? You will not tell me anything about him? Not even his full name? Also, I'm amazed that you have orchestrated all these meetings without any of us knowing a thing!"

Ophelia sighed. She stood to face the mirror, fingering the skirt of her dress. "You know that I can be tenacious and secretive when I wish to be. D has told me I can't reveal anything yet. It would only hurt our chances. I can say he tells me he is an officer or at least he somehow works with the police, and he is so handsome. He has the most perfect teeth."

Anna chuckled at that, and Ophelia continued, "It would be unwise just yet to say more. I will when the time is right, I promise, and Mother and Father will just have to accept my decisions. I hate how we cannot be together openly simply because of money or society which both drive us to separation. Although he doesn't sound 'lower-class' as it were to me. He speaks very well."

Anna smiled. This was why she loved her cousin so much. She didn't have quite the same rebellious spirit as Anna, who had never been in love and had no desire to be, but they both railed against their constrictions. Anna clasped her hand as Ophelia walked by, stopping her gait.

"They are silly rules, cousin, and perhaps one day, they will be changed, and women can do whatever they please. I hope I can meet this young officer of yours sometime. And learn his actual name?"

Ophelia moved to her chair and sat down with a flourish, her taste for performance coming out. "Oh Anna, he is just what a man should be! We share many of the same interests. He even desires to travel! He says we may go somewhere new once we are married! Anna, I just know you will like him."

"I'm sure I will like him, if you do. But I'm sad I won't get to be at your wedding ceremony, if you must do it in secret. The wedding of society princess Ophelia Marshall to be held in...who knows where."

Ophelia chuckled. "Finally, not a whole to-do about something that I am involved in. I would rather get married in a barn to this wonderful man than have a big white wedding with an utter bore."

Anna crinkled her nose. "You're sure about this? Your life will be completely changed."

Ophelia nodded, her curls bobbing and her earrings making a light tinkling as she did. "Yes, Anna. I see that familiar crinkle between your brows. You may disapprove, but I am certain of it. For what is all this," she motioned to her room and everything in it, "without love?"

Anna looked around. She was no stranger to finery, but she wasn't sure she could get rid of everything she held dear for something so ethereal and changeable as love. For ambition, education, adventure, yes. But not love. It was a foolish thing. The stuff of novels and dreams.

"You will always be by my side, Anna. I know many will desert me at my choice of husband once it gets into all the papers. They will hear about it all the way in London, I'm sure."

Anna shook off the worry that was beginning to grow. She nodded. "Yes, Ophelia. I will always be with you. Until death do us part." They both giggled and Ophelia sighed with contentment.

"I will soon be a Mrs. Mrs. D." She held out her left hand to imagine a ring there. "'Til death do us part."

CHAPTER

4

That evening, the elites of the city came to gather at Lord and Lady Croft's Hamilton mansion. Many of them were British expatriates, having felt the need to leave ever-growing England and make their fortunes in the ripe soil of America. But some were also Americans, who had procured enough wealth and status to be invited to such an event. In America, everything was for sale. All the owners of the major businesses in the city had received their golden invitations. Not the least of these were Mr. and Mrs. Marshall, owners of the mill, along with Lord and Lady Wincherton, who were partners in the mill, and of course the owner and managers of the cigar factory, the tannery, the printers, and many more.

The carriages and the bristling horses were lined up outside of the rather large, ostentatious home, putting Anna in mind of the Gothic novels she had often read as a young girl. Tall, pointed turrets and heavy gray stone gave the house a sort of mystical, dangerous air. Although now, she preferred detective stories, whenever she could get her hands on one.

Anna was happy with her choice of gown, but she approached the ball entrance with slight trepidation, knowing that her mother would be watching her every move. Her parents were behind her as she entered, her gloved hands unable to stop their nervous movement. She could debate a topic of interest for hours on end, but she was uncertain of herself in a ballroom. They gave their cloaks to the waiting footman, and now her gown was in its full glory as she wandered into what could never have passed for a London ballroom but would suffice for small-town America.

Her mother whispered in her ear as she approached her hosts, ready to make her greeting. "In England, Lord and Lady Croft had been a Duke and Duchess, but some horrible scandal had forced them to flee to the United States and hide their true identities. But mind, they still expect deference."

Anna nodded, amazed at such news. She relished the idea that Lady Croft was once involved in some sort of scandal. Anna would have liked nothing better than to question her about it in front of all her guests. What an expression she was sure to see on Lady Croft's face.

In front of their hosts, the three of them greeted them respectfully. Lady Croft said to her husband, who looked even large and more bird-like than his wife, "My dear, this is Lord Edward, the Earl of Wincherton, and Countess Regina Wincherton, and their daughter, Lady Anna Lovelace."

The last introduction she said with slight distaste, and her mouth turned down as if regretting to have to say the words. Anna did her best curtsy, for she noticed her mother watching out of the corner of her eye. Lord Croft bowed his head with a few bumbling words and then looked beyond them at the next group. Once they were past the pair, Anna breathed a sigh of relief.

"Thank goodness," she whispered to herself and received a sharp glance from her mother and a wink from her father.

Ophelia had arrived earlier, and when Anna spotted her across the room, she rushed to her side, glad to have found a friend amongst the heap of wealthy strangers her mother called "society". Ophelia spread her hands wide as she surveyed the occupants of the room, quickly growing in number.

"Take your pick, Anna. Just look at all of the eligible young men there are on offer."

She winked, and Anna laughed. "I suppose you will not be looking with me?"

"Certainly not, dear cousin." She leaned in to whisper in Anna's ear. "I have plans to meet him later this evening in the church graveyard."

Before she could respond, a handsome man approached them and stood in front of Anna, bowing his head low, his hands behind his back.

"Would you care to dance, Miss?"

Anna blushed, surprised at the invitation. So soon, and she had not even had a chance to sip at a glass of champagne to ease her nerves. Desperately, she wanted to reject his offer, for she would much rather have stood speaking to Ophelia, but she caught her mother's warning glance from across the room.

"Of course, sir," she replied, and allowed herself to be pulled onto the dance floor for the very first song of the evening.

After a few more gentlemen had asked her, two of them too old, and one with such piercing eyes they were almost frightening, Anna finally found some reprieve. She was confronted again by a young man on her way to the drinks table. She couldn't help but notice his handsome features, so very different from the other men who had come her way.

"Will you dance, Miss?" He asked kindly, and with a tinge of disappointment, Anna reluctantly agreed.

At least Ophelia was also dancing at that point, and she could not have spoken to her anyway. The man took her into his arms and smiled down at her as they moved in time to the music of the waltz, Anna's dress swaying with each step. Her feet were sore, but it was a relief to dance with a handsome man as opposed to an old man seeking a young wife, which one of her suitors had most certainly been.

"I must ask your name, Miss."

Anna could spy her mother beaming in the corner as her daughter danced with such an eligible gentleman. He was tall, well-dressed, and commanding. Anna realized he had asked a question and rushed to reply.

"Anna Lovelace. And you, sir?"

"Ah, I am Frederick Mason, My Lady. You must forgive my use of Miss. I do know your father a bit, as we are both businessmen in such a small town."

Anna wanted to snort with distaste and frustration.

Lovely, so perhaps Father coerced him into asking me to dance.

Although Anna was quite pretty and fashionable, she was often left alone in the corner, for her mother told her that her face gave off an air of rejection. Many of the people in the society circles of the town felt her to be just a little a bit odd. At least the women. She had been an English lady, but she was not like a lady with her questioning glances, abrupt manners, and outlandish statements that she had no qualms about sharing in public. And so, she had mostly stayed at home or with Ophelia to avoid such harsh looks.

Anna realized that Mr. Mason was an excellent dancer, and Anna felt like she was floating along in his embrace. After their introduction, she looked up fully into his face. The dim lighting of the dance room had done well for his features. He had a strong jaw, a well-clipped mustache, and still had all of his thick, brown hair. He had good teeth, which he was often displaying in a wide smile as he spoke. Anna could feel thick muscles underneath his coat, and by the lightness of his feet, she could tell she was dancing with an athlete.

She used this time to ponder what life would be like if she was a different woman. She might have jumped at the chance to receive such a man's attention. Her mother would have been so pleased. A handsome, young, presumably wealthy businessman? Yes, he was quite suitable, if untitled, and if she was not mistaken, he had the hint of an English accent as well. It sounded as if he'd lived for a long time in America and had forgotten his roots. But what was it about marriage that seemed so distasteful to her? If it was to a man like this, she was certain he would be quite kind, although there was a lurking sensuality behind his eyes which unnerved her.

Marriage seems like such a dull prison. One gets married for connections and wealth, has a few children, and then lives the rest of one's days in idleness, not allowed to pursue any true invigorating interests or expand one's horizons.

If only she could be like everyone else. It would all be so easy. Yet, she wouldn't trade who she was for anything in the world.

She smiled at Mr. Mason. "So, I suppose you did know who I was after all."

He had the good manners to look slightly sheepish, but he did not take his light brown eyes from hers.

"Yes, I suppose you're right. But it would not have been gentlemanly of me to have introduced myself in such a way. What would a lady such as yourself think?"

Anna rolled her eyes. "Away with such rules, Mr. Mason. We are in America now. I would have thought you were quite normal, although I would have been very curious as to how you would have known me."

Mr. Mason laughed, a refreshing sound in such a strict atmosphere. "This is a small town, Lady Lovelace. Although it pretends it is growing into a city, it is still just a working man's town, and so we would have seen each other eventually."

"How have you come to be here, Mr. Mason? May I ask what business you are in?"

"My parents were English, but moved here to make their fortune, as is so common these days. I am in the business of my uncle, leading working men in a trade along with another relative. He is around in this room somewhere. I confess I do not enjoy the work, and one day I wish to be rid of it and find my fortune elsewhere. Perhaps return across the sea." The friendly expression of earlier twitched into one of resignation and anger, but it disappeared in an instant.

Anna was thrilled by such talk. A man who did not enjoy his

employment and wished to live elsewhere, foregoing a position in strict, decent society? It made her every muscle come to attention with excitement. She was still curious about his business, but it appeared he did not want to share further.

"That sounds all very wonderful, Mr. Mason. It's most unusual that someone of your status would wish to leave, when there is so much money to made here, as my uncle is forever telling me."

Mr. Mason sighed. "I do find myself being the unusual one. Perhaps you could understand me, Lady Anna? I do not mean to offend, but you do not seem like the other females that fill these halls, not so many frills and coquettish manners."

He looked around him grimly but returned to her face with a smile. Anna blushed with pleasure. Finally, someone had noticed and instead of criticizing her for it, had embraced it. "Yes, I'm afraid it's true, much to the dismay of my very proper English mother."

Anna glanced in her mother's direction, and Mr. Mason looked that way, catching her mother's eye who smiled and then looked away politely. The song ended, and couples were moving apart to find new pairings.

Mr. Mason let go of Anna after lingering for a moment, and then said, "Let me fetch us a pair of drinks." He was going to turn towards the table, but a servant walked by, holding a tray. "Ah, thank you, my good sir," Mr. Mason said to the servant, and Anna was taken aback.

Kindness to a servant? A wealthy man of business who had peasants of all sorts in his company? And a man with English parents? Her heart fluttered with excitement at the potential of having met a kindred spirit.

With another large smile, he handed her a champagne flute. "Thank you," she replied, trying not to stare too openly at him, but at the same time trying to puzzle him out. She was so grateful for the drink, she had to try to keep from gulping it in one fell swoop. She could see Ophelia coming towards them from across the room.

She was about to open her mouth to speak when he flushed a little and said, "Well, Lady Anna, it was a pleasure to meet you. I hope we shall meet again. As for being unusual, to me, you seem perfect."

With that, he bowed his head, and Anna was left dumbstruck on the edge of the dance floor which was now refilling with new couples. Ophelia stood at her side squinting towards the back of Mr. Mason as he disappeared in the crowd.

"Now, that didn't seem so bad," she said slyly. "I didn't get a good look at him, but by your expression, it seems he surprised you. In a good way."

Anna was still surprised but shook herself back to attention, trying not to let his words fill her with too much pleasure. Was she such a silly-headed woman to be so affected by one compliment?

"You could say that, I suppose. It was not too bad. Not at all."

Perhaps she understood the idea of falling in love just a little bit better, even though at the same time, she felt entirely befuddled. Perhaps not all men were so bad, desperate to catch their victims into traps? Who was this unique stranger?

CHAPTER

5

Rubbing a hand over his tired face, George knew he needed a shave. It was late, and he and a fellow policeman, Ned Barnum, were making their way home from the station. The sun was beginning to hide behind the taller buildings, but the orange, yellow light of the sunset crept between cracks and alleyways, making Lancaster look almost heavenly.

Strange, when the devil walks amongst us.

"What a day," Ned said, yawning. He pulled at the straps of his police cap and removed it, showing a thatch of white-blond hair. "It wasn't what we expected was it?"

"No," George shook his head. "But that, I guess, makes it a little more interesting."

They crossed the street, watching for the late-night weavings of carriages, trying to avoid piles of horse excrement the street cleaners failed to scoop up. On the other side, George reached into his pocket for a cigarette. As usual, he offered one to Ned who always refused.

"Never thought we'd see women fighting, you know. That was a strange sight. And all for something small. A letter looked like to me. I couldn't tell from there. They would have nearly bludgeoned each other bloody by the time we got there."

George nodded. He threw his match to the ground and pulled a big puff from his cigarette, removing his cap with his other hand and tucking it under his arm. He wasn't sure either what it was that had the two factory girls so riled up, but he had seen one of the women slip something white into her pocket after they were torn apart.

He said finally, "They weren't happy to be stopped either. I've never seen women put up such a fight. But I'm sure a night or two in prison will sort them out."

Ned frowned. "Not really. I'm sure they'll be back to it as soon as they get out. It doesn't solve the problems that've come up with the workers' strikes. I suspect the fight today was connected."

George looked at his friend. Ned always was a sort of champion for the people. George hated to admit it, but Ned kept him in line. Normally, he was apt to dismiss criminals and those who didn't behave as they ought as not worth his time. If it was easy enough for him to behave, then why couldn't they? But Ned was right.

Ned kept talking. "I always hate to go up there, you know? To the factories. They look like one of the circles of Hell. I'm not surprised that the strikes are going on."

George shuddered. The sight of the factories when he had the occasion to go inside were the kind of things one saw in nightmares. Dirty, ragged people surrounded by dirty ragged things. Machines creaking, the heavy scent of blood and sweat, and the soullessness in each of the workers' faces.

"You're right, Ned. I wouldn't want to be one of them. I can tell you that right now. I'm very happy with my room at the boarding house, tiny though it is."

They turned onto Marietta Avenue and quickly turned back onto Orange, the houses growing in size and elegance. The streetlamps were lit, and at the corner of Marietta, the faint sound of an accordion wafted through the air. In the shadows, George could spy an old man swaying along to his sorrowful music.

Ned nudged George back to face him. "Come for a drink, George. We've had a long one. The pub at the corner of my place and yours. It'll do us good. It always does, doesn't it?"

George chuckled. "But Ned, you've got a young, pretty wife at home who probably wants you to return, not sticking around with me until the late hours."

George pulled at the buttons of his coat, ready to be free of its constraints. Besides, the deep blue sight of a uniform tended to make bartenders uneasy.

"Oh, Laura likes it when I stay away a bit. Gives her time to chat to the neighbor women, once she's done with the washing. She doesn't need me coming home with all my weary stories and getting underfoot as she calls it." Ned grinned. "One pint is all, of course. Ain't got time for no more. We've got an early morning. But I shouldn't be telling you that, Senior Officer," Ned added, in a teasing voice.

Laughing, George replied. "True, true. One pint then it's off to my bed. I want to think of nothing for a whole eight hours if possible. No factories, no blood, no stench of sweat."

As they ascended Orange Street, they could hear the sound of waiting horses in the night and spied a line of carriages next to the well-lit Hamilton House. Ned whistled.

"Looks like there's a big to-do up at the new place tonight. All the fancy sorts, you know. Lords and Ladies and them." He elbowed George. "Now that you're promoted, maybe you should show face there sometime."

George rolled his eyes, and Ned laughed heartily. "I don't think I would much fit in, Ned."

"But the ladies there are probably the finest things you ever did see. All the society misses, I'm sure."

George could see it. Long dark-colored gowns, the movement of gloved hands, the sparkle of jewels. He would never be allowed at such a venue, even though his fiancé Jenny would dearly wish it. She had ideas, he knew, of moving up in the world.

"No doubt Jenny would be dying to go. I'm sure I'll hear about it soon enough."

"You probably will, George. Women are always talking about these kinds of things. I can't wait to tell my Laura. But first, to the pint."

"The pint," George said, giving Hamilton House another doleful look as they turned off onto their street.

***

A surprised Ophelia guided Anna over to the refreshment table and found her own glass of champagne. She turned back around to look at the dancers, leaning close to Anna's ear.

"Why Anna Lovelace, you look positively bowled over. What could that young man with the extremely handsome back of the head have said to upset the balance of my solid, well-balanced cousin? Drink the champagne, dear. You may need two glasses."

Ophelia giggled into her own glass as Anna sipped hers.

"Well…" she began slowly, eyeing Mr. Mason as he spoke with a group of gentlemen in an opposite corner. He glanced over at her and smiled once more with his perfect, white teeth. She hurriedly looked away. What had he really said?

Perfect. He'd said perfect.

But she didn't reveal this to Ophelia. It was far too…personal.

"Nothing that a glass or two of champagne won't fix, Ophelia. You know I could never succumb to the attentions of a man, no matter how handsome he may be." She sighed. "It is not in my nature to fall in love, and I find it suspicious of any man to try and make me do so."

Ophelia lifted her eyebrows in surprise. "He must have said something! You looked shocked, as if you'd seen a ghost."

Anna waved it away feeling as though the moment had passed. She was now in possession of her full self, even if her interest was piqued in finding more out about this man.

A kindred spirit is not something to sneeze at.

"Oh, Ophelia, it was only some sort of flirtation. Surely, you receive those frequently from your *many* admirers." Ophelia rolled her eyes as Anna continued. "But perhaps I was overly shocked to receive my first one. You saw the rest of my dance partners. Old and decrepit or so terribly shy they could barely stammer out a word. I had a mind to reject each and every one of them, but it appears that Mother Dearest is watching like a hawk from afar. I did promise my father I would be nice and make her happy. At least for a time."

Ophelia sighed. "Anna Lovelace, you are hopeless. Sometimes I don't even know how we get along so well. I wish to hear as much gossip as possible, and here you are, on the brink of it, and you won't even share it with me! Your own cousin!" Ophelia made a pained face, and Anna laughed aloud, drawing the disapproving attention of a few of the older society women.

"Again, so dramatic Ophelia, but how about this? I shall reveal to you what he said and did, but you must let me meet your D before you wed."

Ophelia's face brightened, and she clasped Anna's hand. "Agreed!"

Anna leaned forward and whispered into Ophelia's ear. Ophelia gasped and pulled away, delighted. "Anna! What a compliment! You are sure to hear from him again soon. Your mother will be delighted. Oh, if only I could tell boring Miss Hawkins and idiotic Miss Jordan your story. They are always out for blood and deserve to be knocked down a bit. Oh look! Miss Hawkins seems to be dancing with your elegant man at the moment."

Ophelia motioned to the dance floor and was standing up on her toes straining to see. She squinted her eyes, trying for a better view, but

Ophelia's eyesight was not very good, but she flatly refused to wear spectacles. "I'm annoyed that I cannot get a good look at his face, Anna. You know that I am quite the appraiser of handsome men and wish to place my seal of approval on him."

Anna nudged her cousin. "Why should you? I have no interest in him whatsoever, Ophelia, even for all his lovely compliments." Anna sipped at her glass again, her eyes wandering to the smiling Miss Hawkins and the white teeth of Mr. Mason. She could tell he was using the same charms upon his new dance partner.

Men, such creatures of habit. I knew they couldn't be trusted.

Ophelia opened her mouth to protest, but a dark-haired footman approached her. "Excuse me, Miss Marshall. This note is for you."

Ophelia took it swiftly, her cheeks flushing. Anna's gaze was drawn by the sudden change in Ophelia's expression. "Who is it from?"

"I'm not sure, Miss," the footman replied. "A maid approached me with it."

"Thank you."

Ophelia opened the note and could barely contain her excitement. Anna looked over her shoulder to read, *Meet me in the graveyard. D.*

"Oh, Anna, it's him!" Ophelia said in an excited voice, sipping the last of her champagne as quickly as possible without appearing too unladylike. It amused Anna, but a flutter of fear washed over her.

"D?" She whispered.

Ophelia nodded and clasped Anna's arm. "Anna, please tell Mother and Father that I have left early with a headache. I won't be long. I'll be back in the house before they return."

Anna nodded, but she was nervous. She held onto Ophelia's hand just a little longer. "Are you certain, Ophelia? To meet in a graveyard at night. It could be dangerous, and you're practically leaving me to the dogs in here! You're certain you do not wish to return to the ball after your rendezvous?"

Ophelia kissed Anna on the cheek and said, "When you are in love, Anna dearest, you will know just as I feel. Nothing could keep you away!"

She was gone in a flourish of fabric, attempting to conceal her departure as best she could. Soon after, Anna was approached by another gentleman to dance and in order to stop thinking about what was happening with Ophelia, she allowed herself to be whisked onto the floor. She was too busy with her own worries for her cousin and trying to remember the steps that she didn't notice another pair of eyes watching Ophelia's departure with interest.

***

All clutching, grasping whores and greedy beggars, the lot of them. But I must keep up appearances and so have done my duty at the ball. Especially after that ghastly display at the factory. Two bitches fighting, causing all kinds of problems, all for something insignificant. All controlled by their cravings. I was glad the police handled the affair and were gone before I got there, so that I did not need to sully my hands with the nonsense. At least it was not related to that horrid strike. I have little enough patience as it is for their foolishness.

Thank goodness, I have no one anymore to push me in any direction I do not wish to go. Mother is now gone and has naught to say to me from her grave. I am my own instructor, my own guide, and others must do my bidding.

Mothers are eyeing me as they always do at balls, their mouths watering with excitement, hoping their daughter will catch my eye. I dance and please, but it is merely a game. Such a good player I am!

However, maybe one of the young ladies already has, but not in the way the mothers hope and imagine. Their daughters could be made better by my hand released from their constraints, but again, not in the way they envision. I have already found my next muse, the holder of the next heart for my collection. She is beautiful, she is frivolous, and her lovely red hair and pink lips draw my attention and have for quite some time. I have heard of her beauty, and in person, it exceeds my expectations. My skin quivers with the thought of seeing her pale face against the ground, devoid of blood, silently and peacefully sleeping forever, the most beautiful she has ever been.

Ah, I see she leaves to meet her lover, the obstacle in my path, for that is what these women always wish to do. If only I could part the crowd like Moses and find her easily. She is so careful not to attract suspicion, but you do, my dear, you do! You are so gentle in your movements. No one else would notice but no one else is as shrewd as I, dear Muse!

Now is my chance to collect a rare, bloodied rose. A woman in the dark, desirous of discretion? She is perfect, well-suited to my needs. I wasn't sure it could happen this evening, but no matter, I have been waiting for a fresh victim and everything I need is close by. What fun! Since she will be harder to acquire, the more time I shall spend with her, making her utterly perfect. She will thank me. Her heart will thank me. I am grateful to the one who brings her to me. The one who does not realize what he's done.

I must follow her now and take my chance. There! She slips out into the night, thinking she is unseen. I am stopped by an odious man about the factory. I brush him off quickly. "I will return in but a moment," I say. "I am in need of fresh air", I tell the interfering mothers who try to detain me. I exit the home, the crispness of night upon my face. I see her. Her figure is nearly ghostly in the moonlight rushing across the road to the graveyard. I motion to my waiting carriage to the side of Hamilton House. He knows my plans.

It appears fate has smiled on me this evening. This truly is a sacred calling. Blast! Someone is watching, smoking against the wall. I cross the street and turn the other way around the church, hoping I was not noticed. There is another entrance to the graveyard. I move quietly, ever so quietly! I am just as the mist, creeping forward slowly, unheard, floating across the ground in search of what I seek. There she is! Looking into the darkness, whispering to the night. But wait! Him! Does he not know that he interferes?

When he is least aware I jump from the shadows, a rock in my hand. He crumples. Oh, how devious I am! His unconscious form disgusts me. So animalistic, so beastly, nothing of what a woman's figure makes in such a position. She has not heard. Thank the supposed Heavens, she is unaware. I see her, creeping around the gravestones in search of her man. So, I will he be.

CHAPTER

6

The next morning, Anna awoke feeling exhausted and slightly despondent. The rest of the party had been a bore, with multiple men coming to ask her to dance after Ophelia had left, and not one of them had been as interesting or memorable except for just how exceptionally dull and ugly they had been. The room was rather crowded, and so she had not seen Mr. Mason for the rest of the evening, nor however, had she seen Ophelia, but she hadn't expected to.

Anna sat in front of her looking glass, leaning her head on her fist. When would it end? When could she stop appeasing her mother's wishes and do what her father said she would do? Find a way out. She could not simply attend balls forever. Anna longed for the day when it would be unbecoming for her to do so, once her age was beyond a certain number.

To be a spinster was to be free. Then, she could pursue her own pleasures and with the money which would have been her dowry, or if she could earn her own money, she could live a life devoid of balls, strict rules, and limiting factors. Since they had arrived home late last evening and she had not gotten much sleep, she was feeling a little irritated with Ophelia. She had made excuses for her, and while her Aunt Louisa had not been pleased, she did not question it. It seemed that Ophelia had had plenty of headaches of late, and her mother would be calling the doctor soon.

Besides Ophelia, Anna had no female friends who were as close as her cousin. She couldn't seem to quite fit with the young women in America. She was running away from wealth and consequence while these young ladies seemed to be running towards it. When she spoke to other women her age, it was like they were all eyes and ears, waiting to see what she would do, waiting to pounce on anything that would make them appear better and more marriageable. She wished she could tell them, "You are! Go forth and take as many men as you desire, for I do not want them."

So, at the ball without Ophelia at her side, Anna had spent an idle evening in the arms of uninteresting men and in conversation with vapid young women. She had also unfortunately been subjected to speaking with her mother's friends whose minds were only filled with marrying off their daughters and granddaughters.

After a soft knock, her maid, Norma, entered Anna's bedroom holding a tray of tea. Anna could never get used to the American style of drinking hot coffee. Tea would always be her beverage of choice. Norma was shaking as she entered.

"My Lady, there's a terrible disturbance downstairs. Your mother and aunt would like to see you, but I thought you might need some tea before you went down."

Anna sat up hurriedly, her mind rushing instantly to thoughts of Ophelia. Norma put the tray down while Anna pulled her silk dressing gown from the back of her vanity chair and tied it around her waist.

"What is it, Norma? What's happened?"

"It appears that Miss Ophelia is gone, My Lady. She didn't return home last evening and even this morning, your aunt found her room empty."

"What?" Anna blanched. "She hasn't returned?" She asked in a soft voice, inwardly chastising herself for allowing her cousin to do such a foolhardy thing as meeting a man in the dark.

Norma tried to smile. She moved to Anna's wardrobe.

"Here, Lady Anna, let me help you get dressed, and then you may go and see for yourself."

Anna's mind raced with fearsome possibilities as Norma laced her into her corset and helped her into her day dress. She sipped at the tea trying to calm her nerves. If anything happened to Ophelia, it was all Anna's fault. She closed her eyes and took a calming breath.

But certainly, Ophelia is fine. She must have just gone with her young officer somewhere and will be back later. Ophelia is always pulling such tricks and changing her mind about plans. That must be it. There must be an explanation.

Anna nodded her head, trying to reassure herself, but then a new thought occurred to her.

She wouldn't get married without me, would she? She promised.

For some reason, she knew that wasn't it, and a dark feeling crept over her despite her attempts to self-soothe. It all seemed so strange and oddly secretive. Her cousin hadn't even been able to give her the man's name, only a letter. She didn't even know if it was the letter to a first or a last name! Anna finished her tea while Norma assisted her with her hair, and then she was down the stairs as quickly as she could manage.

She entered the drawing room and saw Aunt Louisa, clutching a handkerchief to her eyes and quietly sobbing. Two glasses of sherry were placed on the low center table, and her mother was comforting her dear sister with one arm about her shoulders.

Anna said, "Mother, Aunt Louisa, what has happened? Where has Ophelia gone?"

Aunt Louisa struggled to get a hold of herself so that she could speak clearly in response. She wiped her eyes and glanced at Anna. There was a coldness to her gaze, and Anna felt the guilt swirling in her belly.

"You told us she had gone home with a headache, Anna, and so we did not disturb her when we arrived back home. Her door had been closed. But then, this morning, she did not appear at breakfast. I sent the lady's maid round to her room, and it was empty. After questioning the servants, we found none of them had seen her arrival last evening, and I did not think to ask them last night. Oh, what will I do? My dear, dear Ophelia. Gone! But to where? She did not even leave a note!"

Anna paused, thoughtful. Ophelia was wild and often reckless, but she was also sometimes strangely conscientious. If she had been thinking of completing the marriage last evening, then she would have left a note for her parents explaining all. She would have most definitely written to Anna.

"I don't believe it. Foolish Ophelia!" Anna breathed, covering her mouth in surprise, feeling the sting of tears in her eyes.

"Foolish? What do you mean?"

Anna blushed, realizing that she'd spoken aloud. "I mean..." she trailed off."

"Do you know something?" Aunt Louisa narrowed her eyes. "I know you two talk about everything. Is there something you know? Your uncle and I are desperate to know. He is out combing the streets with your father as we speak! He will also visit Lord and Lady Croft to question their servants."

Anna hesitated, knowing just how her aunt and mother would take the news of Ophelia's secret. Her mother's voice lowered to a dangerous level. "Anna, this is no time for secrecy. Ophelia could be in danger."

Danger. The thought of her dear beautiful cousin in danger chilled Anna to the bone. But this town was a quiet one. So quiet in fact, it bordered on being utterly dull, save for the recent string of murders. She paused, her every muscle tensing, hoping against hope that what she secretly feared was not true. She did not want to see her cousin's name in the newspaper. Could it be that she was the next victim?

Anna stammered out a reply, her newest thought having thrown her into confusion and fear. "I'm sorry, Aunt, Mother, but there is a secret. I can tell you that I do not know where she is, but I do know where she was going or rather who she was hoping to meet."

"Who?" Aunt Louisa cried out, clinging desperately to the arms of the chair, her tears forgotten now, her face twisted in both anger and pain. She looked almost ten years older.

Anna hated to betray Ophelia's confidence, but her silly cousin had caused all kinds of worry and could be anywhere now with anyone. Anna shuddered.

"She was meant to meet with a man after the ball, someone she called D. She received a note from him at the ball, asking her to meet him across the street at the St. James graveyard."

Aunt Marshall looked at her sister in confusion. "D? Who is this D? I'm certain that I do not know anyone by such a name."

Anna shrugged. "I don't know him myself. Ophelia just told me about him and only mentioned his initial. Apparently, he is somehow affiliated with the police, and she and him are in a sort of relationship."

"What?" Aunt Louisa went white and threatened to faint, laying back against her chair. Her sister laid her hand on hers, patting it softly.

"Sister, all will be well. We will get to the bottom of this." Her mother stood up and pulled Anna to the side, out of earshot of Louisa. "Anna," she said sharply, "How could you keep this from us and lie to us?"

"Mother, you know that I would never wish to put Ophelia in danger, but I wanted to help her in this case. She was so earnest. I know now that it was a foolish plan."

"Quite right." Her mother nodded stiffly. She glanced back at her sister, sniffing quietly, dabbing her handkerchief at her eyes. "I expect you to be just as forthright with the police, Anna. When they come."

Anna nodded. "You called them?"

"Yes, I sent a messenger around as soon as we heard the news. We will soon get to the bottom of this." Her mother walked back to Louisa, grabbing her around the shoulders again.

Anna watched them from a slight distance, leaning against the mantelpiece, feeling the heat of the fire on her legs. She swallowed nervously, worried about her aunt's pain and her cousin's fate, and yet, something new occurred to her. Despite the police's involvement, Anna could be the one to save her cousin from any danger and find out just what had happened to dear, sweet Ophelia. She had a dangerous yet exhilarating feeling that perhaps her chance had come at last.

***

Sweet, sweet red-haired maiden. She came so willingly after I told her I'd seen her supposed lover injured at the entrance to the graveyard. She did not even question me at my sudden arrival from the darkness. I had pulled my cigar from my pocket, so she'd assumed I was smoking in the cool evening air. With a sound of surprise and fear, she rushed over, gathering her skirts to avoid them catching on the moonlit gravestones.

I followed her, gathering my wet cloth of chloroform for her sweet lips to breathe. It was there in my pocket at the ready, for who knew when one's victims might come? The woman bent down over her foolish lover, her fear touching. Ah, but men look so beastly and ugly when lying like dead. I hate that I had to even do such a thing in order to draw my prize.

It was worth it, and all part of the plan, of course. For a prize she was. She did not even notice my subtle hand. I am oh, so quiet when I wish to be. I covered her mouth with the cloth, and while there was a slight struggle, and I was given sight of her beautiful wide eyes, they soon closed, and her body relaxed. I pressed my lips to the side of her neck to feel the quickened pace of her heart. "Soon you will be mine, my sweet," I said to it. "My treasure."

It was dark enough to carry the woman through the back of the graveyard and to my waiting carriage. The driver did not even look back as I loaded the woman inside. I have paid him well and threatened him enough to avoid betrayal. It is easy to involve anyone for the right price. Into the night we return.

She breathes sweetly and softly beside me. How long will this woman be for this world? I have been waiting long enough for her, the obstacle now out of my way. Perhaps, for a little excitement, I can draw out the time longer and longer. That will make the police go wild with their hunt, believing in their good skills to find her. But, oh, they shall never find my trove of treasures for forever mine they shall remain.

CHAPTER

7

George Ford had a fitful night's sleep. He hadn't seen Jenny in a few days, and after seeing the wealth and brightness of Hamilton House the previous evening, he felt a guilty ache in his belly at the thought of seeing her, knowing that she would talk to him about it. He could never give her that, and he was fearful that she would realize it one day and leave him.

Back at the station, almost as soon as he arrived, a note was thrust into his hand from one of the secretaries he'd met on his way in the door.

"Sir, a servant of Lord and Lady Wincherton sent this just this morning. Since you're meant to be on duty today, I brought it to you."

She shrugged and returned to her desk. George moved to remove his hat, but he paused, unfolding the note instead. Reading it, he called out to Ned who was returning to the front desk, a few papers in his hand.

"Come with me, Ned. We've got a call to make at the Lovelace home." Ned came around the desk, and George whispered, "Girl's missing."

Ned went a little pale as he pulled on his police cap, and the two of them hurried off towards Orange Street. The street was busy, everything open and alive again after the stillness of the night.

"No cab, George? We could make it faster."

"No. We'll be there quick. Don't want to waste the time hailing one. Besides, I don't see any around."

His voice was tense, and Ned walked nervously beside him. George had a feeling deep in his gut that this was another abduction by the killer. Soon they would find the body, if it was not out and displayed already. He secretly rejoiced after having waited too long for anything interesting to happen.

Perhaps the sergeant might consider me for a promotion if I do well on this?

Although to use a murdered woman as a way to launch his detective career felt wrong. But he couldn't help it. The killer was fascinating and intriguing in a way that Ford had not met with before. He wanted to know everything about him and why he did what he did.

But there was no murder victim yet. Just a missing woman. The house was not far, so it didn't take them long to reach it on foot. At the base of the stone steps, George eyed the house critically. Finally, one of the blue bloods getting hit by crime. Usually, he was dealing with the poor and desperate. The mobs and strikes at the factories or petty thefts were all that filled his day, especially when he'd been just a junior officer.

He could understand the strikers to a point, begging for a better wage and better working conditions. Too many children were employed there as well, and they were continually getting struck down with illness because of the long hours.

His grandfather had been one of those men, and he died after a lifetime of brutal work. Both George and his father had been lucky enough to secure different employment. Employment which at least garnered a bit of respect.

The men scraped their boots on the iron bar below the stairs. The streets were dirty today, with carriages flowing like a growing tide around the narrow streets, leaving horse droppings in their wake. George hit the knocker twice and looked around. This would be the first inquest he was to begin, if it was for the murder case.

Normally, officers were sent for first to do the preliminary interview. If the case was something "worthwhile", then the detectives would take it up. He tried not to appear too nervous as he waited. He adjusted his uniform, and Ned coughed.

Damn it, it's taking a long while. Attempting to make us wait, no doubt.

Suddenly, the door flung open, and a footman allowed them entry, taking their hats. They waited until they'd been announced and then entered the room with as much authority as they could muster. He could do this. He nodded to each of the ladies.

"Good morning, ladies."

He spotted a young blonde woman in the corner of the room, standing by the fireplace. While the two older women looked away as soon as they made their initial greetings, she kept his gaze, and it gave him an odd feeling. He swallowed and looked away, feeling his nerves take over again. He cleared his throat, attempting to reestablish equilibrium.

"Officer, would you like some tea or coffee?"

He heard Lady Wincherton's lilting English accent and knew he was among the old gentry, those who had lost their fortunes in England but had found them again to some degree in America. He tried not to let that fact color his opinion of the victim.

"No, thank you, Madam, My Lady." George hesitated, feeling suddenly awkward, but Lady Wincherton did not seem to notice.

"Please, do come and sit." Lady Wincherton motioned him to a soft, rather ornate chair in front of their hearth. He waited for the striking young woman to sit before he did and nodded to Ned to stand nearby. "I am Countess Wincherton, and this is my sister, Mrs. Marshall. This is my daughter, Lady Anna Lovelace. And you are?"

George followed her motioning hand to each of the women and found himself entrapped in the young woman's gaze again. It looked as though she was scrutinizing him, measuring him, and he looked away quickly before he lost all of what he wanted to say. He remembered that he'd been asked a question.

"Ah yes. I am Senior Officer Ford. I am the officer on duty today. This is Officer Barnum. Lady Wincherton, please tell me what's happened. I'd like to ask you a few questions along the way if I may, as well."

Lady Wincherton nodded weakly. "Of course. I am sorry that Lord Wincherton and Mr. Marshall could not join us at the moment, but they went to Lord and Lady Croft's in order to question the servants there." She cleared her throat. "It is really my sister's child who is the reason we have called you. Louisa, will you tell the officer?"

Mrs. Marshall looked nearly identical to Lady Wincherton, except for the fact that she looked rather tired with tear-streaked cheeks. When she spoke, her voice was quiet and weak.

"My daughter Ophelia did not return home last evening after a ball at the Croft mansion. My niece knows a few details about what has occurred." She burst into a fresh set of tears and clutched at her already damp handkerchief. George held tightly to his notebook, and he clenched his jaw. Tears made him uncomfortable.

"I know my daughter, Officer Ford, and while she can be a bit headstrong, it is not like her to vanish into thin air!" Then Mrs. Marshall could no longer speak, and Lady Wincherton had to attend to her.

"I am sorry, Madam. We will do all we can to find your daughter," George replied rather lamely, unsure of how to react in the face of such feminine emotion.

He wondered how difficult it must be for women to live everyday with such lack of control. He found it to be a weakness, and he was happy to have been born a man: strong and full of conviction. He turned reluctantly to the niece whose eyes found him again, displaying their wit, intelligence, and strength of character, such a contrast to the other women clutching to each other for support.

He had never seen a woman look so. She was lovely, to be sure, with curled blonde hair, sensual lips, and a lovely dress of deep mauve. Her arms were crossed over her chest, and he saw the glinting of a golden pocket watch hanging from the base of her bodice. Women were meant to be demure and shy, not staring at a strange man as if they knew all his secrets. He squirmed rather uncomfortably under her gaze, but resolved to not show weakness to a woman, especially one such as this who made him feel both lacking and unsteady.

He looked down at his small notebook where he had scrawled a few beginning notes. "Lady Anna, what can you tell me about what's happened?"

Anna straightened her shoulders and began speaking in a clear, controlled voice. She looked distressed about her cousin's disappearance but at the same time seemed full of a strange sort of determination.

"All that I know is Ophelia had planned on meeting a man outside of the ball. When telling me about him earlier in the afternoon, she had referred to him only as 'D', and he was to meet her in the St. James graveyard late at night during the ball. She also told me she believes him to be somehow connected with the police. She received a note telling her it was time to meet. Perhaps you know him, Officer Ford?"

She raised an eyebrow, looking at him hopefully.

D. There were many officers whose names started with D. It could be anyone.

As far as he knew, none of them professed to have known or wished a meeting with Ophelia Marshall, one of the most well-known and supposedly beautiful women in town. And none of them would have had an invitation to the Croft ball, unless of course they were of very high status.

George had never seen Ophelia, but Jenny had mentioned her as Miss Marshall's actions were often mentioned in the newspaper.

"I will have to inquire, of course. It's a popular letter for a name, you must understand, though."

His weak attempt at lightening the mood was not well-received. The patch of skin between Anna's eyebrows twitched slightly at his remark, and he cleared his throat in response, raising his pencil to write a few more notes.

"What is the nature of their relationship? Had she known him from before?"

Anna colored slightly, and without looking at her aunt she said, "I do believe they wished to get married one day, officer."

There was a crow-like outcry of pain from Mrs. Marshall at the news. Anna glanced at her sorrowfully but continued.

"It is possible that that is why she is gone. They could have...eloped."

"I see."

He scrawled down a few more things. A woman attempting to meet a man at night, with all that had been happening. It seemed odd. He was certain he knew the culprit. Well, did not *know* him, but knew of him by his work, and somehow, he had lured Miss Marshall out of the Croft ball.

George glanced at the tearful older woman. "Excuse me, Mrs. Marshall, but would you happen to have a photograph of your daughter? We will begin our search for her right away." He stood, preparing to leave, pushing a hand through his slicked-back hair and replacing his cap.

Lady Wincherton nodded.

"We do." She called for a maid to bring her what she sought. "She was recently in the newspaper, Officer Ford, and they have placed her picture in the society pages."

The maid quickly returned and handed him a folded paper. In it, he saw a picture of a lovely young woman smiling back at him. He suddenly felt guilty for wishing for a murder victim just for something more interesting to do.

"What color is her hair?"

"Red, sir. Very distinctive," Mrs. Marshall replied.

"Thank you. I shall take my leave. Lady Wincherton, Mrs. Marshall, Lady Lovelace. You will hear from me with any information. I promise you. Oh, and please have Lord Wincherton and Mr. Marshall send me any information they wish me to know, but I will go to Hamilton House myself."

"Thank you, Officer." Lady Wincherton said, her face drawn as she guided her sister out of the room.

George moved to the open door, where the footman was waiting. With a rush of skirts, George heard and felt Anna Lovelace by his side just as he was about to step out into the bright sunshine. She touched his arm lightly, and he looked down at it, confused.

Her fingers were long and elegant, and he couldn't help but feel a frisson of warmth at her touch and nearness. He looked up to be faced with her green eyes once more looking at him, filled with questions. And he even dared to glance down at her pair of pink lips, which were slightly open. Despite himself and despite the existence of his betrothed, he considered briefly what they might feel like to kiss.

"Mr. Ford," Anna said, and George was forced to look at her eyes again. He swallowed, attempting to recover himself, but she didn't seem to notice his attention on her features.

"Yes, My Lady?"

She lowered her voice. "I have been following the recent happenings in the newspaper, and I fear that my cousin may be the next victim." She looked around to make sure her mother or aunt were not still within earshot.

George had had the same feeling, but he didn't need anyone else, especially not a woman, to point it out to him. He suddenly felt protective of his position. And why was a woman, such as this, sullying herself with the sordid happenings on the street? Jenny would keep away from things like that. He stood taller and spoke sternly but politely in reply.

"Well, you shouldn't worry yourself about such things, Lady Anna. The police will handle this. I'm certain your cousin just lost her head for a few hours but should be back soon. You know how women can be. We'll do our best to make sure she returns safe and sound."

There, she can consider herself sufficiently scolded.

Anna abruptly moved her hand as if it pained her to keep it on George's arm.

She straightened as well and tight-lipped, lifting an eyebrow, she replied, "My cousin is not the type to 'lose her head' as you so put it, an affliction only given to women in your mind. Let's hope the police do not 'lose their heads' as they attempt to make a search for her. Good day, gentlemen."

She huffed and moved away out of the foyer and disappeared through a side doorway. George winced slightly at the loud slam of the door behind her.

Ned spoke as he donned his police cap and left the house. "My Lord, is she a wild one. Have you ever met a woman like her, George?" Ned chuckled, his eyes bright with merriment.

George's mouth was tight with frustration. He was an officer of the law, come to aid this woman and was to be given lip for it?

"No, I haven't, and thanks be to God. Aren't you grateful Lancaster isn't overrun with angry, headstrong, and loose-tongued women?"

Ned laughed again as they walked back towards the station. George could see his friend eyeing him.

"Not so much," Ned said. "My wife likes to speak her mind. I'd say it frustrates me, but if I'm honest, it keeps things interesting. Who wants to marry a woman without a thought in her head?"

George was subdued for the moment. He knew Ned was right, but he would be the last to admit that Lady Anna Lovelace had brought things up in him that he hadn't felt before. It only served to make him angrier and lose focus, when all he needed to do then was focus on his first real case.

CHAPTER

8

Anna fumed. She had satisfyingly slammed the door after leaving the officers, and then raced straight to her bedroom. She didn't want to return to the drawing room, afraid her agitation would disturb her mother and her aunt.

I hope to God that arrogant man heard the door and understood what it meant. He is the reason why the world is so backward!

She paced back and forth. Officer Ford was exactly why she could never marry. Never mind that Mr. Mason had been kind and flattered her at the ball. She was certain that all men were this way deep down. It was like they all came from the same seed.

But while Mr. Mason had been smooth and well-groomed, Mr. Ford's appearance was rather rough and untamed, very much a man of the world it seemed. However, she couldn't deny that he was well-formed, with a strong jawline and straight teeth, great strength hidden underneath his uniform. He had unique hazel eyes that seemed to watch her with interest, until they turned to look at her in scorn instead. She scoffed in disgust at her own moment of weakness and threw her arms in the air.

"Forget that he's handsome! It only serves to infuriate me further! He was rude, insolent, prideful, and of course believes that women are mere ornaments who serve no purpose whatsoever. We are all out and about 'losing our heads' as he says!"

She sat down on the bed with a huff, hopeless and helpless. If his thoughts about women were thus, why should he feel any need to search for Ophelia?

Perhaps he would think that one less woman in society would do us well, she thought unfairly.

"Ophelia, dear Ophelia, where could you be? Why would you leave me so?" she whispered.

A tear fell down her cheek, and she brushed it away quickly, knowing her cousin would need Anna to use all of her mental powers to find her and not waste any time on useless tears.

The letters.

She must try to find the letters D had written to Ophelia. That was her first step. Invigorated with having something to do rather than sitting around and waiting for the officers, she hurried from her room to fetch her cloak. She would need to go to Ophelia's house at once.

While she was downstairs, in a rush explaining to the housekeeper about her plans, she noticed a white card on the front table. She went to pick it up.

Mr. Frederick D. Mason
Chestnut Street

The housekeeper, Mrs. Bonds, cleared her throat, "Ah yes, My Lady. Mr. Mason came by to see you, but you were upstairs, and with the news, I thought it best to send him away until a better time."

Anna kept gazing at the card, remembering her time with Mr. Mason from the ball. It seemed so odd that he would call at such a time, but then, the rest of the world was moving, was it not?

"Yes, yes, of course. Thank you, Mrs. Bonds. You did the right thing. I shan't be too long. Please have the carriage brought around. I wish to visit my cousin's home."

She placed the card in the pocket of her day gown, not wanting her mother to see it.

Perhaps if she doesn't know he came, she won't press me about him.

Mrs. Bonds looked concerned, but she made no objections and called for a footman to alert the driver.

"You're certain, Miss? Could it not be dangerous?"

Anna smiled and placed a hand on Mrs. Bond's arm. She had been a kind woman to Anna in the last few years, despite the extravagances and whims of her mother on the poor woman.

"Thank you for your concern, but I shall be quite safe. Please explain my absence to my mother. Tell her simply that I went for a bit of air."

She only had to wait for a little while before the carriage was brought to the front of the house. She hoped that she would be able to sneak away while both her father and uncle were still at Hamilton House. As she was whisked away towards the Marshall house, the blood was now pumping quickly through her veins. It was worry, yes. She was afraid for her cousin. But this was the first time she had a mystery of her own to solve.

Anna's thoughts were spinning as the carriage approached Ophelia's wide drive. Since her aunt and uncle were elsewhere, Anna hoped she could be allowed to roam freely without sharing any further details about her fear for Ophelia. The maid who answered the door kindly let her in having recognized her.

Once she was safely inside, she removed her hat, and asked the maid, "Would it be possible if I went upstairs to Miss Ophelia's room? There is something there I have left behind."

The maid looked a little wide-eyed with the shock of the recent news but replied, "Of course, My Lady, but you do know that your aunt and uncle are not at home?"

"That is no trouble. I am only here to fetch something. I won't be long!"

Anna's hand smoothed over the banister as she ascended the stairs with speed, hopeful the letters would be easy to spot. When she reached Ophelia's door, Anna stood in front of it for a moment.

"Ophelia, help me to find you. You cannot leave me here alone." She placed her hands on the door, wishing more than anything that Ophelia would be behind it once more, waiting for her with a laugh and a smile.

When she opened it, the room was bare of her cousin, but it still felt like a warm and comforting place to Anna. Full of color and life. She shut the door behind her, her eyes searching the room for where Ophelia might have placed her beloved letters. She shuffled around hurriedly, rifling through shelves and books and diary pages. Finally, she remembered what a sentimentalist Ophelia was and taking a chance, she overturned the pillow to find the stack of letters underneath.

"Ah-ha!" She said, her heart beating with excitement.

She untied the ribbon keeping the letters together, so that she could try and read an address on the top. She didn't want to break her cousin's confidence by reading them just yet. However, none of them contained any hint of a return address.

Of course! Anna could have yelled in frustration at her own stupidity. *If they were to be discreet, they would not have dared to reveal anything about D's location.*

She slammed the letters back down under the pillow, and then began her search anew by Ophelia's writing desk, hoping that there was an unfinished letter or some sort of notation as to this mysterious D's whereabouts.

She squealed with delight. Finally, she had come across Ophelia's address book. Ophelia was always very good about writing letters. She had a beautiful hand, and she was very prompt in replying. She was also very organized about her address book, and she would not have any letter recipient that did not warrant a notation in that book. Anna flipped through and found a line marked "D". It was the only entry that did not contain a full name.

"This has to be it."

Taking a pencil from Ophelia's desk, Anna scribbled down the address on one of Ophelia's white stationary pages: 42 S. Shippen Street.

Rather from the lower side of town. Perhaps he is more penniless than I might have thought?

Anna placed the note inside her pocket and just as she was about to leave, she paused by Ophelia's bed and then reached under the pillow to take out the letters from underneath.

"It's best they stay with me for now. There is no sense in anyone else reading the private letters at the moment and causing a scandal from here to England. I certainly wouldn't wish for that police officer to get his grubby hands on them." She hurried to the door and closed it quietly after her.

Besides, there may be even more clues to her man inside these letters, and I want to be the one who finds the information first.

She inwardly apologized to Ophelia about perhaps having to read them as she left to meet her carriage driver.

Anna thought very briefly about going to the police with her new information, seeing as finding this mysterious man could prove difficult or dangerous, if it was the killer from the newspapers. But then Officer Ford and his snooty expression came to mind.

She jutted out her chin with defiance, brewing up a different plan. She would go tonight to find D herself to see what he had to say, and then go to the police after that. Perhaps they could bring him in to question him once they knew of his whereabouts.

"He would be more likely to speak with me as opposed to an angry, blustering policeman, standing in his doorway. If D loves her as much as Ophelia claims, then he will want to help."

She nodded, trying to fill herself with a little courage before her nighttime adventure. She clutched tightly to the letters in her hand, anxious to read them, but hesitant to intrude.

As she rode home, she said, "I will only read them if her lover is not at the address. Yes, that is a good compromise, I think," It was one of her quirks to speak to herself, especially when she was thinking through a problem.

Her mother told her it made her look mad, and no one would want a wife or mother who was insane.

"Insanity is the crutch of the weak and the poor," Her mother had said.

Anna merely rolled her eyes at the time but would reserve her habit of speaking to herself for times when she was alone.

Once she returned home, she sat back in her own personal parlor, hoping to avoid her mother and aunt until she had more time to think. She could hear her father and uncle's deep voices from downstairs, just arriving back, and she was eager to hear what news they'd uncovered, but it could wait for just a few moments.

She pulled out Mr. Mason's calling card and turned it about in her hand, thinking about the evening before. There was something about him that had alerted her to something, and she wasn't sure what. Was this desire? Interest? Fear? She couldn't exactly tell. He certainly was different from the rough edges and manly huskiness that exuded from Mr. Ford. Anna grimaced. Why had that man come into her head again? He was neither polished, nor polite, nor worth any time! She looked down at Mr. Mason's card again and she thought with dread, *Will he be calling again?*

"I wonder if Ophelia's D is like Mr. Mason. Mr. Mason is just the sort of man Ophelia would like, if she had gotten a good look at him at the ball. Perhaps I should have introduced them."

The reminder of Ophelia's dire situation made Anna feel sick. She lay back in the armchair, staring at the fire in her parlor grate. Tears threatened to well as she thought about what her cousin must be feeling right now if she had been taken. Anna shivered at the possibility. She didn't get the feeling that Ophelia was yet dead, but if she was in this killer's hands, then there were precious minutes to discover her whereabouts, and Anna needed to think hard and use her time wisely. She decided to wait until dark and late in the night before she snuck out of the house to find this D. From there, she hoped a next step would present itself.

"Hopefully."

***

My dear sweet girl rouses from the place where she lays in my lair. Such obvious beauty. It is enough to make any man swell in more ways than one. Yet it is the steady mechanism inside her that stirs my blood. I watch her chest rise and fall in that beloved rhythm and have been watching her since I brought her to me. My fingers itch to touch, to begin my work, but something holds me back.

"Are you weakening?" I ask myself.

Surely not. It is the police who hunt me that are weakening. Something else that lulls me into hesitation. Something about this woman. I have trapped and killed many, but she is different. She is so high above the others, according to society, and yet I have ensnared her. She has fallen for the tempting elixir of frivolous passion just as the rest of them, and yet, I wonder why I hesitate.

Never before has a victim so intrigued me. I reach out to push away a lock of her red hair, and she jolts awake, her eyes fluttering in surprise.

She stutters, "Who are you? Where am I?" and I can see the fear in her eyes, oh that delicious, familiar fear.

Beware my dear! Do not give me what I so desire, or you shall fan my thirst into its deadly flame.

I shush. I soothe. "Do not worry, Miss Marshall. You will be given your higher purpose. You must not fret. I shall set you free."

Her eyes are wide as she tries to take me in, to make sense of it all. Her mind will be too earthly for such sacred understanding, and it is cloudy from the drug.

"What purpose? What's happened? I was at the ball, and then I left to meet..." She trails off, and I watch her with a smile. Her eyes open even wider as she remembers. "You put a cloth over my mouth. But why? What purpose could I have here? Why have you done this? Where's D?"

Her eyes rove over my chambers, my secret lair, and they land on my trove of treasures, standing dutiful watch nearby. I am grinning now. My little treasures. No one alive has seen these beauties, and so she will have to die of course, But not yet. Not yet.

"Ophelia, Ophelia, wherefore art thou, Ophelia? Ah, quite the wrong play," I say with a chuckle. "You were Hamlet's lover. What a beautiful name, yet tragic. Surely your parents knew you would be given a tragic fate with such a name as that. You must calm yourself. Now is not yet your time. I am feeling a wave of mercy this evening. D is safe. He is gone now, now that he has done his duty. You will not need him any longer."

I reach out a hand, and she pulls away roughly, her eyes narrowing. What spunk and feistiness! I lick my lips. The prize will be very well-won indeed. Patience, patience.

"How do you know my name?" She cries out indignantly. "If you do, then you certainly know that people will be after me, hunting for me. You will not be able to escape the gallows!"

I chuckle. Victims were often similar in so many ways, always bargaining, always clinging to hope.

"My dear girl, of course I know who you are. We run in the same circles, and I have seen you many times. D has brought you to me. He has brought you into my sphere, even if he did not wish it."

So caught in her own surprise, she sits upright and begins to breathe quickly. Her face is a shadow now, its former firm expression crumbling. "What do you mean 'brought me'? You are a friend of D's?"

"Of course. We are business associates, of a sort. Even more than that." I then change the subject to lighter topics and light a cigar. We might as well spend our time pleasantly since I have decided to be merciful for a little bit longer. I say, "Your cousin is rather a lovely woman, Ophelia. We danced together at one point, and I heard her enjoyable conversation. She intrigues me."

Ophelia's face becomes a delicious mixture of anger and hopelessness. I almost clap at the sight! "You're the man she danced with?" I bow my head, ever the gentlemen in my manners. "You won't hurt her too, will you?"

Oh, the weakness. More pleading looks. I shake my head. "I suppose I can reveal everything since you will not get the chance to tell anyone else. No, I will not hurt your cousin. Anna, is it? She entertains me. And besides, she is not so weak as to have the craving for the midnight oil of which you and all the women before you have sunk so low as to desire. You fell so easily for the man as well."

"What? What're you talking about?" she asks, so beautifully ignorant of her wrongdoing, of her failings.

I pause, ignoring her lack of admission. An idea was taking shape in my mind, a lovely germ of an idea, slowly blossoming.

"Ophelia, my dear, I have an idea. I do believe I will send your Anna a letter."

I sit back, savoring the beauty of my own thoughts. They never disappoint me. What an excellent idea! What a fun way to add to my little game! I stifle my chuckle.

"I shall write a letter to her, Ophelia, to let her know all about you. She might wish to play my game."

I tilt my head and watch the young beauty's tear-streaked face. She cries so silently! It could weaken a man's resolve, but not me. I brush one tear aside with my thumb, and she trembles under my touch.

"Dear, dear Ophelia. Have you any message for your cousin? I would be happy to pass it on, of course. But do be sensible with your words."

Ophelia's mouth opens slightly. She is surprised! I am too, for I have never treated former victims with such manners. I am quite the gentleman. Mother would be so proud! I suppose the need for my manners increased when I realized the high status of my victim. An old habit, I'm afraid.

"She'll find you. Anna's the smartest person I know, smarter than any of the men

in the police force."

Ophelia's tears stop their flow now, and her chin juts out in anger and resolution. Her voice has taken on a tone of menace. I stand, tutting her lack of manners.

"Ophelia, you must try to calm yourself, or I will need to find a way to keep you contained." I flash my eyes towards her in warning. "But I do not wish to do that." I go to my writing desk. "I think I quite agree with you about the police force. They are rather a bumbling lot. They haven't caught me yet, despite the many deaths, the many letters and clues. I'm enjoying taunting them, but the game has grown tiresome and lackluster." I look back at her.

"I think you will help add to its enjoyment. Bringing your cousin into it will give me that pinch of thrill I've been lacking lately. Life is such a bother sometimes, you know, with businesses, societal rules, and the like. I have been getting a little bored. Hence, my trove of treasures."

Ophelia's eyes turn once more to my gallery of jars. Her trembling is increasing, and she's wrapping her arms about herself now. I smile.

"Again, do not worry. I will write to your cousin at once! And do take the shawl on the bed. You look a bit cold, my dear."

I sit with my pen to my lip. An old excitement begins to well up in me. Such fun! I might actually be sending a letter to someone with a scrap of intelligence. I will have to word it just perfectly, for I do not want her to spoil the game.

"Dearest Lady Anna Lovelace…"

I scribble down and read aloud. I glance over at Ophelia, whose watery eyes are watching me, and her lower lip is quivering. Hmm....she will soon begin to feel sick from the lack of her dangerous medicine. I shake my head in disappointment at her. What weak creatures women are...

CHAPTER

9

That evening, George sat with Jenny in a tiny, ill-lit pub. He looked around the room at the shine of the old wood of the walls and the rough look of the other customers. The pub was just barely above the line of respectability. He wished he could do more for Jenny, like buy her dinner at the fancy hotel in the main square, but these were difficult times for everyone, even thirty years after the war. He was better paid than a factory worker, yet he couldn't give Jenny all of the things he wished he could, and the worst part was, he knew she wished he could too.

They ate in relative silence, and George sipped his frothy ale. He could feel Jenny's eyes on him. He knew she did not approve of alcohol, having been brought up in a strict Quaker home, but he was allowed some indulgences. He convinced her that his work was hard enough to warrant such things. He glanced up at her, and her face suddenly colored with excitement, her dark eyes sparkling.

"Oh, I forgot to tell you, George. My father says we can be married as soon as we would like. He's found the money to pay for a reception party and the use of the meeting hall. There would be no alcohol, of course."

Her eyes swept to his pint glass, but he ignored her insinuation. He wiped his mouth with the napkin before he spoke.

Placing his hand atop hers, he said, "Well, that's great news, Jenny. But we've just gotten a new case of a disappearance at the station, and I need to finish that before I can be a proper husband. I fear even after we're married, I'd hardly be home during difficult cases. I hope you know that."

George felt an odd sense of relief at the fact that they couldn't marry right away. He could still focus on his work, and he wouldn't have to think about the wedding. Not just yet. He loved Jenny, and he knew that a proper life with a wife would suit him, but he didn't want it to be all settled for them just yet.

Jenny's face fell. "It's that society girl, Ophelia Marshall, right?"

George nodded. "How'd you know?"

He hoped Jenny hadn't been following the case in the newspaper as closely as that interfering woman Lady Anna Lovelace did. He clenched a fist on his lap. Why was he thinking of her now? Jenny didn't seem to notice his sudden irritation. She shrugged and pushed her food around on her plate.

"It's all over town. She often appears in the lady's magazines and society pages. Everyone always wants to see what she's wearing. There isn't enough to entertain us in this city, I suppose."

She sighed, and George felt the weight of her disappointment. However, he wasn't sure if her disappointment stemmed more from the delay of their wedding or the fact that she herself was not Ophelia Marshall.

"Yes, it's her, but you know I can't discuss details of cases."

Jenny lifted an eyebrow. "Not even with your future wife?"

George shook his head and took another sip, hating the way their conversation was going. There had been some small part of him that hoped Jenny would be proud that he'd been assigned to interview the Marshall and Lovelace family. It was an honor.

With a little ire, Jenny said, "She's the cousin of that English girl, Lady Anna Lovelace or some British title nonsense."

George nodded, annoyed at the image of a pair of bewitching green eyes that suddenly flashed across his brain.

"Did you speak to her? I hear she's rather strange," Jenny asked.

"Yes, I did. What do you mean, strange?"

I'm not sure if strange would be the word to describe Anna Lovelace. More like 'intriguing' or 'unusual', I think.

Jenny's disappointment was replaced by her excitement at the prospect of a bit of gossip.

"I hear that Lady Croft does not approve of her, and her mother is also disappointed in her. No man will take her for she is far too headstrong, and she has such manly pursuits."

George took another sip of his ale and tried not to let his curiosity show when he asked, "Manly pursuits?" He was glad that Ned was not there to poke fun at his sudden interest in female gossip, especially when it focused on a certain blonde-haired beauty.

Jenny smiled. "Yes, all the girls say that she's been unusually educated by her father, able to speak German, French, and Latin and is an avid reader. She often argues with people at social gatherings about politics and more. She is a bluestocking through and through. I think therein lies Lady Croft's disapproval of her."

"How do you know all this?"

George regretted his question as soon as he said it. Jenny was not poor, but her family was not of a high enough status to be invited to society gatherings such as the Croft ball where poor Miss Marshall had disappeared. It was always a source of anxiety and anger for her.

Jenny's lips tightened, and her shoulders straightened. "Despite the fact that I am not high society, George Ford, I do hear things. I do have some connections; I shall have you know."

She exhaled with frustration and looked away. He had upset her yet again. It seemed to be always like this. Especially lately, when his mind was so full of the killer's doings. He had the niggling thought that maybe she would want to be free of him, since he wasn't of as high a status as she wanted. He was a policeman, but he came from a lowly background, and she was always trying to elevate her station. It was almost a strange thing that she had even agreed to be courted by him in the first place. However, he couldn't think of it now. There was the new information about Lady Anna to think about.

Anna.

With the name came a sharp, vivid image of her, even stronger than the one before, leaning against the mantle in her home, defying him with her strong look. So, she defied societal norms. That seemed to fit his impression of her, so strong-willed, nearing on rudeness. It went against everything a young lady should be. He would normally have recoiled in disgust, but those eyes, those lips.

Lady Anna Lovelace was a beauty, even if she seemed to care nothing about what others thought of her. This enraged him. He was meant to be caring about Jenny's opinion and working towards making her life more comfortable and easier, preparing for their upcoming nuptials, not spending time thinking about another woman.

"George?" Jenny called to him, trying to get his attention.

Her arms were crossed now, and he realized he hadn't responded to her angry tirade.

"Ah, I'm sorry, Jenny." George rubbed the back of his neck in discomfort. Jenny's dark eyes narrowed. "It's just this case. It has me distracted."

Jenny frowned. "Well, I suggest, George, that you take some time to think about when you would like to get married to me as well. I want to be a wife, not just a girl who sits and eats with her beau in darkened pubs for the rest of her life."

She stood, even though George was not yet done, and the gentleman in him forced him to rise as well. A few stray eyes moved in their direction, and he wanted to avoid any sort of embarrassment.

"You're going?" he asked innocently, even though he knew very well that he was at fault.

Jenny sighed. "Yes, please take me home, George. I had hoped to eat my evening meal with someone whose attention was focused on me, but alas, that is not to be."

She placed her gloves on and donned her cloak without George's assistance. George felt sorry, but what was he to do? This was not a good time for conversations of love or marriage. He had a case to solve, and he wanted, no *needed*, to be the one to do it.

He spoke to the bartender, letting him know he'd be back to pay the bill. Arm in arm on the dark streets, George and Jenny could feel a biting wind beginning to lift. The lamplighter had lit the lamps nearby, but they could still see his stilted form in the distance continuing his duty.

"George, when do you think you'll be made police sergeant? Or even detective?" Jenny asked idly as they walked slowly back to her parent's modest home on Plum Street.

George felt the weight of her words. "Detective is what I'd like to be one day, but that could take years. Years of solving cases, years of hard work, Jenny. Why?"

"Just wondering. If you become a detective, we could surely move to a large home on Orange Street, don't you think?" Her expression was excited, her mind full of plans.

"I don't know..." George trailed off, and he wished that they were already at her parent's house, and he could let go of her arm and go back to the pub for another drink, left to his own thoughts. They walked the rest of the way in silence. He was becoming increasingly inepter at dealing with his fiancé, it seemed. Once she was at her door, he kissed her on the cheek.

"Good night, George," she said stiffly.

A stray lock of her brown hair had fallen to brush her cheek. In months gone by, he would have been eager to push it away, thrilled to get a chance to touch her, but instead, he stayed his hand. The tension was high between them, and he could never seem to lessen it, especially lately.

"Give my regards to your parents. I will call again soon."

"See you."

Once Jenny was gone up the stairs, George felt lighter. He walked briskly back to the pub and ordered another drink to sip alone and as slowly as he pleased. There was no news yet that they'd recovered a body, so there was a glimmer of hope that Miss Marshall had simply run off to marry her lover. The only problem was, there were nearly thirty men whose names started with D who worked at the police station, and he had no idea where to begin finding out which one was Ophelia Marshall's lover.

***

After a solemn dinner with her parents and Ophelia's, Anna left for the quiet of her own room. At dinner, no one had much of an appetite, and they ate mostly in silence, but her mother felt that it was an important ritual to uphold. She did not want the servants running about town letting everyone know that the Lovelace and Marshall family were too weak to eat their suppers.

At dinner, the only words that were spoken were about the failure of her father and Uncle Jack to find out any information at the Crofts.

"Nothing, nothing," Uncle Jack said angrily, clutching his wine glass so tightly, Anna feared he might break it.

She didn't even want to think about the pain her uncle was experiencing at the moment, at the loss of his dear daughter. At the sight of his face, Anna's tears were desperate to come, pressing behind her eyes, but she kept them back, trying to remain strong for her family.

Her father shook his head. He looked worn out as he said, "The servants didn't see anything, apparently. No one seems to know how that note for Ophelia arrived at the ball. It was simply on a hall table, and the servant brought it for Miss Marshall. And I can tell you, the Crofts were none too pleased with us questioning their staff."

"I don't give a damn, Ed," Jack replied gruffly, slamming a hand on the table. "I want my daughter back, and it was at their house that this happened."

After that, the group remained silent, unsure of how to respond. Everyone had retired early, her mother clutching her aunt's arm to bring her up to the guest room. Her uncle had left to return to his own home, leaving his wife to her sister's care. Anna was certain that most of them would not be sleeping that night. They would be anxiously awaiting the senior police officer's new information, hoping that with a new day, new clues or positive outcomes would arrive.

Anna was glad that she had business to do that evening, so that she would not have to suffer through the night, attempting to sleep while thoughts of Ophelia's pain and suffering filled her mind. If Anna even tried, she knew that her eyes would remain open all night, staring into the darkness, and there would have been no point at all in laying down on her bed.

She waited and waited. Once the clock downstairs struck the midnight hour, she felt it was safe enough to quietly descend the stairwell with a long, black cloak on, grasping tightly to the scrap of paper with the scribbled address. She had memorized it, but she held it like a physical reminder of her duty and her goal. Closing the door behind her, she hoped that none of the servants would be awakened by her movements and question her.

Once she was out on the street, she let out the breath she'd been holding. She placed the hood of the cloak on her head and walked on. The gas lamps were lit, and she hoped they would stay on for the duration of her journey. She wasn't sure if they had gas lamps on S. Shippen Street, or even if they would last the night, for she had never had any reason before to be out that late. The thought of cold, darkened streets made her shiver with fear, but she set her teeth and continued forward. S. Shippen Street was not far, but she had never been there, having been told that south of Orange was not an area for well-bred young ladies.

It was a haven for the poor, such as factory workers and people in service. Anna had never had much experience with poor people; her parents would have never allowed it. So, she felt a slight sense of independence and rebellion as she headed south, squinting at the street signs, hoping that she was on the right path. Not only was this her chance to try to save Ophelia, but it was also her chance to try to see a little bit more of the wide world. She had felt a childish thrill as she studied a map of the city before leaving the house, having found it in the library, knowing her mother would most certainly not have approved.

It took about 15 minutes of quick walking for her to find the entrance to the street. She had not seen many people along the way. There were a few policemen wandering on street corners, and a few other cloaked figures, but she was glad she was not spoken to or acknowledged in any way. As she peered down her desired street, she wrapped her cloak more tightly around her. Shippen Street seemed darker and eerier than any of the others she had passed through on her way. With slight trepidation, she passed the hollow shell of the darkened building at the corner and proceeded.

There was still no one about, and her surroundings sent a prickle of fear down her spine. There weren't as many gas lamps compared to Duke Street, and so the shadows that were there were long, adding to the street's eeriness.

"So, we must keep the poor in the dark and add to their wretchedness?" Anna whispered as she crept along.

Her mother would have disapproved vehemently to such a commiserative statement about the poor, but Anna felt like in the air around Shippen Street, it was safe to say such things. It would agree with her. She was no longer on her side of the world anyway.

In the dim light, it was hard to discern house numbers, and she wondered regretfully why she had chosen midnight, for surely the occupant entitled D would also be lying abed at such a late hour. Given there was no other time that it would be acceptable for a woman like her to be seen on this road, midnight would have to do.

She spotted the house she was searching for at long last, just at the bend in the road, and because a piece of the number two was missing on the door, she had passed it a few times already. The house was narrow but made up for it with its height, appearing to have three floors. She hesitated about walking towards the front door, since she was certain that she would wake the others who slept inside with her knock.

Staring at the house's tattered siding, crooked porch, and thin curtains, of which she could see but little, Anna both hated her money yet knew that she must be grateful for what she had. What a horrid life it would be to live in this hovel at the end of an unknown street, trapped in darkness. She lingered at the base of the stairs for a moment.

"You can do this, Anna. Just a bit of courage," she reminded herself under her breath.

But just as she was resolved to walk up the steps and knock on the door, she heard the clearing of a throat behind her.

CHAPTER

10

A few minutes earlier, George lit a cigarette and leaned against the shadowy outline of the Eastern Market building, shut up and ghostly in its nightly repose. The embers flashed brightly in comparison to the dim lighting of Shippen Street which lay just to his left. He'd returned to work after the pub, itching to forget Jenny's displeasure and to keep working on the case. He was fearful that his sergeant would soon replace him for one of the active detectives if he didn't solve this thing and solve it fast.

While he was making his inquiries at the Lovelace's home, the sergeant had sent officers to the scene of Miss Marshall's disappearance. When George had returned to the station after the pub, he'd been told they had found no leads at St. James Cemetery. And earlier that day when he'd spoken to Lord and Lady Croft, he and Ned had also come up empty-handed. With this news weighing on him, he had unintentionally wandered off into the less-lit areas of town.

He wanted to wander about until something would make sense. The other officers, including Officer Barnum, had gone home hours ago, and he could imagine Ned's chastisement if he found out that George had not gone home to rest but had begun to walk the Lancaster streets aimlessly. As he pulled on his cigarette, he thought about what the officers who'd visited the cemetery had said. There was no body, no blood, except for one tiny spot of blood towards the entrance of the cemetery, along with a bit of cigar ash.

That could have been from any of the visitors to the graveyard in recent days. Or it could have been recent, seeing as the ashes weren't blown away by the breeze yet, but that still tells me nothing.

Normally at these recent grisly scenes, there would not be much blood. The killer's usual habit appeared to be that he took the ladies to his abode to do the deed before replacing them in graceful display.

Why does no one ever see him? How could he pass through the city and do "his sacred calling" as he put it without anyone knowing? Are we all so blind to the activities of others?

George was tired, and he took of his cap and mussed up his dark brown hair in an act of frustration before gently pushing it back again under his hat. He exhaled, and the light wisp of smoke moved away from him, disappearing just as George reached out his hand to intertwine his fingers with it. It felt just like the very man they were intent upon catching. He smiled morbidly. Smoke or mist was just how the killer had described himself in his letter to the newspaper. He couldn't quite remember which it was. The fatigue was getting to him, and he grumbled with frustration.

Will the man never be caught?

George suddenly felt the weight of a city on him. It was his job now to pursue this killer and eventually find him and make him pay for his deeds. Before he'd left the station that evening, he'd spoken to his sergeant about allowing him to take control of this case. Sergeant Donaldson had hesitated, but since the other detective was currently too ill to work after spending countless hours hunting this same killer down in the past months, he'd agreed.

"You've done well lately, Ford. But don't let it get to your head. Not yet at least."

George was delighted, but now he knew that everyone, especially the upper crust, expected him to bring the man to justice and remove him from their perfect, spotless society. He realized grimly that of course they would want the mystery solved if it involved one of the higher classes. They couldn't bear the thought of one of their own being taken away and so cruelly.

He heard a sound coming from down at the bend of the street, which broke his reverie. He straightened and squinted into the darkness. A dark figure was standing in the street, staring up at a house. Due to the smaller stature, he assumed it was a woman. He also assumed at first that she was going home, but the way she had paused and looked up made it seem as though she was waiting for a clandestine meeting with someone. To see a woman out so late at night was suggestive of something either sinister or salacious.

Curious, he slowly wandered towards her, if even for a bit of interaction before he returned home to think about the case as he lay in bed. The closer he got, the more he became intrigued by the figure. She still had not moved from her spot, and she didn't seem to notice his presence either. That meant this person was either used to the street and unconcerned with its passersby, which was unlikely, or they were a stranger to the area.

As he moved up behind the still form, he heard her mutter something to herself. He cleared his throat to get her attention. The woman gasped and turned around to look him full in the face.

"Lady Lovelace," he uttered with surprise as his mind registered those fierce green eyes and all-too-lovely features in the light of the closest gas-lamp.

He dropped his cigarette and stamped it into the ground, glad to have an excuse to tear his eyes away from her for a moment. Her presence unnerved him, and since he never expected to see her there of all places, he'd had no time to prepare.

His expression was grim when he looked back up at her. "What in the world are you doing out here? And talking to yourself, I might add?"

He was surprised at the sharp edge to his tone, and he moved his hand to the back of his neck, suddenly a little embarrassed. Anna looked shocked for an instant, but then her calm expression returned.

"Officer Ford," she breathed quietly into the night. She crossed her arms and eyed him suspiciously. "I could very well ask you the same question, well except for the talking to yourself part."

George chuckled grimly. "Refusing to answer a police officer's questions? That could be deemed an offense, My Lady."

To his continued irritation, he could have sworn he saw one corner of her mouth turn up in a smug smirk. He was about to speak again, but then Anna shushed him. He was incredulous. How dare a woman have the gall to do such a thing to a man, and a police officer no less?!

"My Lady, I am a police officer, how dare---" but he was cut off by her hand on his arm, and a pleading look in her eyes. He breathed in, surprised by the feeling of calm that came over him at her touch.

She stepped ever so slightly closer and removed her hood from her head. George smelled the faint scent of flowers, but of which variety he couldn't identify.

"Officer Ford. Please listen," she begged. "I'm here for the sake of my cousin. Look at this."

She shoved a paper into his hand, and he looked down at a scribbled address.

"What's this?" he whispered back.

"I found it in Ophelia's bedroom. Remember, I told you she was to meet a man the evening of the ball. She told me he was her betrothed and referred to him as 'D'."

He sighed. "Well, I don't remember you officially telling me that they were engaged. I don't appreciate you keeping that part from me. But as for this D. My Lady, I've checked in the police force listings for the whole of Lancaster City. There are about thirty men with Ds to start their names, both first and last. It will take time if I must question each and every one of them. One doesn't go around questioning police officers. I don't yet have the jurisdiction for that kind of thing, anyway. At least I don't think so. I'm only filling in for the time being while my colleague is ill. And it doesn't seem like the right course to me anyway. It could be a huge waste of time."

Anna shrunk back slightly at the news. "I see. What was Ophelia thinking of? Perhaps this man had deceived her as to his occupation? Well, he did only say that he was somehow connected to the police, not that he was an officer himself. I searched in her address book for any mention of him, and all I found was the letter D with this address. I came myself to inquire about my cousin."

Suddenly, George felt protective, and he reached out a hand to clutch her elbow as if she was in the middle of running right up to the darkened doorway.

"Are you mad, woman? You can't simply wander the streets at midnight by yourself visiting random people in the dark. Especially not men. You don't know what happens along lonely streets such as this."

Anna stared back at him boldly. "Officers clutching onto women and scolding them with frightful looks?" George sputtered in response but couldn't think of anything clever to say. She chuckled. "I have an idea of what goes on, Officer Ford. But I would risk anything to find the truth about my cousin's whereabouts. I wouldn't want the police department to *lose their heads* and suddenly forget to look for her."

She lifted an eyebrow, daring him to reply. George was angry at having his words spat back at him once again.

He leaned a little closer to her and whispered gruffly, "You don't trust the police department? We can handle this matter for we have the power and training to do so. We don't need others to intrude, especially not a Lady with a fancy title who is not even American! I'll put everything into finding this killer of women who roams our streets. I can guarantee you that."

Anna smirked. "So, you do believe that it could be the killer from the newspaper whose chilling words continue to ring in our ears? The one you told me not to worry my pretty head about?" She laughed, a clear, lovely sound that surprised him.

"I didn't say you were pretty," George replied without thinking and then was stuck in her gaze.

He hadn't realized how close to her he'd gotten. His hand was still on her elbow, not grasping her but merely touching, the warmth of her skin emanating from inside her cloak. As he looked into her laughing green eyes, he felt a strange desire he had not felt in a very long time. The feeling overtook him, and for a moment, he thought of how her laugh made him feel somehow like he was something special. Yet her wit reduced him to nothing. The tiredness from the day really was getting to him. He felt almost like he was in a dream. Then he realized the words he had just uttered. He pulled away quickly.

"Forgive me, My Lady. I didn't mean to be forward or crass. I'm just not used to a woman becoming involved in police matters and being so *forceful.*"

Anna kept her eyes on him as he looked down and pulled on the lapels of his coat trying to set himself to rights. When he looked up, he could see the shadow of a satisfied smile on her face.

"Nothing to forgive, Officer."

He cleared his throat again. "So, let's approach D together then. But I'll do the talking."

I have to regain some ground, don't I, after that idiotic display?

Anna nodded. "Agreed. Far be it from me to argue with an officer of the law."

George made a scoffing sound in his throat that almost turned into a laugh.

Damn this woman.

She argued with him at every turn, and with each moment that passed in her company, he found her even more interesting, and he hated to admit, desirable. What was going on with him? He walked up the steps towards number 42 and knocked on the door. While he waited for a response, he turned around to see Anna shivering behind him.

"You should have worn more than a cloak, My Lady."

"As you have probably guessed, I don't have much experience frequenting darkened streets at night. In future nighttime ramblings, I will take your advice." Her tone practically dripped with sarcasm.

He was about to let her know that she should not in future do any other ramblings of the sort, but a man answered the door and prevented him. The man was tall, older, with greasy dark hair and a misshapen beard that covered his face in patches. He reeked of sweet smoke and gin, and George had to keep from heaving at the scent of him. He'd smelled such things many times before, but it all seemed so strange, especially since a very well-smelling proper lady was standing only just behind him.

Resuming his police stolidity, George said, "Sorry for the hour, but I'm Officer Ford with the Lancaster City Police Department. We want to ask you a few questions, Mr. ...?" He held out his badge to be appraised.

George's voice trailed off, but the stranger did not seem eager to fill in his missing moniker. The man leaned against the door jamb and crossed his arms. "Aye? But the lot down this way donnae take kindly tae officers intrudin' upon their personal freedoms at such an hour. If ever."

George lifted an eyebrow at the man's insolence. "Well, since there are women's lifeless bodies being discovered on the streets of our fair city, and they're not just the bodies of women from the higher class and are from everywhere, we thought we might come and take a look at the 'lot down this way.' We're here to ask about the latest disappearance."

George surprised himself at his easy use of the word 'we're', but he didn't want to take the time to turn to see another satisfied smile on Lady Anna's face. The man harrumphed, and to George's chagrin, Anna stepped forward, her eyes wide.

"Sir, I am Lady Anna Lovelace. It's my cousin Ophelia Marshall who has disappeared, and I found this address in her address book. She said she was meant to meet someone named D. Are you D? And do you know my cousin, perhaps?"

George watched with scrutiny as the man's expression changed from one emotion to the next at the sight of Anna, her face lit by the candlelight from the grubby hallway behind him. George clutched onto Anna's elbow again to keep her from going forward even more. She looked at him with frustration, but she didn't move.

The disheveled man fumbled in his pockets and found a cigarette. He lit it, keeping his eyes on Anna. George was losing patience, but he didn't feel he could be forceful with Anna there, in case things got ugly. The man took a deep puff of the cigarette and blew upwards out into the street saying,

"Yer a bonny lass, are ye nae? Ye donnae look like ye live on this street. I would have remembered ye." George watched with disgust as the man's eyes searched Anna's frame, sliding over her body as if he was going to eat it.

George had had enough. He wasn't used to such patience, but he had hoped to conduct the interview with a bit of decorum since a lady was present.

Never mind that now.

He grabbed a handful of the man's dirty jacket, and the man nearly dropped his cigarette in the process.

George said, "Just answer the question. There's no time to be looking the woman up and down as though she was here for your entertainment."

His voice was gruff and menacing. Their noses were practically touching, and the man's odor became overwhelming. It was a mixture of gin and some kind of sweet, cloying smoke. George let his coat go, and the man returned to his casual leaning posture against the doorframe, as if nothing had happened. He took another calm puff.

"Aye, I know her. She comes here sometimes tae meet with someone. And I am nae telling' ye who! Get paid too well for that!" His anger suddenly rose, but he calmed soon after, brushing ash from one of the lapels of his dirty coat, as if it could have made the jacket appear any cleaner. He glanced at Anna. "Aye, me name begins with D, so I suppose ye could call me that, lass, if ye like. But it's a common enough letter."

Anna pushed towards the man again, but her movement forward was impeded by George's arm. She looked at the supposed D with confusion. "Are you betrothed to my cousin?"

The man smiled, and George recoiled at the sight of multiple black and yellow teeth when D grinned. "Betrothed tae that beauty? Nae a chance. I donnae ken of any betrothal, but I do know she was hangin' around with David F. He runs the place."

"David F?" George looked at the man, his patience wearing impossibly thin. However, he was relieved that D had forgotten his earlier promise not to tell them who Ophelia had been meeting with. He thanked the potential consumption of too much gin for that.

Another mystery name to solve.

Anna was silent as she took in his words.

"David F. Is he an officer?"

The disheveled man burst into throaty laughter. "If so, he's been doin' a poor job at it." He began to pull at something on the tip of his tongue. "Havenae seen the man in a couple days, though. Nor the lass. I'm sure he'll be back soon enough. He doesnae come every day, after all."

Anna moved closer to D. George was amazed that she seemed oblivious to the man's overwhelming scent, despite her rather comfortable upbringing.

Her voice was pleading as she said, "Sir, just tell me. Do you have any idea where my cousin has gone?"

D looked down at Anna's eager expression and chuckled. "They all go at some point, and then they drag themselves back. Thought I'd see her last night, thought I'd see the both of them. It was their usual day tae meet. Besides, it's the way of things in this business. We willnae ever run out of customers." He shrugged as he blew out a large puff of smoke. "Donnae touch the stuff meself, but these folks cannae get enough of it."

He hooked a thumb in the hallway behind him. George and Anna looked at each other with confusion, and when they did so, D took the opportunity to shut the door in their faces without another word. With speed, George slammed up against it, shocked that the man would do something so bold, with the police on his front stoop. And if he was going to admit it, he hated that he'd been defeated in front of Lady Anna.

"D, you have the answer, we know it! If you won't talk to us now, we'll be back again!"

Lights began to flicker into life around them in various dirt-covered windows along the street, and he looked back at Anna, who looked smaller somehow. All her former ire and confidence was gone.

In a quiet voice, she said, "Come, Officer Ford. We wouldn't want anyone to find me out here or bring anyone out on the street. I wish to return home."

He nodded and reluctantly pulled away from the door, his heart clenching at the sight of a dejected Lady Anna.

PART II

CHAPTER

11

Anna had been so hopeful when the man said he knew Ophelia. But he had spoken in riddles in his Scottish burr and being that he was more focused on keeping himself out of trouble, he hadn't really told them anything. He'd even added one more mysterious name to her list. Her heart had lifted and then crashed to the ground. They had been so close to getting information, but then D had shut the door on them, and she had felt like something snapped inside of her.

She had left her house that evening so hopeful, so full of confidence that this was going to lead somewhere. But their one tether to information was now cut off, and she was stuck in the increasingly cold night with insolent and haughty George Ford who would rather she never have come out at all.

What other choice did I have? The police would never have known about this place if I hadn't come. Why was Officer Ford out here anyway?

They walked slowly towards Duke Street. Once she'd convinced him to pull away from plastering himself against the old man's grimy wooden door, he'd said in a low voice, "I'll walk you home."

She wanted to protest, but she knew she shouldn't argue. George Ford was apparently moody, similar to a crotchety old man, which was at odds with his youthful features. They were practically the same age, she guessed. He seemed to get angry the most when she would try to interfere or question his ideas, and she was certain it made it worse that she was a woman.

Anna was too tired to argue anyway, and if she had to admit it, she was grateful for a policeman's company as she walked back home in the hazy darkness of the city. She tried to tell herself that her appreciation for the company had nothing to do with the fact that George Ford was a very handsome man. Despite his rudeness, he was becoming even more handsome and somehow likable the more time she was with him, even though they'd only met but twice now.

He was all bluster, until he wasn't, and then he was as soft as a kitten. One moment he was holding a criminal up against the wall by the scruff of his collar and then the next minute, he was watching her kindly and telling her that he would accompany her home.

At D's doorway, his hand on her elbow had been firm, but gentle, and it ignited something in her that only confused and added to her current distress. Those hazel eyes of his. They were inscrutable. Full of anger and bitterness but also intelligent with a bit of loving warmth. It made her brain fuzzy, and that was the last thing she needed as she tried to search for her poor cousin. She would need all the clarity and strength that she could muster, and George Ford was standing in her way.

Men. They are always trying to charm! I must not fall prey to it.

She purposefully ignored the fact that Mr. Ford had not once done anything in an attempt to charm her. She suddenly felt her anger rise at the direction of her thoughts, and she crossed her arms around herself to bring her cloak a little tighter. She needed to speak, to change the subject that was swirling dangerously around her mind.

"Now, were you doing out at Shippen Street, yourself, Officer Ford? If you hadn't come and intervened, I might've learned the information I needed. The man was unwilling to talk to the police, and I don't blame him."

She let her words fall, hoping they would have her desired effect. She didn't look at him but kept her eyes forward as they walked towards the better-lit areas of the city. Even with him by her side now, Lancaster City looked like a haunting skeleton, the dark roads like yawning caverns.

George took off his cap, placed it under his arm, and pushed his dark hair back with one hand. Anna could see his movement out of the corner of her eye, but she refused to turn and look at him, no matter that the personal, intimate motion made her insides feel strangely warm. It also made him seem more human somehow. More understanding.

He sighed, and when he spoke, he sounded resigned. "I was walking around the city, smoking and thinking about the case. I'd been to the pub, and I was not yet ready to go home. Or else I would be lying in bed awake, thinking about it. Then, I saw you. You should be thanking me that I was there to help you. Who knows what that man would have done to you had I not been there? You saw the way he looked at you."

His face was turned towards her, and so she turned to him and stopped her gait. There was no one on the dark streets around them. Their only company was the slight whistling of the cool night wind as it whipped around the stone buildings. They were nearing the wealthier part of town, but right then they stood in a sort of no man's land. She took a deep breath and stared back at him.

My goodness, he is handsome.

The thought came to her unbidden, and she felt even more furious. He was even more handsome than Mr. Mason, but Mr. Mason had not made her feel as though she needed to put her hand up against the wall for support. She shook herself out of her foolish, frivolous thoughts and tried to appear stern.

"I don't know what would have happened, but I might have the answer to why my cousin frequents that establishment and who in the blazes David F. is! Since you are the wise police officer, and have ruined any sort of chance we had, what do you think it all means, then?"

George glowered and thrust his hands into his coat pockets, his cap bulging out from under his arm. Anna could tell he was angry. He moved ever so slightly closer. "Lady Lovelace, I do not know whether to throttle you or to…"

He didn't finish the sentence, and Anna replied defiantly, "What? You would rather have only the throttling option, then?"

Normally she would never have been this bold, but something about George brought out this new anger in her. She didn't seem to care if she was being appropriate or not, not that she ever did really. Despite how infuriating the man was, she also felt safe with him. She was able to make a statement about throttling because she would never believe in a thousand years that he would do such a thing.

All bluster.

He grunted. "Perhaps. I've been assigned to do this investigation, so yes, I should've been there. You could've just given the address to the police, and we would've handled it. I didn't feel as though I was able to use as much force since you were there. Wouldn't want to show any brutality in front of a fine lady."

He looked her up and down, and Anna could see the movement of his eyes in the moonlight. Compared to D's greasy, appreciative gaze, George's sarcastic assessment of her made her tingle pleasantly, and she was worried for a surprising moment that he would find her somewhat wanting.

She again did her best to push thoughts of that nature aside. "Don't be ridiculous! Despite your thoughts about women, I am not so weak that I can't handle an investigation as it attempts to find out the truth about my cousin and all these women who are suffering at the hands of this killer! So, again, what do you think it all means?"

His mouth turned to a thin line. "I think that we should continue walking to your home, and that I shouldn't be discussing case details with a member of the public who doesn't work for the police department - and is a woman!"

Anna was on the verge of flying into a violent rage. Not even her mother's diatribes on decorum made her as angry as this.

Men are all the same, aren't they? Trying to belittle us with the hated reminder of the 'weaknesses of our gender!

She was sure that Mr. Mason with all his charming manners would feel as George would feel, along with other men of her acquaintance. Well, her father was not the same as all men, as he had given her so many opportunities, but she was sure he would still disapprove of her desire to act as detective for her cousin's case.

"Ah, that tired belief that women are useless. I think you use it because you're afraid of what I might do."

"Of course!" George threw up his arms and began walking away. She hurried after him. He was her escort after all. He continued in a harsh whisper, "It's a concern because you women just do whatever it is that pops into your mind without thought! I am worried that you might get yourself injured, kidnapped, or even killed as you progress in your so-called investigation!"

"Ha! You pretend you care for my well-being, do you?" She was now just trying to rile him up. She wasn't sure why, but it gave her much satisfaction, even if some of his words stung. Never before had she had an argument like this with a man. It felt so freeing. Since they were alone out of the eyesight of the public, she felt like she could say anything she wished.

George snorted. "Don't flatter yourself, *My Lady*. Another fault of your sex, I might add. If any of those things happen to you, then it's me that's stuck with all the paperwork!" He grinned at her, and she grimaced.

"Fine then. So, I'm assuming you have no ideas at all about David F, and you're using the fact that I am a woman to weasel out of telling me?"

He sighed and walked in silence for a few moments, his moment of bluster seeming to have passed. "I have my ideas, but I'm afraid that it wouldn't be decent."

Anna pulled on his arm to spin him towards her again. It was the third time she'd touched him during their acquaintance. Her mother would have been horrified at such wanton behavior. She noticed him glance down again at her hand before bringing his eyes up to hers. In a brief moment of embarrassment, she pulled away.

"Haven't we been through this? Clearly, I'm willing to do practically anything to get my cousin back. Tell me your thoughts."

He rubbed the back of his neck as he looked at his feet. "I have seen the likes of it before and heard of it myself from other officers from different cities." He took a breath. "Lady Anna, I believe it to be an opium den, and as this D told us, David F. is the owner."

For what seemed like the thousandth time that night, Anna was bowled over with surprise.

***

George now couldn't wait to get home to slide into his warm bed. He realized his own folly of wandering around at night, but how could he have known he would bump into none other than Lady Anna Lovelace and get into a mess of trouble? She was becoming more impertinent the more they discussed the case. He couldn't wait to drop her off at her house and never see her again.

He knew his hope wouldn't be possible. The vision of her angry face in the moonlight as they argued would be imprinted on his memory. Besides, he was sure she would emerge again one way or another. She wasn't like other women, and it confused him. Jenny, he could understand despite all their disagreements, but Anna made no sense to him whatsoever, and she seemed to enjoy that fact. It was almost as if her impertinence was on purpose for her own entertainment.

She was passionate, foolhardy, headstrong, nothing like what he had been taught to expect in a woman's behavior. He thought them all to be docile and pliable. He hadn't ever known his mother, but his other female relatives had been that way. Here he was in the middle of the night walking her back to her home after both rebuking and being rebuked by her.

He hadn't expected to see her again until the resolution of the case, when he would have had to deliver the sorry news of her cousin's death, once the body made its way to some public setting. He did have a strong feeling that Ophelia was going to be another of the killer's victims, and it was just a matter of time.

But totally unexpectedly, he found Anna out here in the night with him, and her presence was surprisingly like a warm, pulsating light that emanated energy, freshness, and attraction. In the heat of their argument, George realized that what his fellow officer Ned Barnum had told him that afternoon had been right.

While it irked him to be spoken to in such a way by a strange woman, he rather enjoyed the feistiness of it. It certainly made her interesting and jolted him out of recent malaise. Once he went home, he knew he wouldn't be able to keep her words from his mind. He would never admit that to anyone and definitely not to Ned.

Ned would laugh me from one end of the city to the other.

Now he was looking down at Anna's surprised and saddened face. Her reaction to his ideas about the opium den made him feel like he'd just punched her in the gut, and that made him queasy.

She was thrown off-kilter for a moment but then replied, "But that can't be. How could my cousin be involved with opium and a man who owned such an establishment? I feel like I would've known. Someone must have seen her as well. And why would she tell me that she was about to get married? It doesn't make any sense! Could she really desire to marry the owner of an opium den?"

She was looking down at the street. They had stopped walking. George didn't know what to say, but he wasn't sure if Anna was even looking for him to answer her questions. He wished he could yell at her again, but seeing her like this, so shrunken by shock, he held his tongue.

"Maybe she didn't know that he actually owned it, more that he assisted in its ventures. She did think he was a police officer or with the police. Well, that's what she told me, at least. I did find letters from him in her room, a whole stack of them kept underneath her pillow. When I first found them, I was reluctant to read them."

"Well, have you read them since then?" George asked quickly, forgetting his sensitivity.

"No. I promised myself that I wouldn't read them unless I couldn't find D. Since I couldn't find the D that was her lover, whom I suppose is David F., I shall read them once I return home. I'll let you know if they say anything related to the case."

George clenched his jaw. Normally, he would have yelled outright, demanding the evidence, but her sorrowful expression still continued to quell his ire. Instead, he said, "Please give them to me too. Once you're done. They are police evidence now."

Anna nodded. Their interaction had now become so formal.

George said, "All right, Lady Lovelace. We're almost at your door. We don't need to discuss this any longer, especially not out in the cold."

He stopped himself from reaching for her again, and he put his hands back in his pockets with the embarrassing realization that he had never touched a woman so much in one evening. It was growing untoward, and he hoped Lady Anna wouldn't think anything of it or mention it to anyone.

Although, on her part, she had touched him many times as well, and each time he had to squelch the surprising heat that rose inside of him at the contact. Even with Jenny, they refrained from touching each other in public, as was proper. However, even in private, Jenny's touch didn't thrill him like Lady Anna's did. He pushed that thought down as soon as it arose, knowing it would lead him down a dangerous road.

To his surprise, she said, "Yes. I'm too tired to continue thinking about this tonight. It might become clear in the morning. I hope that there will still be time left to think of what to do next." George looked up to the sky and could see faint streaks of dawn threatening to appear.

Having nothing else to say, he said, "Morning will soon be here."

They strolled in silence for a few minutes until they stood before her shadowed doorway. Anna began up the steps, clutching her skirt and cloak in her hands. She paused and turned back to him. His eyes were on her, watching her slow ascent.

"Good night, Officer Ford. And thank you."

George cleared his throat, surprised by Anna's soft tone. "Good night, My Lady. You're welcome." Anna smiled, eyeing him for a moment longer before turning inside.

He exhaled once she closed the door and felt like he could finally breathe deeply again. What did that smile mean? If she expected him to say thank you to her in return, then she was sorely mistaken. With his eye on the impending dawn, George Ford stalked home, growing desperate for the warm space of his bed and a moment's peace away from a pair of bright, fierce green eyes.

CHAPTER

12

The next morning, Anna woke at her usual time, even though she had gotten in so late. She knew that if she did not, her mother would surely come and pound on her door until she crawled out of bed, admonishing her for one reason or another. Besides, her sleep had not been restful anyway, and she was looking forward to having a day to think about her plans for what to do next.

Norma helped her with her corset, and while she yanked tightly, Anna's thoughts were filled with Ophelia and opium. Had there been any clue to her cousin's problem? She still could not believe it.

Perhaps Officer Ford was wrong, and Ophelia was only there to meet this David F. as a lover?

She clung to that hope as her green gown was slipped over her head and tied and adjusted. Norma prepared her hair for the day, but eventually, Anna was left alone in the room, steeling herself for what lay ahead at the breakfast table.

Downstairs, her father was reading the morning newspaper, leaving out the already read sections next to him, so that she might avail herself of them. Her mother sat nervously next to him, tightly clutching a cup of tea as if it might try to escape. Her eyes were red-rimmed, but her appearance was immaculate as usual, not a hair out of place.

"Good morning," Anna said to the two of them, and they responded in kind in hushed tones.

She sat down, collecting the pages in front of her, hoping something might spark her inspiration. She found the article about Ophelia and her eyes moved quickly over the words, desperate to read more and find out some clue.

Disappearance of Wealthy Socialite Ophelia Marshall

It contained nothing more than conjecture and bloated suppositions. Of course, it would be the exciting occurrence in the city at the moment. Ever since the Lancaster "Ripper" had come to call, many of the denizens were thrilled that it would put their tiny town on the map. Anna had very much been one of them, she admitted to herself, and she could understand everyone's interest, yet now, she was sickened by its attachment to herself.

Despite its ridiculous claims, Anna read the article and smoothed the wrinkles out of the page. She looked up at her mother to find her still clutching her teacup.

"I wish you would not read such rubbish, Anna. It does nothing to help bring Ophelia back." Her voice cracked, and her eyes became watery. "Nor does it help shape and improve the delicate mind of a young woman. A young woman who must soon put her mind to matrimony."

Anna did not reply and felt that she shouldn't argue in the face of her mother's distress. Her father folded his newspaper and placed a hand on his wife's. "Dear Regina, do not distress yourself. The police will find her. I am sure of it."

Her mother released her teacup at long last and dabbed at her eyes with a handkerchief. "Yes, of course, we must trust in the authorities. Perhaps Ophelia was simply doing as she told Anna she would do, going to marry that commoner and leaving her family behind to deal with the consequences. I cannot believe that I am saying I would prefer that outcome."

Her mother's words began with grief and ended in disgust. Anna sighed. Her mother was a born and bred aristocrat. There would be no changing her low opinion of the huddled masses who filled her father's and uncle's mill despite her recent fall from society in London.

"Mother, all will be well. Ophelia is smart. Once she hears of her family's distress, she will return."

Anna glanced at her father in whose eyes she saw a little gratitude. She did not believe the words herself, but even so, they helped to ease her own worries somewhat. They gave her a flicker of hope that things would turn out well.

But on the other hand, her fear was growing as the minutes ticked by. Last night, George gave away his concern that it was this "Ripper" who had taken Ophelia. If that was the case, what hope did they have of ever seeing Ophelia again? This thought thundered down upon her, and Anna felt her chest tighten and a pressure build behind her eyes.

No, she would not cry. She could not. She would not be a woman like her mother, too busy with grief and prejudice to find a way to fight back and think about solutions. She wanted to approach this situation with logic and knowledge and not let emotion cloud her judgment. She didn't know yet what she was to do, but she knew that neither her mother nor George Ford would like it. That made her smirk. The thought of George puffing himself up again as he tried to combat her lack of femininity that she displayed by deigning to ask questions that others might not ask filled her with pleasure.

Despite his harsh words, George had been tender at times last night, once he revealed to her his thoughts about the opium den and its connection with Ophelia. He had watched Anne ascend the steps to her home and accepted her 'thank you' with grace. He did not say thank you in return, but that was to be expected.

How very like a man to think that only he was the one to provide useful help. I will be hard-pressed to ever get a thank you out of Officer George Ford. But his face was kind in that moment.

Anna found her mind straying as she chewed idly on a piece of buttered toast.

What is George Ford truly like?

She seemed to bring out the worst in him, but she wondered if he had a sense of humor or if he smiled. Her face heated at the imagined picture of a smiling George looking at her. A smile would transform his face, she thought, for he was very handsome even with his permanent scowl.

Anna and her parents finished their breakfast in silence, and Anna excused herself to the library to begin a plan of action. She took what news articles she had kept, including the letter from the killer, as well as a few sheets of paper and a pen. She also brought the letters that Ophelia had left under her pillow. She had promised not to read them unless Ophelia's supposed lover was not there, and he was not, was he? She would sit at her usual place of study and think. Right now, that's what Ophelia needed. While the police force had other cases to tend to and daily problems to fix, at least Anna had the luxury of a clear schedule.

Sitting in the library, she wrote down a few notes, trying to think back to the snippets of answers they'd received from the reluctant D in the doorway. She was hesitant to open the private letters, and she dragged out the time with notetaking in order to avoid them as long as possible.

D in the doorway--opium den
David F.- the owner?
Ophelia was often going
Why did she really go to the cemetery?
Did David take her?
How long has this been happening?
Is the engagement a lie?

After what seemed like too short a time, her mother rushed into the room, still clutching the handkerchief from before. But this time her face was alight with excitement and energy.

"Anna! Come quickly! Mr. Mason has come to call! Why did you not tell me he'd left his card yesterday? Foolish girl! Mr. Mason is quite the catch, and your father has spoken well of him often enough."

Anna's stomach fell, but she dutifully dropped her pen and stood up. Her mother looked her up and down.

"Your dress is fine but be sure not to bring up news of the killer or Ophelia, or any of your ideas about politics." Her mother was pointing a finger at her, her face scrunched up with admonition.

Anna sighed but groaned inwardly. "I understand, Mother. I shall be just as delightful as you desire. Are you sure you wish to receive guests during this time?"

"Yes! We will not miss this chance for you, my dear! Mrs. Jordan will certainly hear of it and tell all our acquaintances of what an opportunity we neglected to take up." Her mother turned to go but then spun around again. "You know I have only your best interests at heart. Now come quickly. We do not want to keep the gentleman waiting."

They walked down the spiral staircase towards the parlor where they met visitors, and despite the energy of her mother, Anna moved slowly, her reluctance making her feet heavy. Now a man was attempting to foil her plans once again. Here she thought she'd have the whole of the afternoon at her disposal, but now it would have to partially be taken up by the frivolous visit from a man!

Her mother entered the foyer with a flourish, and Anna could hear her voice bouncing from the walls, light and cheery, changed from the hasty harshness she had used upstairs with her daughter. It made Anna want to laugh. It was all a business of image, this bartering of pleasantries in exchange for services rendered. Her mother was kind to Mr. Mason because she felt he had the qualities of a suitable husband for her noble-born daughter. It would bring the Lovelaces the status they wished to maintain. It was an arrangement. Anna hated it, but she knew how to "play the game" to some extent.

Once her mother had spoken, Anna entered the room, not so much with a flourish but with sense, her green gown making lovely swishing sounds as she walked forward. Mr. Mason stood erect, his hands clasped behind his back, with his perfect teeth once again set into a wide smile. He was smiling at her mother, but once Anna entered the room, his eyes lit up, and he bowed his head.

"Lady Anna, what a pleasure to see you again."

Anna felt a slight annoyance at the handsome man's attention. Since the day of the ball, she forgot that he did have an air about him that would make women feel rather warm on the back of the neck and weak at the knees. It was a different kind of feeling from what she experienced with George for Mr. Mason's attractiveness was obvious and evident, with his lovely brown hair and tightly clipped mustache. He wasn't smug about it, but he did not appear unaware of his charms.

Contrarily, George is completely oblivious to any sort of effect he might have upon a woman besides irritation.

Anna's thoughts were wandering, and she envisioned a hand threading through a swash of dark hair before being covered by a navy police cap. She was roused by a jolt from her mother's elbow.

"Anna, dear. Mr. Mason has spoken."

Anna blinked away her thoughts and replied as hurriedly as she could. "Oh, do forgive me, Mr. Mason. My thoughts were running away from me. Poor sleep, I think. Welcome to our home." She curtsied low, and Mr. Mason grinned back at her in a strange, proud sort of way.

"You are forgiven, Lady Anna. Per our discussion at the ball, I did not expect you to behave as other ladies behave." At her mother's horrified stare, Mr. Mason continued, "Which I most appreciate and consider a refreshing change." Anna tightened her lips to keep from laughing at her mother's expression when it changed to stark relief.

Motioning to the inner parlor, her mother said, "Please come and join us for tea, Mr. Mason. Or would you prefer coffee? I know Americans are much more partial to the darker drink."

Mr. Mason chuckled, and Anna was surprised by its lightness. "No, madam, I much prefer tea. Perhaps my accent is now too slight, but I am an Englishman." He winked, and to Anna's surprise, her mother blushed a little. He added, "So, I'm afraid coffee is not my beverage of choice."

"Excellent," her mother replied, satisfied for the moment. She called for tea and then sat with grace on the cushioned chairs in the guest parlor.

Mr. Mason was the last to sit, and Anna noticed how smooth and perfect his hair and mustache were, slicked back so that not a hair was out of place.

So fastidious about his appearance, Anna thought idly. *Mother most definitely will approve of that.*

"Tell us more about your family, Mr. Mason. Are your parents still with us?" her mother asked prettily.

Anna knew her mother was attempting to model appropriate female behavior for her daughter, and Anna tried her best not to roll her eyes.

"I'm afraid not, Lady Wincherton. They passed many years before." He looked a little solemn, and Anna felt pity for him.

Her mother continued. "I am sorry to hear that, Mr. Mason. But you were raised in the United States?"

His smile returned. "Raised in England until I was a young boy but spent many years here. My parents did their best to instill their English virtues. I also inherited a part of a factory from my uncle."

"Oh, Mason, Mr. Mason, of course!" Her mother shook her head. "You must forgive me. I have met you once, I believe. You often speak with my husband."

"Yes, I do. I mentioned it to Lady Anna at the ball that he and I have met often on business matters. I remember you well, Lady Wincherton, but I did not wish to presume that you would have remembered me."

"Oh my," her mother said, with a fluttering hand to her chest. Anna could tell she was embarrassed. "I think my mind has been elsewhere of late. But do continue, pray."

Mr. Mason gave a comforting nod with his head. "I have called this place home for many years. However, I do not know that I will always stay in Lancaster."

Anna's eyes brightened, and she spoke up. "I remember you mentioning something like that at the ball. I wish I had had more time to ask you about it. Do tell us more."

Anna could see out of the corner of her eye that her mother's perfect facade had cracked slightly at the mention of leaving Lancaster City, doing something outside of the normal. But for Anna, it flamed her curiosity and her desire to prod him further about it, knowing that her mother disapproved.

The tea arrived and was placed on the table between them. Her mother began to pour a cup for each of them, her fingers moving deftly to complete the delicate task.

Chuckling, Mr. Mason said, "I admire your direct questioning and your open enthusiasm, Lady Anna. It is what kept you in my memory since the night of the ball. It's not many women, Lady Wincherton, who will speak so directly," he said, glancing at her mother.

Her mother arched an eyebrow, and her voice had lowered a bit. "Yes, it is not many women."

Anna could hear the disapproval in her mother's voice, but she didn't care. Despite her feelings about marriage, she wondered if it could be her escape from such a hum-drum existence, if she was married to a man such as Mr. Mason.

The conversation flowed in other directions. He first told her of his plans. Then, they spoke of England, and her mother found a connection between herself and one of the Mason relatives. They even discussed the politics of the current times and the struggles of owning a factory, which Anna's father could understand, but then the topic of Ophelia was broached.

"It was a shame to hear of Miss Marshall's disappearance. I read about it in the newspaper. I do hope she is well."

Quiet fell over the room, and Anna could hear the note of solemnity in Mr. Mason's voice. The only sound that was heard for a few moments was the clang of her mother's teacup against her saucer.

She cleared her throat. "I am very concerned for Ophelia. She is my niece, and my dear sister is struggling to cope."

Anna glanced at her mother, surprised that she would be so open with a stranger. She placed a hand on her arm. Mr. Mason began to look uneasy.

He said, "Do forgive me, Lady Wincherton and Lady Anna. I'm sorry for my lack of sensitivity. I should not have brought up such a traumatic thing for you and your family."

Anna smiled. "Please do not apologize, Mr. Mason. There is nothing to forgive."

Her mother recovered herself. "Please do not worry, Mr. Mason. It is in the good hands of the police."

Or is it?

"Yes, of course. They will handle it, I'm certain." He still looked uneasy, but his old smile had returned. "I shall trouble you no longer, and I will take my leave. Thank you for the tea."

Her mother looked disappointed, but she did not argue. The ladies both stood, following Mr. Mason, and they accompanied him to the door.

"Thank you for coming. You would be most welcome at any time." Her mother curtsied to him, and he bowed his head.

Thank you for your kind hospitality, Lady Wincherton. I would be happy to accept your invitation another time. I do hope it will be under better circumstances."

He bowed low and took her hand in his. He turned to Anna, and she felt a pang of guilt at the way he was leaving. But she knew her mother should never have allowed him entry when all this business with Ophelia was afoot.

He gently took her hand in his own and laid a kiss upon the back of it. Anna breathed in sharply at the surprise of the feeling which burst up through her from her belly. He lingered for a moment, and then he glanced at her with his brown eyes. They seemed darker and deeper than they had the night of the dance.

He is a skilled charmer, indeed. George Ford couldn't have done that as prettily.

Anna stated her goodbyes even as the embarrassment of her thoughts began to color her cheeks. Her cousin's life lay in the balance, and she was thinking about warm, tingling feelings?

I'm so ashamed. Forgive me, Ophelia.

With one more glance, Mr. Mason was gone, and things returned to normal.

"Well, he is very pleasant, is he not, Anna?"

"Yes, Mother. He is and well-practiced in the art of charming young ladies, I think. However, it was still perhaps too soon to have company."

Her mother pursed her lips, and Anna expected a rebuking, but she was disappointed. "You are right, Anna. I was thinking too much of our family and not of what my sister must feel at this time. I shall return to her house to see how she fares. Will you come?"

Anna nodded. This would be her chance to look in Ophelia's room once again for any more clues.

"Yes, but let me gather a few things first."

Her mother nodded and called for her own coat to be brought. Anna rushed upstairs for her notebook and the stack of letters. She wanted the time to be alone and to think of solutions, but she hoped that by looking at Ophelia's room once more, she might find another piece of evidence to bring to George. She would also have the time to cut open the pile of letters and finally figure out what her cousin's correspondence with D was all about.

CHAPTER

13

That day, George and Ned sat in George's office, smoking as they leaned back in their chairs. Ned was a lower officer, but George was not one to leave behind his friends so easily, even if he was gliding through the ranks as he had for so long hoped. Once they'd both reached the station earlier that morning, George had told his friend all about the events of last eve. In the bright morning light, they seemed strange and almost unbelievable.

Ned scratched his chin and asked, "Have you told the Sergeant about this opium den, George?"

George shook his head. He wasn't sure why, but he felt a sudden possessiveness of the news. It had been his own discovery, along with Anna, of course, but she certainly couldn't get all the credit for it, not when he'd been the one to interrogate the dirty man in the doorway. His conscience prickled at his unfair thoughts, remembering full well the way she'd boldly asked her own questions, unafraid of the man's responses or lewd glances. She was also the one who had gone to the address on her own before he'd luckily found her. George shuddered to think about what would have happened to her if he hadn't shown up.

George exhaled. "The sergeant won't take lightly to anything that looks like distractions from the case."

"But he ought to know. How is it a distraction? You've got a lead!"

"And how should I tell him that I came across this den? I don't want to bring Anna's name into the mix. It wouldn't look good for her, a high society lady like she is."

George crossed his arms and kept the cigarette hanging from the side of his mouth as he leaned his neck backwards.

Ned laughed. "Oh, it's Anna now, is it? Now that you've met in the dark streets, you're on first name terms?"

George flushed against his will, and Ned continued to laugh.

Damn it. This is why women are trouble when they try to get wrapped up in men's matters.

"*Lady Anna,* then. Ned, you're insufferable. *You* are a distraction to the case. I shouldn't have told you about her."

"Yes, you should've. She sounds pretty exciting to me, and I wish more than anything I could see that fiery woman out on a case, putting you in your place, for that's what she did, I'm sure."

Ned laughed again before taking a draw from his cigarette.

George sighed. "I need a pint, that's for certain. As soon as work's finished, you will find me at the bar, begging the barman for more and more."

Ned stubbed out his cigarette. "Come, George. You've got to tell the sergeant. If there's a link between the opium den and the killer's victims, then you've got to find out what it is. You know you have to begin to interview the other families."

George nodded. "Yeah, I know. It was tough to find the information about them. Some victims were very poor and had no record of family. But I'll do my best. You'll come with me to question them?"

"Yes, but first you need the approval of the sergeant. Even if you are a temporary detective." Ned winked. "Go on, go get it."

Ned hooked a thumb towards the door, and George groaned to his feet. He wasn't sure why he was so hesitant, but Ned was right. There was no getting around it. Did he not want to solve the case? Was that not his deepest desire? He could see it now as he walked across the bustling office towards the head of police.

Typing women were in a flurry as they shuffled papers and punched typewriter keys. They buzzed and moved quickly. They were so numerous, it almost made them nondescript. None of the officers paid them any mind, unless a woman was unlucky enough in the office to have a beautiful, enticing face.

He knocked on the door and adjusted his uniform. He could see it in his mind's eye: **George Ford, Senior Officer brings the 'Lancaster Ripper' to Justice.**

He smiled to himself. What Jenny might think of him if that came to pass. Anna would be so grateful to him. What a hero he would be. His self-congratulations were interrupted when a loud voice barked from inside.

"Come in!"

George swung open the door, and he spotted the gray-haired sergeant looking at him from behind his desk. "Ah, George, what can I do for you?"

George shut the door behind him and stood in front of the desk, his hands in front of him. "First off, thank you, sir, for allowing me to take up this case in Detective Barclay's absence. There's been a bit of new information with the Ophelia Marshall case."

"Of course, of course." The sergeant waved away George's gratitude. Then he said, "So, what've you got?"

The older man leaned back and laid his hands across his large belly.

"Well, I was given information from a source about the location of what I believe to be an opium den. The proprietor or assistant to the proprietor of that establishment claims knowledge of Miss Marshall and told us she was a regular attendee there or at least a visitor. The man we met with gave the name, David F., as the owner. Miss Marshall was going to meet him. She had given her cousin the initial 'D' as the name of the lover she was meant to meet in the cemetery the night of the ball, so this is likely him." Donaldson started to scratch at the growing beard on his face. George continued. "There may be a connection between that den and the other victims. But I need your permission, of course, to begin any interrogations in that quarter as well as with the families of the other victims."

Sergeant Donaldson pursed his lips and swung in his seat for a few moments, taking everything in.

"So, you found that den, did you?"

George was surprised at the sergeant's knowledge but not completely. He knew some people knew about it, as he had asked questions in the police force, but for some reason, the fact that his superior had known about it and yet had done nothing was a little disappointing. It felt like he was a little boy finding out that his father was not all he'd hoped. The sergeant was just a regular man like he was, subject to whims and vices.

"So, you knew." He sat down in the chair in front of the desk, a little deflated.

He wasn't sure if it was only the moral issue or the fact that he wasn't the one to bring the sergeant this groundbreaking news.

"I knew, but I couldn't quite get a handle on it. I thought if it didn't cause any trouble to us, why bother? But you say you think it's connected to the victims?"

George nodded. "I do. I just have a hunch because of the connection to Miss Marshall."

Sergeant Donaldson nodded. "You mentioned an 'us'. Who was the source that gave you the information about the den? Did you go with someone?"

George's heart did a nervous flutter. "I was out searching the streets, when I came upon someone who knew of this D, this person connected to the den. They led me to the address."

The sergeant drummed his fingertips on the desk, lifting his eyebrows expectantly. "And who was it?"

George shrugged. "I can't say. It's someone connected to the victim, and I don't want to say or else their reputation could be ruined."

The sergeant nodded. "I see. Does their identity affect the case at all? Or could they sway your judgment?"

George shook his head. "I don't think so."

Anna could make him confused about a lot of things, but he didn't feel that she would affect his decision-making when it came to the case. She wasn't the type to distract so that the focus was on herself and not the matter at hand.

The sergeant waved his hand in the air. "Fine. Do what you must do. But I'm telling you, Ford. I need this case solved quickly. The upper crust of the city is at my throat, hoping it won't be them next. We need to give them something. Some assurance that it won't be their daughters splayed out in the square. But keep things hush-hush."

George stood. "Thank you, sir. And as for the den? Do I leave it for the time being? Or arrest those involved?"

"Leave out any arrests. Just ask your questions. Besides, the people there might be more willing to talk to you if you aren't on the brink of arresting them."

George returned to his office, passing through the hall of typing women, all looking exactly the same. If Anna was working there, he was certain she would stick out of the crowd.

Once he got back in the office, he pushed open the door and said, "He allowed it! He's given permission! Let's hit the streets."

Ned put down his fresh cigarette with a smile and jumped to join his friend.

***

Anna had finally torn herself away from her aunt and mother in the Marshall living room to explore Ophelia's bedroom. It had not been easy, but she had been honest with them, and she told them that there might be something there that could lead her to find out more information. Information she could share with the police. They surprisingly hadn't put up much of a fight, and she hurried up the stairs with the thought that they might change their minds.

Her aunt was in such a pitiable state, she was likely to change her mind at any moment. Anna reached Ophelia's room, and when she entered, it was so utterly silent, that it gave her pause at the entryway. Nothing had changed, not that she'd expected it to. It suddenly had the aura of someone who had passed, and it made Anna feel sick.

"Ophelia, please be alive. Please be alive!" she whispered to the room, hoping something, somewhere had heard her earnest plea.

There was no more evidence in the address book or the various letters which were scattered over her desk. In her pocket, she felt the weight of the stack of letters she had retrieved from under Ophelia's pillow. Now would give her the chance to read them in peace.

She had fulfilled her promise. Now, it was imperative that she read the letters.

"Ophelia, please forgive me for this intrusion."

Anna ripped open the first envelope. Inside, the letter read,

Cemetery. Plum Street. Midnight. D.

Anna's heart began to race, and she tore open the next one.

St. James. 10 o'clock. D.

So, it was a common meeting place for them? Anna didn't have the stomach for anymore. This was either evidence for her cousin's predilection for opium or a lovers' meeting. Despite her continuing to disbelieve in George's opinion, she had a feeling at least part of it was the truth, and she would have to give him these private letters in order to prove it. But if they were not lovers, then why did Ophelia keep them under her pillow? It was such an intimate gesture. Perhaps only because she didn't wish anyone to read them and now Anna was doing just that.

Taking a breath, she thought she would try one more letter. It read:

42 S. Shippen Street.

I can't wait to see you.

D.

That was dated a few weeks back. Anna's heart sunk even further, knowing this was the address of the supposed opium den, but she puzzled at the last sentence. Perhaps Ophelia really was telling the truth about being in love? It gave Anna a flicker of hope. But what had opium to do with all of this?

Frustrated, Anna pulled out a drawer and took out a fresh piece of paper. She would write to George right away, even if he wouldn't listen. Anna made another promise to herself. If she received no reply, she would show up in person. She knew that George would not like that, and a part of her hoped he wouldn't reply, just so she could see the expression on his face when she burst into his office.

Anna wrote 'Dear' and then scribbled it out. She almost tossed the paper to the side, but then she thought, *What did it matter if her letter to the police was full of scratches and rewrites?*

~~Dear~~ Officer Ford,

I have read the letters. I will bring them to you if you ~~so desire~~ want. They merely contain the addresses and times of meeting for some purpose. I'm sure you know what purpose it might be. D is the supposed author of all of them.

~~Lady~~ Anna

Her pen had been poised to write out her full name, but she thought better of it, and crossed out her title, leaving only Anna. She hurriedly folded up the letter, and then slid it into her pocket with a pat. She would not risk mailing it from her aunt's house and rile her mother up to no end. She would ask a messenger boy outside of her house once they arrived home. The pile of opened letters on the desk was an ominous reminder of what she had to do. She gathered them up and placed them back into their ribbon.

"I am sorry, Ophelia, but the police have to know. It is the only way I know to get to you!"

She left and kept her tiny bundle hidden as she took herself into the drawing room, entering to the dreadful, heart-wrenching sounds of her aunt's wails.

CHAPTER

14

George and Ned sported long dark coats in the cool, early spring air. It still held the last bite of winter's chill.

"Who's the first victim?" Ned asked as he lit up a new cigarette and waved the match out before dropping it to the curb.

George pulled out his notebook, pushing his own cigarette to the corner of his mouth. "Emily Wilson, 39 E. King St."

He put the notebook back into his pocket, so that he could take the cigarette in hand.

"When the family was first interviewed, Emily still lived with her mother, so I hope her mother's home at this hour. From the looks of the address, they're probably a working family, so she might not be."

He glanced down at his pocket watch.

"No harm in trying," Ned said. "This is the best course of action. What else could we do? Hmm...we could always sort out a work riot at the factories? Or talk to Mayor Edgerly about why the police department could use more funds and equipment?"

George scoffed. "No, thanks."

His cigarette was finished by the time they arrived at King Street. They could have hired a cab for the afternoon, but George preferred to walk. It gave him more time to think things through, and he hadn't quite gotten used to the privileges of being a senior officer or temporary detective.

"I for one am so glad the other detectives are taking a bit of leave. Barclay and that lot. Idiots. They look down their brow at you as if it wasn't the two of you on the same street growing up."

Ned shook his head, and George laughed. "I agree. I know just the look you're talking about, and I would've seen it today after Sergeant gave me the go-ahead. But they'll be back in a few days, I'm sure."

After another ten minutes, the two of them were stood in front of a door marked 39. King Street in that direction was nearing the poorer side of town, but as the killer said in his letters, he did not discriminate in his victims. He simply chose women who were available, and George wanted to find out if all of the victims had opium in common. What had made them so available and perhaps so desirable for the killer?

He knocked on the door and adjusted his coat. He had waited a long time to do something like this, follow up on a lead, and he tried to keep his heart from racing as he waited for Emily's mother to answer the door.

You're a smart man, George, you can do this, his mind tried to reassure him, but for some annoying reason, he wished for Anna Lovelace to be by his side at the interview. He had a feeling that she would have a soft way about her when dealing with a victim's family.

He was grateful that no more time was allowed to spend on thoughts of Anna, for Mrs. Wilson opened the door. She squinted into the sunshine, and George could see it was dark behind her.

"Yes?" she croaked, and it sounded like the voice of a woman much older than the one who poked her head out into the afternoon light.

"Mrs. Wilson?" George asked, placing a hand softly on the door, so as to encourage her to keep it open. "I am Officer Ford, and this is Officer Barnum. We don't want to frighten you, and we're sorry for the intrusion, but we were wondering if you had a moment to talk with us? We'd like to ask you some questions about your daughter."

"Sarah?" Her eyes narrowed further, and she tilted her head in confusion.

"No, ma'am. I apologize again, but we want to ask you about your daughter Emily."

Mrs. Wilson's grip on the doorknob suddenly tightened, and her eyes opened wide, so that George could see that they were a lovely shade of blue.

"Emily is dead," she replied in a strangely flat voice.

"Yes, I know, ma'am. That's why we want to talk to you about her. We think there might be a connection to all of the incidents going on around town. We'll be talking to all of the victims' families once more."

"Victim, she was." The woman said to herself and pushed away from the door and began making clinking noises inside the house's gloom.

George glanced at Ned, who shrugged back at him. They stood frozen in the doorway, unsure of how to proceed when Mrs. Wilson called out,

"Come in. What have I but time now? Not working any longer."

Normally the phrase could have offended, but it was said in so casual a voice that it made Mrs. Wilson seem bitter, resigned to some tragic fate.

George and Ned entered and took off their caps. Mrs. Wilson motioned to the table.

"Sit. Coffee's hot."

They followed orders and soon, two cups were before them steaming upwards and looking inviting but smelling more like old dishwater. George clasped onto his politely, hopefully she wouldn't be looking at him to drink any of it. Ned took a sip, seemingly not bothered by the odd smell emanating from the cup. Mrs. Wilson sat down with her own cup between her hands.

"Mrs. Wilson, I know that you spoke to the police before, but I have a few questions. Was there anything your daughter was involved in? Did she say she knew any men? Anyone she would meet with at nighttime in the weeks leading up to her death?"

Mrs. Wilson reddened, and even in the dimness of the kitchen, George could tell he had asked the right question. Her fingers clasped together tightly, and she looked pained as she spoke.

"Yes, I think there was someone, although I never saw the man. Sarah hinted at something, said that Emily was going out somewhere at night, meeting someone. But I don't know where."

Mrs. Wilson put her face into her hands and began to breathe deeply, as if trying to avoid tears. George looked at Ned, fear in his eyes. Crying women always made him acutely uncomfortable. His mother had died so early, and he wasn't used to dealing with what his father used to call "women's emotions". He decided to continue his interview and to ignore whatever was going on.

"Mrs. Wilson, would you think that your daughter was involved in any sort of outside activity? Besides there being a man, do you think she might've been consuming opium? Going to an opium den to get it?"

Mrs. Wilson shot up. Her eyes narrowed, and the former fatigue she had shown was now gone.

"Opium? My dear, sweet Emily? Certainly not." She stood and began to tidy away the coffee cups.

George knew then that something was amiss. He knew he had struck a nerve. Mrs. Wilson may not know the truth, but she could have suspected.

"Do forgive us, Mrs. Wilson, but we have to persist in this line of questioning. It'll only help us find the killer before he gets even more women. If there's a connection to the opium den and the killer, then we need to find it. Please say you'll help us. There's a victim with him as we speak. We're certain of it. Surely you've heard about the missing Marshall girl."

George looked at Ned again, feeling a little guilty for stretching the truth, for he didn't know the whereabouts of Ophelia Marshall, not officially anyway. Mrs. Wilson stopped her movements in the sink basin. She did not turn around.

"Like I said, she was gone a lot at night. I was too busy to notice, going to work, getting supper on the table and all that. I should've noticed. She was my little girl, and now she's gone."

George feared by the slope of her shoulders, that she would start to cry again, but she was merely silent.

"I had a feeling that there was something more than a man. Emily was changed. She was sick a lot, and I was worried that she might have been coming down with consumption, but nothing ever happened. Nothing came of it. She would go out at night, and then she would return a little bit better, but it got worse until she went out again. I wasn't sure what it was. It could've been opium, but I know nothing about it. I swear it."

George nodded, so relieved that she was giving him just the information he wanted. Now, he just needed to link it to the other victims. "Thank you, Mrs. Wilson. You've been most helpful and hospitable."

Ned stood and said, "Thank you, ma'am."

The two of them headed for the door, and only then did Mrs. Wilson turn back.

"You'll find him won't you, boys? To me, he seems like the mist itself, flitting and floating around the town, uncatchable."

George clung to the door handle in surprise. Her use of the word mist discomfited him. "We'll do what we can. You know, ma'am, mist is the same way the killer described himself in the newspaper. Did you read that?"

He was surprised, for in an area such as this, most people, especially women, would not be able to read nor did they need to. She shook her head.

"No, I didn't. I wouldn't want to hear anything from that devil."

George said goodbye and shut the door behind him. It gave him an odd feeling to leave a woman like that in the dark, left alone with her grief. Outside, the light of the afternoon sun felt like it was out of a painting, so bright and yellow. George was almost dizzy with it.

He smoothed his hair and placed his hat back on his head. "On to the next."

Ned nodded next to him. "How was Emily Wilson found? Maybe we can find some connection there too. If the opium connection is the same, and the fact that he kills women and takes their hearts is the same, then maybe other things are. What do you say?"

George nodded as he lit a cigarette again and watched as the smoke lifted up to the painted-yellow sky. "Could be something."

Looking around at the Lancaster streets this time of day made it seem like the killer was far away and no one was really in danger. It almost felt like they were making it all up, all joining in on a game that the killer was leading. He had the strong urge to laugh.

"Let's go. Market Street this time."

They headed back towards the center of town until George stopped and put a hand out to stop Ned.

"What?" Ned said, looking confused.

Across the street, George saw Jenny and another young man come out of a coffeeshop. Her arm was in his, and she was laughing with her head back as if she hadn't a care in the world. George went cold, his stomach suddenly tying up in knots. He checked the time. It was nearing 5 o'clock, and so some of the men and women would be finished their work for the day and heading out into the town. Now the town held more 'delights' then he'd ever realized.

For Jenny too, apparently.

Ned looked at George's face and paused with him. He turned to the direction of George's gaze, and said, "Eh, isn't that Jenny? Who's that with her?"

"I don't know, but be quiet, I don't want to be seen."

Jenny and the man turned in their direction, so he yanked Ned into a side alleyway and pushed him back against the wall. They listened to the pair of footsteps and could hear the couple's laughter as they strode by. Their voices were hushed, so George couldn't catch any words, but once they passed by, he pushed forward into the street to watch their backs, shock and surprise filling his every vessel.

Ned said clumsily, "I'm sure it's just a relative. Someone come to town to visit. Uh...guess you've never seen him before."

George shook his head, and his cigarette dropped to the ground from his loose fingers. "Damn it." He reached for another from his pack. "No, I haven't. If it's not a relative, there she is, parading the man about in the light of day! She didn't even have the respect to do it at night when at least their faces could've been hidden."

Ned patted George on the shoulder. "Come, let's go to the bar. I'm sure it's nothing. We'll have a pint, talk things over, then return to the work. I could use a break, anyway. That house gave me the creeps. What about you?"

George didn't say anything, but he let Ned take him to the public house at Central Market in the center of town. It was warm, comforting, and familiar. The faces sitting inside swam before his eyes as he thought about Jenny and that other man.

What was she doing?

He knew that she was frustrated that he was not yet made detective, and that he wasn't yet ready to begin planning the wedding, but surely, she wouldn't simply choose another man and so easily! She was practically flaunting it in front of his face! The man was also very handsome. George could see the shine from his bright white teeth all the way from across the street.

Most people in town knew of George's and Jenny's engagement. At least those in their circle.

What an embarrassment to be so cuckolded!

Well, they hadn't been together in the Biblical sense, but George hated the idea that Jenny had simply dropped him without even speaking to him. He stewed to himself as Ned ordered the lagers and placed a tall pint in front of George.

"Here, drink that, old friend, and see if you can't shake off all the things we came into contact with today."

George took a large drink, hopeful for the sweet bliss of oblivion. It was frustrating, but the real problem was and what really made him angry was the fact that he wasn't so upset with Jenny for leaving him, but he was upset that he felt a huge sense of relief. He even could feel a tingle of hope that it was true that she'd moved on to another.

If it was true, then he wouldn't have to go through the business of hurting Jenny by breaking things off. It had crossed his mind, more than once. However, he knew he didn't want to do with the social awkwardness of it, and he wouldn't want to put Jenny through it. And yet, the sighting of Jenny today spoke volumes.

She's a good woman, and my parents would've been happy for us, but there's nothing between us anymore.

That realization hit hard, and the fact that he was finally allowing himself to believe it made him almost wary of his surroundings, like someone could see the truth on his face and tell Jenny before he had a chance. He took another large gulp of the pint until Ned stopped him.

"Whoa, friend. Why drink so fast? We have time."

George dropped the pint to the counter.

"Ah, you're right. I am on duty after all. What is it about women, Ned, that drives you insane and makes you want to do mad things?"

In that moment, he spoke freely and thought not of Jenny but of Anna. Now that he'd admitted to himself that his engagement was over, fresh thoughts of Anna spilled in, and he realized he was open to them now. He couldn't turn away from them now that the pleasant tingle of ale was moving through his veins. He wanted to see her again, if even just to talk to her, to be near her. He'd not stopped thinking of the sound of her laugh and how it had made him feel strong, capable, and interesting.

Ned laughed. "They've a way about them. One minute you're spouting sonnets, and then the next they're raging at something you did or said. It's in their blood. I think they enjoy torturing us a bit." He laughed again. "What will you do, George, about Jenny? That's who you're talking about, right?"

George swallowed nervously, knowing he couldn't dare share his thoughts with Ned.

"I don't have the faintest idea. I suppose I'll have to talk to her, but what am I going to say? I saw you in town with a man? Sounds ridiculous."

Ned turned to him, his face earnest. "Think of it like an investigation. You have the evidence. You know what time it was, what street, what coffeeshop. You have a description of the man. Confront her with the evidence. You don't have to accuse. You can ask."

George nodded, but he didn't even want to consider that conversation right then.

"Right. Well, let's get on with the questioning the other families. There's not much time left before we need supper."

Ned hopped off the stool while George paid. For the rest of the afternoon, they attempted to interview the other four victims' families. One was hopeful, mentioning strange behavior before the murder, but the next two seemed to not even exist, the address falsely written down, and the last one, the family of the most recent victim was too grief-stricken to speak. George told them he would come back another time.

One of the most difficult barriers to work as a policeman was the fact that one still had to follow social rules, or else the boss would be up his back. People would no longer trust him, and he wouldn't be able to get his job done. Sometimes, he wished he could bash doors down and demand answers from people unwilling to speak. In an interrogation room, that was different, but in their homes, he couldn't do something so rough.

In this case, especially, he felt his anger rising. Time was ticking, and he knew he'd come across a body soon if he didn't figure this out. He was actually surprised they hadn't already. The killer seemed to be lying in wait for some unknown reason. George almost regretted secretly desiring the killer to strike again. It was thrilling, but it was draining, and he practically felt like he was going to fall down, once he and Ned entered the station again.

"Bye, George. I'm off."

"Thanks, Ned. Good work today."

He waved to him and entered his office to sit down. His eyes were desperate to close, but he knew he had to make a few notes first before he could eat dinner and slip into bed with a whiskey in hand. He began scribbling when Mary, one of the office clerks, knocked and entered. He always remembered her because he'd helped her family with a domestic disturbance a few years back.

"Sir, this letter's come for you a while back."

She passed it to him. "Thank you, Mary. Could I have some coffee if it's not too much trouble? You should go home then. I didn't expect you to wait."

"Of course, Mr. Ford. It's no trouble at all."

She smiled and left the room. Mary was pretty, and the fact that he felt free of Jenny made him wonder if other women were interested in him too. Maybe there was a whole world of women out there who he could be with instead of Jenny. The thought excited him but made him feel guilty too.

Deep down, he knew that he didn't mean all women. He meant Anna. What had this woman done to him to make herself so often in his thoughts? He'd just met the woman! George looked down at the letter in his hand and was shocked to see it came from the Lovelace address.

CHAPTER

15

H e tore it open, his curiosity increasing with each moment.

"So, Anna's read the letters, then. They confirm my theory."

He spoke to the air, feeling the earlier fatigue take over. He hadn't gotten a full-night's sleep in days, and now after seeing Jenny and that man, he was even more tired, knowing what the future held. It was time to go home, but there was more, so much more to do yet. If all of the victims were opium addicts, then it must mean that Ophelia's D and the killer were connected somehow? Or perhaps the killer was D and D was David F.? It was all so confusing. What if, at the den, he had just been close to the killer and to Ophelia and he'd done nothing?

But this D or David is a businessman. Why kill his own patrons? It'd only serve to lessen his business and make others fear to come in the doors.

Then what was the connection? It couldn't merely be a coincidence. It was true that he hadn't been able to interview all of the families, but still. There were too many strange occurrences for them not to be related.

Anna would know.

When the thought came to him, he knew then that he was growing delirious. He was paying for his lack of sleep today. He wanted to forget the thought for the stupid, random thing that it was, but deep down, he wanted to talk to her about the case. She would have ideas, ideas he could use. She'd be able to think clearly about this. He wanted her here. Now, he really was going mad.

Nothing that a hot bath and a whiskey can't fix, he thought as he stood up and pushed her letter into his pocket.

Suddenly, his door burst open, and as if the fates had heard his request,

Anna Lovelace stood in his doorway, attired in purple velvet, her eyes wide and her breath quick. George tried and failed miserably to wipe the surprised pleasure off his face.

"Lady Anna! What're you doing here?"

Anna shut the door behind her. "Forgive me for the intrusion at such an hour, but I've news that I had to bring myself."

She placed a letter into his hands. It was clean, expensive paper, and a flourishing hand had penned 'Lady Anna Lovelace' on the outside.

He took it, his eyes narrowed with confusion. He looked back up at her and noticed the way her cheeks were pink with haste and her eyes fiery with curiosity.

"Take a seat."

He pointed to the chair across from his desk, and she did so, adjusting her skirts. He sat down and opened the letter.

"Can I read it? Or do you want to tell me yourself since you're here?"

George nearly colored from the way his voice had filled with softness. He was so cowed by her sudden presence, and he wondered if it was because of their time outside the den and walking back alone together in the moonlight. Now that his feelings for Jenny were clear, ideas had begun to open up to him, and he felt uncertain about his words and his movements when Anna was around. How much had happened in the course of one day.

Anna bit her lip, and it looked as if tears were about to spring from her eyes. "Read it, please. We can discuss it once you're finished."

George nodded and began to read, his eyes widening with each new word:

Dearest Lady Anna,

It is my absolute pleasure to write to you, dear heart. The idea just came into my head once I spoke to your cousin. Yes, you have guessed it, I have your cousin, Ophelia, with me. She is beautiful, one of my finest victims. However, do not concern yourself. She is perfectly safe. I found out that you were her cousin, and my mind pulsed with interest. I met you before. Do you not remember?

We spoke briefly, swaying to soft music, but from that moment I could see the intelligence in your eyes and the desire inside of you raging for a different life. I could give you that, my dear, if only you'd let me. I too rage for newness and intrigue, for this life that plagues us is unutterably dull. Play this little game with me. The police force is a group of uneducated rabble. They have nothing that interests me. Clearly, for I have flaunted my actions in their faces, and they have yet to find me. I am bored.

Indulge me, will you not, my dear? I can see you are intelligent and could find your cousin if you so tried. I implore you to search for me. Find me-- the killer. I will reward you ever so much, and I will thank you for the game. If you can find me, then your cousin will be returned to you. Her heart is tempting and yet, I fear this game tempts me more. Do not tarry. I may change my mind.

X

***

George put the letter down and smoothed over its folded lines with his thumbs. Anna watched his hands, strong and manly, used to work, and she noticed ink stains on his fingertips and knuckles. It comforted her in some small way. George was silent after he read, and she too wasn't sure what to say. The killer had found her. He knew who she was and most likely they'd met at the ball. It seemed they were acquainted, but as she'd walked to the police station from her house, racking her memory, she could not think of anyone that she had spoken to that night who had made an impression on her besides Mr. Mason. All the other men were either so dull or so fawning, she could barely pay them any mind.

Mr. Mason couldn't be the killer, could he? He was so handsome, so kind, and so polite. It wouldn't make any sense.

It could have been any number of men that she had briefly chatted with out of politeness. Or it could have been a man from many weeks before at a different ball.

But why send the letter only now if he had known of me then?

"George, certainly I would know a killer when I saw one, wouldn't I? He claims we've met before."

She was about to return to musing when she blushed at her realization. She had just used George's Christian name without even realizing it or asking him. She knew he was a man of manners and old traditions, and while they irritated her, she needed to be polite, or else he may be unwilling to help her. However, after their night of adventures last evening, she felt strangely at ease with him. As if the day had brought with it a new familiarity.

"Oh, I'm sorry. I was simply thinking aloud. Officer Ford." She didn't look at him, fearful it would make her blush even more, and she didn't want to show George any sign of weakness.

"No." She looked up and saw him smile weakly and shake his head. He looked tired. Dark circles were under his eyes, and Anna wondered briefly what his home looked like, and if he enjoyed returning to it night after night. She colored even deeper.

Why should I be thinking of where the man lives? Or where he rests his head? Foolish girl, Anna! You are just as bad as the other ladies.

Thankfully, he continued. "I think I prefer it this way. Officer Ford sounds far too stuffy." A sly half-grin crossed his tired face. "I hate to presume, but since I can imagine we'll be seeing a lot of each other, what do you think about me calling you Miss Anna? My Lady seems far too formal for us *lowly* Americans."

He chuckled, and Anna noticed the boyish way he rubbed the back of his neck as he spoke, as if he felt nervous for asking her a question. Who was this man, so changed from the stern one from last night? She remembered that he would switch from softness to hardness in a moment, and she supposed this was one of his soft moments. Even so, it made her insides go warm and tingly when he did so, and she wished he would return to his hard self.

That self she could understand, and it was easier to deal with. Anna smiled far wider than she intended to.

"Yes, of course, although I would prefer it if you called me simply Anna, if I'm to call you George. We are to be on equal footing."

She straightened her shoulders with resolve.

He sputtered out with a sort of laugh, "Equal footing? I'm merely a police officer and you an English lady."

"I'm determined to forget social class, George, especially now that I reside in America. It irks me, for it serves no real purpose than to denigrate the poor masses who fill the darkened streets of our town and many others."

"Well," he paused in mid-speech watching her for a moment. She had worn her best hat, and her gown seemed more appropriate for a ball rather than a cordial visit. She was embarrassed at the effort she had made simply to come visit the police station, for it was one of her best dresses. It seemed silly, now that the letter had made its way into George's hands, and there were more important things to consider. But she had wanted to look well. Perhaps she hoped it would help him take her more seriously?

He continued haltingly. "The letter. I'm sorry that you've been dragged into this, Anna. I hope you're not afraid, now that we can see the killer's interested in you."

"I know. It's rather disconcerting, but I'd like to take him up on his offer. I know you'll try to dissuade me, but I'm determined, George."

She nodded firmly, bracing herself for his arguments.

He nodded. "I understand."

Anna's lips parted in surprise. Even though he was in one of his soft moods, she still did not expect him to agree to her helping to solve the mystery.

"Do you? No arguments, no bellowing?" George smirked as he shook his head, and Anna grinned. "Well, then I'm glad. But I wanted to get your opinion on the manner of the letter. Does it sound like the killer? Or could it be simply someone else who wishes to taunt me? Trying to make me believe they have Ophelia?"

George frowned. "I can't think of a reason why anyone would want to taunt you in this way. Besides, it's not as if he's designated a meeting place or forced you into any money. In my opinion, it sounds just like the killer's notes he's been sending in the newspaper. Rather lofty and confident in himself."

"Yes, I agree. I've kept those printed letters and have read them over and over. I hoped it would give me an idea of the kind of man he is."

George leaned forward on his desk. "Why am I not surprised that you would do such a thing, Anna?"

Anna's breath caught for a moment, lost in George's laughing eyes. He was so close to actually and fully smiling, and she remembered her theory about what it would do to his face, how it would transform him into the most handsome man of her acquaintance. She hoped he wouldn't ever fully smile because she needed to focus.

To her relief, he continued without smiling. "Well, he said you've met before. Do you have any idea who it could've been?"

Anna sighed, shrugging her shoulders in frustration. "I haven't a clue. I remember speaking with many men at the ball. Any one of them could have been him. Or it could have been from another ball. There is no possible way I could've remembered him unless he stepped forward, stating that he was a murderer."

George snorted, folding his hands over his stomach as he leaned back. "He's clearly well-educated, and I'd guess that he's English or connected in some way to England, for all of his letters have a sort of…" George waved his hand in the air as he tried to think of the word. "Flowery feel to them."

"Yes, I suppose you're right, although I'm not sure whether to be offended or entertained."

"Well, I'll leave that up to your preference Anna," he said with another smirk. "I apologize if I've offended, but it's been something I've been thinking about. Think for a little while about those you saw and spoke with at the party. Were any of them particularly well-educated, had this manner of speech, or were English? Clearly they got to speak to you more than briefly for he noticed your intelligence."

Anna smiled, and George looked away from her and pulled his cigarette case from inside his jacket.

"Or so he says," he amended, cigarette in his mouth.

There he goes again, removing his compliments once he's said them.

"Those at the ball are gentlemen. It would be like finding a needle in a haystack if I had to think about finding an educated man. They are all formal and educated. A couple are English, but still. Many of them, even Americans, if you can believe it, could write in this fashion."

George frowned at her words, but he said nothing. She thought about the night of the ball, flipping through the faces in her mind. There had been Mr. Bermondsey, but he seemed rather too old to fill the position of dangerous killer. There had been Mr. Weston, but they'd only spoken for about five minutes and in the presence of her mother. There were many more, but she couldn't remember all of their names. And then she felt her stomach sink as she thought about the last option, despite her earlier dismissal of him. He was English, educated, and rather alluring: Mr. Mason.

CHAPTER

16

"Do you mind if I smoke, Anna?" He looked at her, and she shook her head, her blond curls trembling as she did so. After lighting up, he blew a cloud of smoke into the room. "What is it?"

Anna was slightly pale, and her brows were knit together, creating a lovely crinkle between them.

"There is someone. A Mr. Frederick Mason. We danced at the ball and had a long conversation. We discussed how different we are to others. It seemed to bond us, for he called at my house only yesterday to begin a sort of courtship, I suppose."

George felt irritation at the thought, but he kept his face placid.

"I see. You think this could be him?"

"I don't know, but he's well-educated, is English, and he is rather," she swallowed, a little embarrassed about her confession, "attractive and charming. I could understand why women eager to please would wish to do what he says or follow him somewhere."

George tapped his fingers on the top of the desk. "Ah. So, the killer must be attractive then? I think you're right. He convinces these women to meet with him in certain places after dark, but I think he's making some sort of connection to opium. He could be meeting with them, promising to supply them? Or they are already drugged and so are more amenable to suggestion?"

"Perhaps. Ophelia went to meet her D in the graveyard, after she received a note at the ball, but I'm sorry, I cannot remember if Mr. Mason left at that time. I don't remember seeing him. Once my cousin left the ball, and after I'd danced with Mr. Mason, I had no real connection to anyone else there. I had to dance, of course, but no one kept my interest. I only wished to go home. And I never saw him after that."

George was reminded of how Jenny had spoken of Anna when they were eating in the pub, telling him that Anna Lovelace was very different. *Good Lord. Jenny.*

The memory of the afternoon flooded back to him. He would have to deal with her soon. In the excitement of the letter and Anna's arrival, he'd forgotten. It had been a blissful half an hour. It was too bad that police officers continued having to deal with their personal life while their work life, and killers included, took no notice, continuing on as they had been.

There was a knock at the door and George tensed, hoping it was not the sergeant come to reprimand him for hosting a female guest at this hour in his office. But it was only Mary, and she opened the door, holding out a cup of coffee hesitantly. "Do forgive me, sir, for interrupting you, but I wanted to see if you still wanted that coffee."

George nodded. "Thank you, Mary. I'm sorry to have kept you waiting. You may go home now. Have the night officers begun their rounds?"

"Yes, sir. They left just a bit ago."

"And the sergeant?"

"He left as well, once the night officers had been dispatched. He asked about you, but I said you were in an interview relating to the case."

Mary laid the cup on George's desk, and George took it gratefully. Despite Anna's presence, he could feel the warm fingers of fatigue wrapping around his brain. He would need coffee to help him continue on for just a bit longer.

"Thank you."

Mary glanced at Anna who smiled at her, and then she left.

Anna turned to George and said with a clipped voice, "Here I hope to wander down new avenues for females and solve the mystery of my cousin's disappearance while the women here are reduced to serving men their coffee."

She watched him carefully, and he wasn't sure whether to burst into anger or to laugh. He felt too tired for anger or laughter, so he decided to answer calmly instead.

"Mary and the other girls here do lots of different things: typing, mailing, etc. We couldn't keep the station going without them."

Anna pursed her lips. "Yet they are never able to help solve cases, are they?"

"No, certainly not."

George took a large sip of coffee and then regretted both the drink and his words, for the coffee scalded him and he dropped the cup hurriedly back into the saucer. He wasn't sure if his mind was playing tricks on him, but he thought that Anna might have smirked.

"I see. Well then why am I suddenly allowed to do so by you, Officer Ford? I don't want special treatment." She stood up, her arms crossed.

George stood as well out of polite habit.

So, it's back to Officer now.

He had rather enjoyed their brief time of familiarity.

"Anna, Lady Anna, you have to understand. It's not a usual occupation for a woman. They don't have the minds for it. Yet in this case, I knew I couldn't stop you. You'd follow me out onto the streets even if I had said no."

After those words, he wished he could shut his eyes and avoid the avalanche that was to come. He clenched his fists, tightening in preparation for her vitriolic response. He could see it in her flashing green eyes, which burned emerald with anger.

"You're quite right in one respect. You can't stop me, for I'll begin my search for the killer. Even before this letter, you could tell I'd decided to do so. But you're wrong in the fact that women have not the minds for it. Women have minds that could be just as useful as a man's, if they were given the time and cultivation that they deserve. Good thing my father wasn't as pig-headed as you, and he'd actually given me a chance to make something of myself, despite my mother's efforts to trap me in the confines of being a decorous lady and push me into the snare of matrimony."

Anna took a deep breath, having not stopped to pause during her diatribe, and George was watching her intently, enjoying the way her face was brightened by her anger. He had never been spoken to like this before, and even though he should have been feeling sheepish, his mind wandered to how bewitching she looked. And how bold she was being. He couldn't imagine Mary ever speaking to him like that. Everything Anna said felt like truth, so impassioned was she, that he knew that anyone who would listen to her would agree with her. Even if it irked them to do so.

Anna continued. "And I won't fall into that trap lightly." She pointed a finger at him. "You've read yourself what the killer thinks of the police officers in this station. He is flaunting his crimes in front of your eyes! So, he asked me, a mere woman, to follow him and try to find him. He will get careless with all this showing off, and then I will catch him, whether you will lower yourself to help me or not. At least my cousin is safe for now."

George had noticed the killer's intent to insult the force, but it hadn't bothered him, for he knew that he hadn't a chance to lead the case before now. It was him at the helm, and it was a chance to prove himself to the sergeant. While he was busy fanning his ego into flame, he had not realized the meaning of the fact that the killer wished Anna to search for him. Why? What game was he playing at? Did that mean danger was around the corner for her too? It didn't seem like it, but one never knew with men who were insane.

He sighed. Anna was still watching him angrily. He hadn't the energy to fight back anymore. Perhaps she was even right. Was he, as she had so eloquently put it, "pig-headed"? She had been requested by the killer to investigate. The killer was right. She *was* intelligent. There was no denying it.

"I'm sorry, Anna. I didn't mean to offend. Let's not fight anymore." He rubbed a hand over his eyes and leaned his fists on his desk. "You can see the way I respected you, knowing that I wouldn't be able to stop you. I just want you to take caution. What does the killer get at the end of this game? Perhaps he wishes to make a grisly trade in victims?"

He waited for her reply, when there was a rough knock at the door, and a tall, dark-haired man entered.

"Uncle?" Anna said, her face paling in shock.

***

Anna had let her mouth run away with her again, but she couldn't help it. George Ford was so frustrating, she could scream! For a few moments, she had hoped that he was different, that maybe she was helping him see things in a new light, after he said he understood her once she told him she would be officially investigating.

Then, there had been his comment about women and their minds. He was like a wily trickster, making women melt to pieces when he turned on his charm and kindness, his hazel eyes watching one with interest. Then, he switched to his hard coldness, full of self-satisfied airs and a rigid view of women and their very limited roles. She couldn't imagine what it would be like to be his wife. She wondered for a moment if he was married. He didn't wear a ring, but that didn't mean much.

If he is married, I pity her then. What an awful life that must be, forced into servitude and not even asked for an opinion of any kind!

But George apologized, and she felt her anger cool a little.

A voice inside her whispered, *Don't listen to him! He could be trying to trick you into it! Into what?* She answered it.

A man who apologizes can be hard to come by, but even so, I don't think I should let it go just yet.

She was just on the verge of replying, when to her surprise, her Uncle Jack walked into the room, his face etched with concern and clinging to the doorknob.

"Uncle Jack? What are you doing here?" Her voice was suddenly small, and she missed the loud, fiery woman of a moment before.

Jack Marshall looked from George to Anna, and his eyes opened wide in surprise as he removed his hat.

"Anna? I should ask you the same question, my dear." His voice lowered in disapproval, and Anna groaned inwardly.

He will tell Mother, and then I will be locked inside forever!

She searched for an excuse. It had to be something good, or else he would not let it rest. He would even speak to her father, and then it would be all over. Any hopes for investigation, any dreams about exploring new worlds in which to test her mind would be lost to her.

George cleared his throat and said, "Sir, you must forgive me. I'm Officer George Ford, and I am the one who called for Lady Anna to join me." George stabbed out his cigarette and came around the desk and offered his hand to Jack to shake. Reluctantly, Jack shook it, his eye still glancing critically at his niece. "I had a few questions about her cousin, and since she seemed the one closest to her and had known about her plans on the night of her disappearance, I thought it would be best to ask her more questions and at the station."

Jack turned to George, and Anna was at a loss for words. She looked at George and mouthed a 'thank you'. She saw the flicker of a wink, gone so quickly she wasn't sure if it had even happened.

Uncle Jack said, "Young man, you do know the hour, don't you? Why, it's nearly dinnertime! A young woman such as my niece should be home, not out, speaking to a man alone in a room, even if he is a policeman. Anna, do your parents know about this?"

She swallowed nervously. "No, I didn't want to worry them. Mother is working hard to keep Aunt Louisa calm, and I didn't think it necessary to say anything." Her uncle's mouth was firmly set, and she knew he disapproved, but there was nothing he could say at the moment. "I was just about to leave, though, Uncle."

"Good. I shall accompany you, but first I came to speak to the officer." She nodded quietly and sat down. Her uncle asked, "Officer Ford, do you think my niece might wait outside?"

George sat down and replied, "I don't mind if she stays, sir, for she knows the details of the case, but it's up to her."

Once more, Anna was floored by George's answers. She narrowed her eyes, even though inside, her heart was beating quickly. Just like Mason, George had said things she had never heard a man say before, and while she felt that Mason had been truthful, she wondered briefly what George was attempting to do. It almost seemed like he wanted to be in her good graces again.

But why?

Jack looked back at his niece. "Anna? You'd like to stay, I imagine?"

"Yes, Uncle. If you don't mind."

She smiled. Her uncle could be harsh, for he was a powerful businessman, but he also had a soft side. Perhaps every man did, and that was the only reason women gave them the time of day. Jack turned back to George.

George said, "Sit down, please."

"I came to discuss with you about the case, Officer Ford. What headway are you making? All I have is a missing daughter and a wailing wife at home, so I have no idea what I am to do. There are people whispering that it is this Lancaster Ripper, and I wanted to come to the officer in charge to see what he had to say about it."

George straightened up. "We haven't had much headway, I'm afraid, but we are finding connections that were not there before. All I can tell you, sir, is that it is good news that we have not yet found...a body, if this has anything to do with the Ripper."

Anna saw George falter at the word, and she shivered as well. It was unfathomable to imagine vivacious, energetic Ophelia cold and pale from death. It was almost laughable and that's why Anna couldn't seem to feel totally hopeless just yet. Now she knew that Ophelia was alive, she could begin to find her. There was hope. The only problem was, she didn't want her uncle to know about that letter. She wondered what George might say to him about it.

Her uncle looked slightly pained, and in his expression, Anna could see the strain Ophelia's disappearance had on him. He was brusque and straight-faced, but he loved his daughter dearly. She doubted that he would ever cry, and this expression now was the closest she would ever get to seeing him upset, she was certain.

"I see. Well, I suppose that is some comfort. Why do you say that?"

"According to the killer's recent patterns, the body would appear within about 12 hours, but that isn't the case this time. At this juncture, I'm hopeful we'll be able to find Miss Marshall unharmed and soon."

Jack nodded. "Did you find out anything about this D my wife has told me about?"

George glanced at Anna, and Anna's breath quickened as she thought about how to explain it to her uncle without giving it away that she had been at an opium den.

"I am working on whether or not he really was involved with the police, sir, but you can imagine the difficulty with a letter such as D. We don't know whether it is a last name or a first name. I'll have to round up those men to question them, but I think perhaps your niece didn't know his true profession. That seems more likely. There seems to be some connection to a man at an opium den."

"Opium?" Jack's eyes were round with surprise and horror. "What connection? What do you mean?"

George swallowed, and Anna felt for him, knowing that he was trying to tread carefully.

"I interviewed a man whose name starts with D connected to the opium den, and he has seen your niece before. Said there was a man named David F., who owns the place, who she was connected with. I don't know if the man D is her man or this David F. Does that name mean anything to you?"

Jack thought for a moment, and then shook his head. "David F.? No. I've met many Davids, but none with a last name starting with F."

"Well," George drawled, "apparently this was likely the man your daughter was intending to meet that night. However, my source wasn't very descriptive. As you can imagine, an employee of an opium den would not be eager to speak to the police."

All the while the men spoke, Anna's mind was racing. She wanted to get back to that opium den to explore it. Perhaps they could find Ophelia stuck inside there! It was her only option at the moment. The killer wanted Anna to play the game and play the game she would. She didn't notice that George had scribbled something hastily onto a small piece of paper and then laid down his pencil.

"No, I suppose not." Jack was thoughtful. "Well, Officer, you will alert me if there is anything I can do, or if there is any lead."

Jack stood, his hat in his hand. Anna followed her uncle to the door, grateful to leave and that George had said nothing about the letter. But she was also saddened for her uncle's lack of answers to his queries. George opened the door for them.

"Of course, sir. You can be certain I won't rest until I know who did this."

George was confident and soothing. Jack looked forlorn and tired, but he nodded and led the way out. Anna glanced at George and nodded to him. While her uncle's back was turned, Anna felt George slip a piece of paper into her hand. She looked down, struggling to believe what was happening, but she saw his hand on hers. It lingered for a split second and then was gone as if it had never been there. George shut the door behind them without another word.

CHAPTER

17

George left the station quickly after Jack and Anna were gone, ready to climb into his bed as soon as he made it home. His mind was filled with two things, and he didn't know which one to focus on. He needed to see Jenny to discuss her being with another man, but he also just gave Anna a note telling her to meet him tomorrow night. And on top of all that, he didn't tell the victim's father that his niece had received a note from the killer.

Am I being an idiot? Am I crazy?

He couldn't really tell who he was anymore. Anna had him all confused. One moment, he was spouting his old beliefs about women and what roles they ought to be playing in his world. But all of his words sounded so foolish as they fell stupidly out of his mouth, especially compared to her eloquent, impassioned speeches. The next moment, he was on her side, defending her against her uncle's suspicions, protecting her reputation, telling her it was acceptable that she begin to officially work on the investigation. George chalked up his odd behavior to being tired, and he hoped his head would be clearer in the morning. At least he hoped so.

***

My young beauty sleeps endlessly, even the night has passed, and a new morning has come. Poor thing, she is spent from all this activity. I know her heart craves for me to do what I must, even if she does not know it herself. She barely speaks and barely eats. I fear that I have broken her. I keep watching her. I have never kept a victim for so long, but I am too excited. I have sent the letter to her cousin, and I await the game. I will know when interesting Lady Anna Lovelace is afoot in town. She will accept my proposal. David will alert me. I have sent him a letter to ask him to look out for her, to make sure she is following my instructions. He seems to be as intrigued by her as I am.

But there is a surprising problem. Miss Marshall has no symptoms, no sickness. She sleeps and is sad, but she does not struggle for breath or scream with craving, as I would have expected with these types. Perhaps she was not one of David's little opium girls that he usually brings me. My curiosity picks and picks at me, until I resolve to speak with David at once. I leave the dear heart to her bed and wander upstairs. I have spent enough time in my chambers today. There is so much more to come.

I call to the maid to bring tea to the parlor. I sit, lost in my own thoughts, touched by the morning sun. Who am I now? Have I broken my sacred calling? I was making these women better, but now I am entranced by something new. I wish one woman to play my cat and mouse game. Will she oblige me as I hope?

And do I really mean what I have written to her? If she plays my game and finds her cousin, will I really let her cousin go? Perhaps. Yet there must be a timeline. I cannot allow Lady Lovelace such ease as to not have to find me within a certain time period. That would certainly be no fun and practically the same as if those foolish policemen were following me.

In the end, I may wish to take Ophelia's heart after all. Who knows when inspiration will strike me anew? I follow the passions of my own heart, but for now, it steadies my hand. It asks me to wait, to toy, to orchestrate. I will tell David to pause any other preparations he was doing for me while this little game plays out.

Tea does me well. It soothes my nerves and irritation. I realize, though, it could all be excitement. Before I was always so in control, following my calling with my lovely, little victims falling into my path, but now I do believe Lady Anna Lovelace has me for her own. She can be the puppet master for a while, and I shall follow the pulls of her strings. What an interesting change that should make.

Where will you go first, My Lady? What will your first step be? You do entertain me so, dear heart. I sigh. I suppose I must return to the real world for a moment and get to the factory. They will be wondering where I have been. As the owner, I should have no need for explanations, but too much absence will become suspicious. I stand and call for my coat and hat. I think about the lovely woman below stairs, sleeping, and lying in wait.

I swear to myself I will not harm a hair on her head until I am satisfied with my newest venture. I tap the top of my hat and am off. From one role to the next. Moving and changing as mist.

***

The next morning, Anna woke, but she was not yet ready to leave the warmth and safety of her bed. Turning to her side, her eyes lit upon the crumpled piece of paper on her night table. It had been smoothed out and recrumpled once she'd found a chance to read it last night.

She pulled it off the nightstand to read it again.

Anna,
Meet me at St. James' cemetery tomorrow.
Come disguised. Midnight.
G

When George had first placed the piece of paper into her hand as she was leaving his office, Anna had sealed her fist shut. She couldn't take any chance that her uncle would see it. The carriage ride home seemed to last a lifetime as she sat across from a fearful and fatigued Uncle Jack, craving to read what George had written to her.

Her cheeks had warmed as she tried to think of what the note could contain. Back at home, she rushed up to her room to unfurl the piece of paper in her hand. Once she read the note, she was pleasantly surprised.

Meet him?

At first glance, it looked like a lovers' rendezvous. However, since Anna knew that to be ridiculous and seeing how he mentioned a disguise, she knew that they were of the same mind.

We will investigate the den together.

She had had the whole night to think it over, her dreams vivid, yet when she awoke, they tumbled away. She was excited but nerves also claimed her for a moment, and she crumpled the paper again, weakening slightly in her resolve. The killer called for her; George wanted her to join him, and Ophelia depended on her. Yet would she be able to find the courage? And would she even succeed?

Her angry, impassioned confidence from yesterday evening in George's office now cowed at the reality of Ophelia's situation. She took a breath and then exhaled slowly.

I will do this. I will meet George tonight, and I will do my best.

Even though she stood by her words, she blushed a little at the memory of how ferociously she scolded George after the comments he'd made. It seemed he was throwing her an olive branch by inviting her to join him tonight, and so she could not let that opportunity go. She had to live up to everything she'd said and not let a man like George, with such old, engrained beliefs, be proven right.

Anna pulled the bell for Norma.

In a few minutes, Norma appeared, young and bright, her curls bouncing, a tea tray in her hands. "Yes, Lady Anna?"

Anna slid her legs out of bed, and Norma helped her into her silk robe. Anna was a little unsure of how to broach the subject, but she knew that Norma would help her.

"Norma, I have rather an odd request of you. It's nothing that will put you in any danger of course," she said when Norma's eyes looked fearful. Her lady's maid was a fragile sort, and Anna hated to ask this of her, but she really had no other option. Norma was the only one in the house who Anna felt would not reveal anything to her mother or the housekeeper.

"I have something I need to do tonight. It's something important, and it will go a long way to helping dear Ophelia. There is a nighttime errand I must complete, but I need to go in a disguise."

"A disguise, My Lady?"

"Yes, and I thought you could help me a little. In order for me to run my errand properly, I'll be needing some men's clothes."

At that, Norma's eyes opened even wider. The young girl swallowed nervously and began to clasp and unclasp her hands.

"Men's clothes, My Lady? But where am I to get those?"

"I was hoping you could find them below stairs, from one of the footmen, perhaps? He wouldn't miss them for just one night. Do not fear, Norma, you won't get into any trouble. If there are any problems with this, I will take full responsibility."

Norma seemed to calm at that reassurance. "All right, My Lady. I'll see what I can do. Will you need me to help you dress in this disguise?"

Anna smiled. "That would be wonderful, Norma, but would you be fine with staying up late to assist me with it? I could manage myself, but it will bolster my courage if you are here to help me, especially with hiding the hair." Anna smiled, trying to keep the energy light and positive, so that Norma's strength wouldn't fail. "I will need to leave the house a little before midnight tonight."

Norma nodded. "Mrs. Bonds doesn't mind what we do as long as we arrive for work, and we're not drunk or too tired."

"Excellent. Come to my room around 11 tonight. We will commence. Bring anything you think might fit me somewhat. Of course, do not worry if it isn't perfect. It's meant to be a disguise after all."

Norma curtsied. "Yes, of course. Now, I will return in a half hour, My Lady, to help you dress for the day."

"Thank you, Norma." Anna sat down on the bed. Now, the only thing left to do that day was wait.

***

As he awoke in his small apartment, George thanked God he was not on duty that day until the evening. This was one of his afternoons off during the week, and it could not have come too soon. Finally, a full night's sleep had changed him into a different man, and he felt strengthened for all that he was to do that day, and even without work, it was a very big day, indeed.

With a queasy feeling, he thought about how he had to meet Jenny this afternoon for a walk in the park and have it all out with her. It was time, and he couldn't wait until it was all over. He didn't want to marry her anymore, and each moment that passed without speaking to her, he knew it even more clearly. She obviously felt the same way, and he hoped against hope that Ned was not right, and that it was not a male relative, but a clandestine suitor.

He dressed, ate breakfast late in the dining room of his boarding house and left, thinking of ways to phrase his words carefully. He never felt he was very good with words. Anna was making that painfully obvious every time they met together. While Anna's speech rolled of her tongue in great swoops and flourishes of well-chosen words, he felt akin to a caveman, grunting and grumbling in reply, hardly getting his point across as clearly or as well as he hoped. He feared that any small mistake today in his choice of words would make Jenny crumple into tears, and he would be left looking the villain. That's why he preferred to take her on a walk with him and not be trapped inside of a restaurant, open to everyone's scrutiny.

If his parents had still been alive, he knew his mother at least would have been disappointed in his decision. She would have liked Jenny, and so did he. She was just the right sort of girl, the best woman for a policeman to marry in order to live a settled and sensible life. But in the space of almost three days, so much had changed, and yet so much was the same, just more evident to him. It was almost like Jenny's supposed indiscretion had come at the best time possible. He wanted to be free of that attachment and explore this new longing that nagged at him.

He couldn't deny that the new longing included a woman who proved her strength time and time again, but there was something more. He just couldn't yet put his finger on it. He was meandering down Plum Street, hands in his pockets, passing by the large Lancaster cemetery. He stopped and lit a cigarette, staring out over the cold, gray stones. He was nearing Jenny's house, and his earlier resolve was beginning to fail him.

He thought about how he had asked Anna to meet him tonight at St. James, the very spot where her cousin had been abducted. Perhaps it was too callous of him, but it was one of the darkest and most hidden places in the city, and they would need to be hidden if they were to meet without notice. It was also close to Anna's house. He didn't like the idea of her walking too long alone in the dead of night.

George turned away from the cemetery, feeling like his feet were leaden weights when he saw Jenny's home loom in the distance. He had seen it many times, and in the first bloom of their courtship, it had set his heart to racing. Now, he realized that it had simply been the excitement and uncertainty of dealing with a woman. It was not love. He was certain it had never been. Only convenience and a sort of friendship.

He slowly walked up the steps and lifted his fist to knock when a breathless Jenny swung open the door, her eyes bright with excitement. She was smiling at the guest in the doorway, but once she saw George, her face fell.

"Oh, George. It's you." In that moment, George felt a sudden confidence. It was all going his way.

CHAPTER

18

He coughed into his fist politely.

"Yes, Jenny. It's me. Were you expecting someone else?" Jenny fluttered and fussed with her hair, and she settled her dress to rights after her mad dash to the door.

She looked past George briefly and then said, "No, certainly not. You just never know who could be at the door. Women are always so stuck inside, waiting for things to happen."

Her fumbled response irritated George. Was she to keep up this charade even when caught in the act?

"Jenny, if you've the time, I wondered if I might ask you to go on a walk with me? There is something I want to talk to you about. Bring a chaperone if you like."

Jenny nodded to the maid inside for her coat. "No, that'll be fine. We can walk in the cemetery. It's within sight of the house."

They ambled towards the cemetery, keeping their usual polite distance. The cemetery was not quite the scene he had hoped for, for his parents were buried in that hallowed ground, and he didn't like the idea of them watching over him in this instance. They walked in silence for a few moments, and anyone could feel that something simmered just below the surface between them. Jenny's quick movements and shifting eyes were enough to disconcert any man. Let alone one who knew why.

He started slowly, trying to emulate what he had practiced in his head on the way over. "Jenny, there's something we need to talk about. I don't know if it matters to you or not, but I happened to see you yesterday. When I was with Ned Barnum on King Street."

The two of them had entered the cemetery path, and George was grateful that it was empty of other walkers. He was watching her shifting expressions and waiting for her to speak. His chest tightened with the thought that it could have been a relative, and then where would he be? He'd have to think of some excuse for why he called upon her in such a manner.

Or you just tell her the truth. Like you planned to, anyway.

Jenny kept walking, but her back stiffened. "I suppose I shouldn't have expected anything less, with you being a policeman and all. King Street, you say?"

"Yep. What were you doing there, and who was that man? Surely as a fiancé, I have the right to ask."

Jenny looked down and colored. "Certainly, you've a right."

She paused and then turned, pulling on George's shoulder as she did so, so that they were standing face to face.

"He's a man I met very recently. He's wonderful and accomplished."

She was talking slowly, trying not to look too closely at George. He could imagine what a painful scene it would be for a man truly committed to his engagement.

How horrible to see a woman struggling to tell you that she no longer wants you and wishes to marry another.

He tried to make his expression as impassive as possible. "I see. What's his name? Are you planning on becoming engaged to him?"

George knew he was being rather blunt, but there was no time to waste. He had to meet Anna later, and he didn't want anything to get in the way. He was done with this tiresome game that he and Jenny had been playing. In this moment, the weight of it suddenly appeared even more starkly on his shoulders.

Jenny looked taken aback. She put a hand to her chest. "There's no need for harshness, George. I'm trying to be kind."

George softened. "I'm sorry, Jenny. But you've got to understand why I ask. It was very strange to see you with a man like that. You were laughing, and you were arm in arm. Very sociable for someone who's not your betrothed."

"You're right. Well, I want to be honest." Jenny bit her lip. "I hope for a proposal any day. His name is Mr. Mason."

George frowned. *Mason. That name seems to be flooding all areas of my life.*

Seeing George's expression, Jenny's voice lifted to a higher pitch, and he could see she was getting flustered. "I planned to tell you, but I knew you'd be busy with the murder, and I didn't want to disturb you with such troubling news."

George knew that was a lie, but he didn't let that bother him. He was certain that there were many other things she would have happily disturbed him for.

"Mason. Frederick Mason?" he asked.

He could have laughed at the possible connection, but he refrained. He wanted to scoff at Jenny's flimsy excuse for her betrayal, but he was grateful for her honesty. Could it be possible that this Frederick Mason was spreading himself just a little bit too thin with the ladies of this town? English, educated, and charming? The perfect candidate to lure women in.

Jenny shook her head. "No, his name is David Mason. Do you think you know him?"

David? Another name that haunts me. Could it be the same David that was with Ophelia? Surely not. That would be just too unbelievable.

He didn't answer Jenny's question. His head was spinning. He felt like somewhere, someone was laughing at him with all these links, these names twisted together in some sort of incomprehensible knot. And he was simply too stupid to figure it all out.

"I'm sorry that you couldn't have told me before, Jenny. I know that it's been difficult with my work and your plans. I couldn't give you what you wanted." He reached out his hand for hers. He could see the moisture in her eyes as she let him take her hand. She was not totally unfeeling after all. He would endeavor to act likewise.

"I think that it's best if we part ways at long last. I won't fight you on this matter. You deserve to be happy with your new fellow. Although do you want me to speak with your father about this?"

Jenny shook her head. "No, I've already warned him of my feelings. He does not object, although he was surprised."

George smiled. He was over the moon he didn't have to speak to Mr. Holz about anything. The man was sour and religious to the point of being condescending. He was not an easy man to deal with.

"I can imagine. I hope you won't hold a grudge against me for releasing you so easily."

Jenny held tightly to his hands. "No, George. I won't. I can say this freely now, now that we are both of the same mind. I care for you deeply, but it was never that way. I had hoped it would happen, especially after we were wed, but now I see that it couldn't ever be. I'd never be able to understand the way you feel about your work, George." She looked down, her earlier confidence fading. "I want to be a man's whole focus, as well as our children. I want him to come home at night and leave everything from his day behind him."

George nodded along. He knew this to be a fault of his. "Thank you, Jenny." He leaned in and kissed her lightly on the cheek. "I wish you both a world of happiness. You'll be much better suited." He held out his arm for her to take as they walked back through the cemetery, their shoes crunching over the gravelly path.

Once he left Jenny at her door, he felt light and free. He turned back towards Plum Street and saw the sun beginning its descent towards the nether end of the sky. It was time to return to the station. For the first time in a long time, he felt a little flicker of hope. Jenny was out of his life. It was finished, and she was happy. He was glad that he would not be thought of as the cad who left his fiancée at the altar, but instead a man who was a little bit neglectful.

He pushed his hands into his coat pockets to avoid the sting of the evening chill, and he thought about why his work consumed him so much that he had no time for anyone else. It had always been that way. Before he'd met Jenny, he and the other constables had spent time in pubs, meeting different women when they were off their shifts. He'd enjoyed it, but it never consumed his whole mind. Even once he met Jenny, there was excitement and thrill, but once he returned to work, that was all he thought about.

He would rather spend the night on the beat, seeing what would come his way than return home to his lonely boarding room or to a dinner with his dissatisfied fiancée. Jenny was everything he thought he was supposed to do, but now that she was gone, he knew he had made the right decision. She wanted things that he wasn't that interested in giving her. Marriage and a family were all well and good and had been the path of many a man he knew, Ned included. However, it was not everything to him, especially not when a case was in the air, and one that was up to him to solve.

Well, both Anna and me.

He could feel the dangerous draw of Lady Anna, and he wanted to ignore it. Even if he felt an attraction to her and was looking forward to that evening more than a policeman doing his work should, nothing could ever happen. They did not make sense as a pair. They were from two very different worlds. Yet something connected and united them. He could see it in their time in the office yesterday evening. He could sense it in the way he jumped to her aid to protect her from her uncle's suspicions. Even in their arguments, they seemed to be somehow enjoying each other's company.

I can only speak for myself I suppose. It's more likely that she thinks me a complete idiot, especially after her harsh scolding yesterday on the merits of the female mind.

Tonight would be an adventure. George was trembling with the excitement of it. But he had to stop thinking about seeing Anna's face again and more about what he was going to do when he got to tonight's destination. What was he hoping to achieve? The station came into his view, and he shuffled into it, feeling a shift in the evening sun. It would be a very chilly night.

***

Anna wrapped her coat about her. Norma had done well and picked out clothes from the youngest footman and therefore the closest in size to Anna. She was amazed at how warm the woolen cap was that covered her hair. It was pulled tight against her skull and even covered her ears. She wished it would be acceptable for her to always wear something like it in the cold months. It was a frostier evening than she'd expected, the last tendrils of winter leaving their mark. That was something she had still not quite gotten used to living in America. The winters were far deadlier and lasted longer than any she'd experienced in England.

It had been simple enough leaving the house. No one was awake to check on anything, and she'd left as quietly as she could and stumbled onto the main street. A cold night always made things seem quieter and lonelier than they really were, and once she was out in the face of the frozen winds, the dark street echoed with nothingness. It was a blank, and while that was a good thing, Anna felt uneasy as she pushed forward towards the shadow of the spire of St. James Church.

She was eager to meet George and had thought about it all day. She wanted answers, and she knew that the den held them. She was afraid, but she had to be strong for Ophelia. She wanted to be strong for herself as well and prove to everyone that she could do this. Even the killer believed in her abilities, at least more than in the police's, and she hoped that he would follow through on his word if she was to discover his real identity.

Frederick Mason popped into her mind as her boots shuffled along the brick walkway. She would see him again soon, and she hoped that she would be unable to connect him to the murderer. He was a kind man, very respectful and polite. She didn't want to believe that he had anything to do with this. She just wished that she could remember if he'd been at the ball after Ophelia had gone to meet her lover.

Anna slowed her pace, seeing the low brick wall and wrought iron gate of the graveyard coming up on her right. She peered around the wall and into the dark stillness. She hoped she wouldn't have to enter too deeply into the graveyard alone in the dark. This graveyard was one of the oldest in the city, and its ghosts were well-known. It was also the scene of her cousin's disappearance, but she tried to push that from her mind for the moment. Opening the gate slowly, she watched the moon bounce off of the silver stones and bit her tongue to keep from thinking about the way the bouncing shadows looked like awoken spirits.

Don't be foolish, Anna! Ophelia needs you!

She moved forward slowly, stepping gingerly onto the main path. It seemed disrespectful to step hastily or loudly through a silent graveyard.

"George," she whispered into the stillness, hating the way the cold made the skin of her neck tingle.

Her heart fluttered with fear as she plunged further into the darkness away from the streetlamps. She whispered his name again, but there was still no answer. Why had the church no lamps to light in the evening? She stopped. She could not go further. She hated that George had asked to meet her here at the scene of the crime. She couldn't not think about it, and Anna shuddered at the image of poor Ophelia, totally oblivious to her attacker as he approached out of the dark, touching her and pulling her away to some faraway lair.

Anna clenched her fists and brought her coat tighter around her body. This was the one item of clothing which was bigger than the rest. The size made her feel more comfortable, as if she was being wrapped in safe protection. She saw an orb of red in the far corner of the graveyard, and into the main path stepped a man with holes in his shirt and jacket. His dark hair was tousled, and his face was covered in dirt. He observed Anna and grinned, and Anna gasped, slowly backing away from him.

Behind her, she tripped over a low stone and was falling backward with a scream brewing in her throat. The grinning man rushed forward and grabbed her around the waist, lifting her to her feet.

This shall be my end, she thought.

"Sorry! I didn't mean to scare you," a familiar voice said. Anna looked up, surprised.

"George! You!" She narrowed her eyes and brushed off her coat. "You could've warned me what your disguise would be. You nearly scared me half to death!"

George chuckled softly, and Anna could see his eyes looking her up and down. He replied, "You know, I could say the same to you. About the disguise."

Anna wanted to, but she refused to laugh. She put her hands on her hips, the bright moment of exhilaration over. They lingered close together for a moment longer than was appropriate, Anna's thoughts full of the way George's hands had been on her waist only a second before. It was such an intimate gesture, rather like a dance, but so brief, it left her wanting more. She stepped away.

"You've done well, playing the part of a down-and-out."

He smirked. "Thanks. I spend enough time seeing them on the street every day. All right now, there's no more time for compliments, although I'm sure you're full of them, ready to send them my way."

Anna rolled her eyes but followed him out of the cemetery.

He's feeling rather chipper this evening, isn't he?

It was strange for George to make jokes so many times in only the matter of a few minutes. But again, he was a skilled professional at drawing women in with his charm until he froze on them again, his hard shell exposed.

Anna kept pace with her dirty companion and couldn't help but keep watching him out of the corner of her eye. Her heart was singing with happiness. She couldn't believe she was here, in the middle of the night with a police officer, right on the edge of solving a mystery. If nothing else, she had bit back her fears and walked out boldly into the night. She couldn't wait to see what excitement the rest of the evening held. With George Ford at her side, she was certain it would be interesting.

PART III

CHAPTER

19

George felt energized and ready for what lay ahead. This was the moment he had been waiting for for such a long time, to be involved in a case where he was the lead, and he could work to solve it. He had a worthy opponent. A woman was missing, presumed captured by the recent killer, and the killer had requested another woman try to find him out. George had flirted briefly with the idea of telling his sergeant about Anna's letter, but it could be all be made up. The killer could simply be claiming the abduction, and he did not want to ruin this chance for Anna. Going to the den was the perfect idea, and it could help rule out a few things.

It was all too delightful, and he tried to keep his excitement at bay because he knew his thrills were at the expense of Ophelia's safety. His delight was compounded by the fact that Anna had agreed to join him and had shown up in his arms in a man's disguise. He felt like laughing, smiling, and making jokes all night long.

The moment he'd held her to him to balance her had been fleeting, but his hands twitched with the memory of it. Now that he was severed with Jenny, his mind was free to think only about Anna and the case. He admitted to himself that those were the only things he was really interested in thinking about anyway. He tried to shake his head to rid himself of his foolish thoughts.

"I suppose you realized where we're going then, Anna?" Her Christian name on his lips made their time together all the sweeter.

He didn't revert to her title as he had done when they'd argued in his office. He wanted that to all be in the past and for them to go back to what they'd decided before they'd fought.

"I'm assuming we're going to the den, just as I'd hoped."

"Eager to sample their wares, are you?" he teased.

George could see Anna's smirk out of the corner of his eye, and he felt even bolder.

"Hardly, officer. However, I can't help but feel just a little excited to see the inside of the place. Oh, what my mother would think if she knew what I was doing right now."

Anna sighed as they slipped down along the dark streets, heading back to S. Shippen, a pair of nondescript figures in the dark.

He kept his voice low. In the empty streets, he felt like his voice was too loud and could be heard by anyone listening in the shadows. "Actually, I was surprised to see that you'd come."

Anna quickly turned to face him. "Why? You know how much I want to solve this for Ophelia, to be a part of something outside of myself. You know the killer asked me. Why would you expect me to back out now?"

A lovely, now familiar crinkle had formed between Anna's eyebrows as she looked at him with consternation, and George felt transfixed by it for a moment. In her brandished fury, a stray curl had fallen out from underneath her woolen cap as well, pale and gleaming gold in the moonlight.

He put his hands up in defense. "I said surprised, not displeased. Don't misunderstand me. I only thought it'd be difficult for you to get away."

She seemed to relax at his reply. "I'm sorry. I think my nerves are on edge. Part excitement, part fear. I," she paused, and he waited with bated breath, so curious as to what her next words would be. "I'm angry that I desire so much to be a part of this because it's at the expense of my cousin's safety. I feel so guilty. Perhaps that sounds foolish."

George nodded in understanding. He knew that feeling all too well. Guilt for the happiness and fulfillment at the expense of others.

"Well, if I'm being honest, then I'll tell you I know exactly how you feel. I was hoping for the killer to strike again to give me a chance to solve another case. I'd hoped my sergeant would allow me the chance. And here we are, both getting the chance we've been wanting."

There was a solemn silence between them as they stood facing each other on the cold street, the wind picking up, threading its way through the holes of George's clothes. He pointed to her hair.

"There's a piece of...You might want to put that away," he began, fumbling over his words as he watched her. She lifted her hand and found her stray lock, pushing it back up into her hat.

"Oh, thank you. Wouldn't want to give anything away, of course. What kind of investigator would I be? Well, we'd better continue."

"Yes," he said dolefully, realizing that he'd enjoyed that moment of openness and honesty and didn't want it to be over. He couldn't remember the last time he'd been that honest with anyone. Not even Jenny knew of his excitement with the case or how he felt guilty at the same time.

"Now, I should warn you. Don't get too bold tonight. It could get dangerous." He patted the bulky frame of the pistol in his coat pocket.

Anna smiled. "I'll do my best, sir, but you know that it wouldn't be possible for me to promise anything of the sort."

George laughed, but when he heard the sound bounce off the walls, he winced.

"See? You're already doing dangerous things." Anna looked like she was about to retort, when he continued. "Look, I've asked around, and it appears we're to enter through the back door to get into the den. We don't want to chance D from the doorway seeing us again, even if we are so well-disguised."

He coughed, feeling a new wave of cold wind, and he pulled his coat tighter around him. "I hope the lighting's dim enough inside that we won't be recognized by anyone, especially if we have a few, um, 'acquaintances' in there."

"Ah, yes, I've a feeling that could be the case for me, not counting perhaps Ophelia. As I've read, opium is often the playground for the wealthy, for they've the money and the time to idle away the hours."

George hadn't wanted to say it, but he was glad that Anna realized it, and she stated it without shame or malice. They slowed as they reached the opening to S. Shippen Street, and George tapped Anna's elbow lightly to turn her towards the small alley to the side. He was amazed at how easy it had been for him to find the location, only by asking around in the police department.

Apparently, the police had known about the opium den for years, as his sergeant had said, but as it brought in money for the town and well-known people of the city were involved with it, they couldn't or wouldn't shut it down.

Anna and George saw someone nearing, their footsteps echoing loudly along the lonely street. He felt cold stone against his back after he pulled them back against the closest wall. He lit a cigarette while they waited, and the person, cloaked and hooded, walked past them without a word or any sort of acknowledgement and shuffled down the narrow alleyway towards the back entrance to the den.

Both George and Anna eyed the figure, and Anna made a move to follow once they'd disappeared, but George grasped her wrist and mouthed "wait" in her direction. He took another drag of the cigarette, turning from side to side to make sure no one else was about and dropped it to the ground. Boldly, George's hand slid down from her wrist and grabbed Anna's hand in his, pulling her towards the alley. He felt a slight tension from her for a second, but then she relaxed. If she asked him later about it, he would explain it away as something to do with safety. Her hand was soft and warm in his, and it felt comfortable there, as if it belonged.

His mind threatened to go in other directions, but he had to focus for the time being. They had a job to do, and he was very glad that Anna was with him to do it. Once they were in the alleyway, it became very narrow, so they had to move in a single file line, but he didn't drop her hand. They could see a dim light at the end, like a beacon guiding them to their destination. He was certain it was for the very purpose of alerting customers of the doorway but not the police, as they could not see the light from the street.

As they continued down, a few shadowy characters squeezed their way past them, and odors of varying revulsion wafted up George's nose, alerting them to the financial status or daily habits of each of the passersby. At one point, Anna made a noise in shock at one particularly malodorous man, and George squeezed her hand in comfort.

The alley ended abruptly with a hastily formed brick wall, the light from a small lamp making ominous shadows along its crude and crooked surface. George reluctantly let go of Anna's hand, remembering that she was meant to appear male. A gruff man in a coat stood sentry, his arms crossed. There was a scar above his left eye, and he looked as if he'd been made for such a job. Warm, yellow light blinked behind him through the open doorway as figures shuffled inside.

The guard looked at the pair of them, lingering too long than was comfortable on Anna's upturned face before nodding. Feeling like they could be caught and thrown into the street at any moment, George pulled on Anna's elbow to nudge her inside. After a short passage, the room opened, and to their joint surprise, it was a lot larger than he'd expected after seeing the building from the street. It looked nearly 50 feet in width to George's eyes, and he felt frozen to the spot, taking everything in.

When he turned to Anna to whisper, "Keep close to me," he saw her surprised expression as well. He could also see a hint of a smile on her lips. Surely as a rich, titled woman, she would never have been given a chance to see anything like it before. He felt a little satisfaction at having been able to give her a moment like this, or at least be a part of her enjoyment of it.

Too bad it is something that isn't all that enjoyable to look upon.

In reply to his words, Anna nodded but kept her eyes forward. He understood, for what a strange sight it was to see. Even as a policeman who had seen his fair share of strange things, this sight was the most unusual. As if they were in an Arabian palace from the Aladdin story, cushions of various sizes were stacked and laid around the dim room, and three side alcoves were sectioned off with gauzy layers of lightly colored lace.

There was a haziness and a sensuality to the atmosphere, and the air was thick and sweet with the flowery smell of smoke. Unfortunately, it also smelled of sweat as bodies lay thickly against the walls and cushions, some of them appearing not to have been bathed in weeks.

At first glance, many of the bodies looked dead until they would move position, long pipes held in their hands or clasped between their teeth. George and Anna moved towards a side wall strangely empty of cushions or bodies, and they hoped to find someone conscious enough to answer their questions. After they passed the first few people, he lost hope that they'd be able to find anyone at all before they began to look suspicious.

Damn.

***

Anna admitted to herself that she was horrified. Oddly, at the same time, she felt grimly pleased that she'd been allowed a sight her mother would never have allowed her otherwise. She had no idea what truly lay under the latticework of a city and certainly not a city as religious and pure as Lancaster City claimed to be. The dark side hidden by shadows. It had always been kept from her for obvious good reason, but now she was seeing what the world actually looked like. She still didn't understand how her beautiful cousin had ever become involved with it.

If Anna had to describe the scene before her, she would have said it made her think of the bowels of Hell like Milton described it, and yet no one looked like they were suffering. Tears threatened to come to her eyes as she noticed the slack faces of the men and women that were piled up around the large room. They all looked like lost dolls, frozen in a thought they couldn't be rid of. As she'd predicted, these men and women were not all as poor as one might have expected. She wasn't sure if that thought comforted her or gave her even more pain.

Some of the people were in fine fabrics and well-built shoes, and others were in rags with dirtied faces. Yet they all looked the same now, immobilized and equalized by smoke and what it did to their bodies and minds. Anna did understand the draw of darkness and of doing things that society might not prove acceptable, but she did not understand the appeal of this nothingness. This desperation to breathe in something that would make one limp and lifeless, dead to the world. If Ophelia had enjoyed the wares at a place like this, then what had drawn her to them?

Could there have been something wrong at home that I never knew about? Have I been too selfish or obtuse to notice? Perhaps I didn't know her so well after all.

As she and George crept along the side wall, afraid to make too much noise to alert the owner to them trying to ask questions. They paused in front of one of the lace-covered alcoves. George quickly peered inside, and seeing it was empty, nodded to Anna to enter in after him. Following him into the narrow room lit only by a small candle on a table, Anna glanced at George as he searched around the room. She was very grateful to him, but she briefly wondered if it was a bad idea that they had come and come together.

He was an officer of the law, and while the killer hadn't given her strict instructions, perhaps he would not appreciate that she had involved the police in her investigation? She shook off her fears. She didn't want to admit it, but she needed George because she didn't know the first thing about performing an investigation, and she certainly didn't know about life on this side of town. George would be her doorway to all of that.

She hoped that George would never see her lack of expertise. Anna had thought of little else since the killer had prodded her to join him in his game. She wanted so badly to prove the killer right, that she was wise, and that she had the ability to beat him at it. She wanted George to see her skills as well.

In the alcove stood a low table and a few dirtied cushions. At least they looked dirty, but Anna thought it might be the shadows from the candlelight playing tricks on her. As she moved closer to the table, she spotted an odd, lamp-like instrument, two long pipes, and two blue ceramic bowls.

George neared her and whispered, "At least it's empty for now. If we're to discuss with anyone, I think we'd better do it in here. I expect someone will have to come and take our payment and light the pipes."

He glanced down at his pocket watch. "They'll be here soon, I'd guess. To service us. Certainly, they've seen us come in."

They looked at each other for a moment before laughing softly.

Anna replied, "Yes, we've perhaps come slightly unprepared in having never consumed opium, but I must say, these instruments are beautiful." She reached a hand out to finger the smooth, shiny surface of the ceramic. "If I had to choose to smoke opium based solely on the beauty of its tools, then I would definitely do so."

George chuckled. "Perhaps that's the real way they gain their customers. Ah well, this is a comfortable enough place to sit while we wait." He leaned down into one of the cushions, and a little cloud of dust came up into the air. He coughed, saying, "Hmm...and here I thought this was a well-visited den, but perhaps not everyone is able to afford such a room."

"And are we?"

"We don't need to pay. We're not taking the wares. We'll simply see if they're amenable to a few questions."

Outside, a pair of voices spoke in hushed tones, and as Anna strained to listen, she could decipher that it was not English being spoken. Anna moved to the lacy doorway and peeked out when she heard the light shuffling of feet coming towards them.

She whispered, "The lighters are coming around to refill the pipes." She stuck out a hand and waved to one of them.

George nodded. "We'll start by asking them."

Anna moved away from the door and settled herself next to him on the cushions, and a young dark-haired, Chinese woman entered the room. She gasped and nearly dropped the tools in her hand when she saw the figures inside.

Anna jumped up and reached out a hand to steady her. "Oh, I'm sorry. We didn't mean to frighten you. We only want to ask a few questions."

"Questions? These rooms are for special customers only. Not you." She pointed to their ragged clothing. "You will need to speak to the boss."

Only a tinge of a foreign accent was heard in her speech, and Anna was relieved that she spoke English. Now that she was in the room, Anna hoped she and George could perhaps find a way to convince her to answer their questions.

The woman made a move to leave, but Anna said, "Please, I need to ask a few questions, if I can have a few moments? I only mean to find out where my cousin is."

George pulled the picture from his coat pocket.

"Have you seen this woman here?" The young woman squinted at the photograph, and then her eyes widened with recognition.

"Why do you ask about her?"

Anna felt a rush of excitement. "Have you seen her then?"

The woman nodded. "Yes, but it is not my business. I will tell the boss you are here. He knows. It is his woman."

Anna tried to stop her, but the woman was too quick. Anna turned back to George, worried about what to do next.

"Oh, I'm sorry. Did I make a mistake? I didn't mean to frighten her. Do you even want to speak to the boss? Perhaps we've bitten off more than we can chew."

George moved to stand beside her. She felt his hand flutter by her own, but he didn't grasp it this time.

"A titled English lady using low-born idioms? I wouldn't have thought it of you, Lady Anna." He smiled encouragingly. "Don't worry. Perhaps it'll be a good idea to speak to the boss, although I don't know how much he'll want to talk to us. At least we don't look recognizable as anyone in particular. You did well."

Anna tried her best to feel calm. She was happy that George was in one of his soft moods, but she feared he might turn angry soon if she did anything which would get them into trouble. Feeling her nervousness grow in intensity, Anna peeked back through the lace to see if the boss would make his appearance in the room. She wanted to get a look at him first, as if that would give her some kind of comfort. It was hazy, but a tall man did appear, the young woman at his side. She was speaking to him in hurried English and pointing towards Anna and George's alcove.

"He's coming!" She steeled herself as the man walked towards them through the heavy smoke. As he approached, a soft "oh" escaped her lips as she recognized the man. George leaned in close to her.

"What is it? Who is it?"

"It's…It's Mr. Mason. My Mr. Mason."

CHAPTER

20

"Your Mr. Mason? Do you mean the Mason from the ball? Frederick Mason?

George wondered why the name Mason was being bandied about Lancaster City as if everyone in town had been titled with the moniker. Anna's face was pale as she turned to him.

"Yes, my Mr. Mason from the ball. He'll recognize me at once. We have to think of something. If he recognizes me..."

"Then all will be lost."

She nodded. "My mother will never let me out of her sight again. He will tell her everything, and we won't be any closer to finding Ophelia."

George could see her mind working feverishly, and the crinkle between her eyebrows returned, this time making her look worried.

George thought quickly. "Pull down your cap and sit in the shadows. I can ask all of the questions. Don't raise your eyes to him."

Anna nodded but didn't seem to hear him. The footsteps of Mason approached ever nearer. It was such a long room, it would take a while to get across it, and she kept watching him, having not moved away from the doorway.

"Hmm...he looks different somehow. But - but I'm sure it's him."

"He's coming, Anna. Be quick. Get to your position. I'll do the talking."

She nodded again, and then her green eyes snapped up to his and her fingers dropped the lace curtain back in its position. He pulled back at the sight of her inscrutable expression.

"I have a better idea, one that will shock and surprise him and distract him so entirely that he'd never think it was me."

George furrowed his brow, curious what she meant. He was about to ask, but she yanked on his coat lapels, bring him closer until their lips met, and George found himself suddenly swimming in a fragrant sea of a fresh floral scent, his mind filling with color.

At first, he tensed with surprise, but then in a flash, he burst into life, and placing his hands lightly and timidly on Anna's waist, he gently pushed her back against the wall of the alcove, and everything around him seemed to fade. Her lips were soft and inviting, and he opened his mouth to hers. She did the same, and they were soon embraced tightly, their mouths exploring one another as if there was no imminent danger and nothing to call them back to the present.

In faded tones, he could hear voices just outside of the lacy alcove, but he didn't care. He was kissing Anna, and right now, that was the only thing he wanted to do or to think about.

With a light swoosh, the man identified as Mason pushed back the lace and squinted into the dimness.

"Excuse me? Oh," he uttered when he spotted the pair of embracing lovers. He cleared his throat, and groggily, George pulled apart from Anna, and she kept her head down as promised. "I'm sorry to you both, but this is not that kind of place. There is a club," another throat clearing, "for gentlemen with your predilections, not too far from here, if you will allow me to direct you."

The man had the slight tinge of an English accent, but it was barely perceptible. George stifled a laugh as he thought about how very unmanly Anna Lovelace really was.

His head was still spinning after that kiss, but he was able to focus enough to say, "No, that won't be necessary, sir."

He turned to the face in the archway and was shocked into speechlessness when the lamplight shone on the man's face in full. This was the man he had seen with Jenny that day on King Street. The sideburns, the black hair. He would have recognized him anywhere.

Swallowing nervously, George asked, "You are the proprietor of this establishment?"

The man's eyes narrowed as he took in George's ripped clothing. "I am. I share the business with my cousin, but I'm the one who's in charge of running things. May I help you? Do you wish to make a purchase?"

Oddly, the man's voice was kind but wary, and George felt like he was on the wrong side of an interrogation.

"Will you come inside? I thought we might ask you a few questions."

"We? Your young partner will ask as well?"

The man pointed to Anna, and Anna lifted her shoulders in confusion. "Ich verstehe kein Englisch."

George looked between the two of them, frozen in laughable surprise as Anna suddenly spouted off in German, with Jenny's future fiancé questioning them.

"Ah, no. He doesn't speak English as you can see. He can wait outside."

Anna left without looking up, and George breathed a sigh of relief. He could focus much better with her gone. Mason stepped inside, and George felt a little subdued by his size. He was thin yet tall and imposing. Mason's voice developed a slight edge.

"I'm a very busy man, so I suggest you ask me your questions and then be gone. These rooms are meant to be reserved for our most special guests."

"I wonder, then, why they are so dusty? Perhaps you don't have many special guests arriving of late."

He saw Mason tense. "It is true, we more often get customers of your caliber, but I cannot allow those of your kind to be in these rooms or else certain things will occur that are not permitted to occur in my establishment, such as what I witnessed a moment ago."

Uncomfortable, George cleared his throat and began. "I am here on behalf of a dear friend. She is worried about her cousin's whereabouts." He pulled the picture from his pocket. "Ophelia Marshall. The man, D, at the doorway told me she's come around a time or two. Your assistant seemed scared that I'd asked. Have you seen her?"

George tried his best to catalogue each of Mason's movements as he heard the news. Mason almost looked like he was going to cry which made George even more uncomfortable. When he spoke again, Mason's voice was thick.

"Yes, I know her. I was very sad to hear about her disappearance."

"What's your name? What's your relationship with her? Your man upstairs in the doorway told me the owner of this place was a David F.?"

He slowed his voice down on the second question, as he remembered he had to pretend that he was not a police officer, feverishly questioning a suspect.

Mason hesitated for a moment. "It appears I will need to speak to Darren so that he does not divulge any unnecessary information to strangers who are not interested in purchasing my wares."

Ah, Darren in the doorway it is then.

He wavered but then shrugged. "Yes, David F. is my name, but that is all I can tell you. This woman came here a few times. We had a sort of relationship, but I have not seen her since her disappearance. I'm afraid I cannot help you, for I've no idea where she's gone."

George tried to piece together who this man was who was paying court to Jenny but also perhaps in a relationship with Anna's cousin? None of it made any sense. Perhaps his last name was Mason and F was merely a middle initial?

"No idea where she could be? We are desperate to find her."

David shook his head and looked down. George felt like the man looked almost sorry he could not give more information.

George tried a different tack. "My friend was told by Ophelia that she was in love with a man named D and expected he might propose any day. She was also told he was connected to the police in some way. Have you seen anyone with her that might fit that description?"

At George's mention of love, David's eyes snapped up to his. "In love? She said in love?" His voice was eager, almost happy, and George felt like this was the strangest situation he'd ever been in with a suspect. To him, this man did not seem like a killer, more like a besotted young boy, sad that he had been caught.

"Ah, yes. She said, 'in love'."

That moment of openness was gone, and a flash of hardness crossed the man's face.

"No, there have been no police officers here. If that is all, I must return to business. Besides, this is not a hotel. We cannot harbor anyone here who does not wish to partake of our supplies."

George nodded tightly. "I understand. Thank you, sir, for your time." David nodded and turned to leave.

He paused and then said without turning around, "I do hope you can find Ophelia. She is a good woman, undeserving of what has happened to her."

"Yes, we will--", he started, but the man left, and George stood alone in the alcove, wondering if he should laugh at the information that had just been so easily handed to him. Anna burst in from the side, an excited look on her face.

"I've spoken to a witness outside who was only slightly coherent. Tell me everything." George looked at her for a moment, her eager expression so inviting. He smelled another waft of that intoxicating floral essence even amidst the fetid air of the den, and he had to keep his hand from coming up to cup her face.

"We've got to leave. We can talk outside."

He led the way out, and without gripping hands, they left the den, navigated the alley, and found themselves in the wide-open street, breathing in the fresh, cool night air.

***

Anna was floating. After the kiss, she felt her blood flowing through every vein as she left the lacy alcove, cowed by the presence of Mason and what had pushed her to kiss George as she had. What had it been? It was an idea, hoping to throw Mason entirely off the scent of her as the young boy in disguise, but it was not exactly necessary. She stood outside of the opening to the alcove, leaning against the wall, hoping that her ears would pick up a little something. She hadn't been able to get a good look at the man since she was forced to put her head down to avoid recognition, but she felt for certain it was Frederick Mason, the man who was paying court to her this last week. The smile was the same and so were the eyes.

But this time he had dark hair, nearly black, sideburns, and no mustache. It was very possible he could have shaved it off since their last meeting, but the dark hair? The appearance in an opium den? It was all too strange, and she couldn't make sense of it, especially since thoughts of George's brief yet passionate embrace were taking over her focus.

"Entschuldigung. Hast du Wasser? Ich brauche Wasser."

A tiny voice spoke from below her, and understanding the German words, Anna knelt down close to the woman. She was young, beautiful, and looking as if she'd seen better days behind her. She was asking for water. Anna could imagine feeling thirsty after sucking from a smoke-filled pipe for hours.

Spying another one of the young lighting women, Anna waved to her. "Please bring this young woman some water." She turned to the German girl, and asked her in German, "Ich habe eine Frage. Hast du eine Frau gesehen? Echt schön, sieht reich aus. Ich denke, sie unterhalt sich oft mit dem Chef." *I have a question. Have you seen a woman? Very beautiful, and she looks rich. I think she often speaks with the boss.*

The woman nodded slowly, surprisingly able to respond despite being in a haze from her smoke. She answered, but her words were so slow, that Anna was beginning to grow impatient. "Ja, ja. Sie war hier. Ich habe sie ein paar Mal gesehen. Sehr schön. Ich habe sie auch in der Zeitung gesehen." *Yes, she was here. I've seen her a few times. Very beautiful. I've also seen her in the newspaper.*

"Kennst du ihren Namen?" *Do you know her name?*

"Ophe...ahm...Ich kenne den Nachnamen nicht." *Ophe...something. I don't know the last name.*

"Spricht sie nur mit dem Chef? Sind sie in einer romantischen Beziehung?" *She only talked to the boss. Are they in a romantic relationship?*

"Weiss ich nicht. Vielleicht. Ich denke, einmal habe ich sie gesehen, wie sie sich geküsst haben." *I don't know. I think I saw them kiss once.*

At that moment, the same lighting girl brought the glass of water, and the German girl drank with gusto.

Anna stood again. "Danke."

She had something to chew on while George was conducting his own investigation. She tapped her fingers against the wall. So, this was likely *the* D, or David, that Ophelia had spoken about. It was just as George had predicted about this David F. But why had her cousin fallen in love with the owner of an opium den?

Had it not bothered her that while she was in the den, there were bodies lying around her, filling themselves with poison as she kissed her beloved? This did not sound like Ophelia at all, but Anna had to admit, it did a little bit. Ophelia was always trying to bend the rules, and if she did so, it was always in a very dramatic and flagrant way. Falling in love with the head of an opium den would very much suit her rebellious desires. Was that why she had lied about David being involved with the police somehow?

Anna watched as the disguised Mason left the alcove, and she took the chance to jump inside to speak to George. She was grateful that it was not the kiss they'd shared which was the latest thing to discuss but the matter at hand.

"Tell me everything."

George smirked and looked solemn at the same time. She followed him out of the den, her heart racing until they reached the street.

Taking deep breaths of clean air, she said, "My goodness, I hadn't realized how thick and choking the air was inside. I'm so glad to be returned to the fresh air. I confess I don't understand the appeal of that kind of place at all."

George breathed deeply beside her. "Me as well. I've never seen anything like it before. It was like a playroom but at the same time a hellhole."

Anna laughed. "Those were exactly my thoughts! It brought to mind images of Hell I've seen in books or in galleries." She shuddered in the cold wind and in the clutches of the strong image. "It was dreadful."

"I agree, although I've not been to any galleries. Come. I'll walk you home."

Anna walked beside him. "Fine, but please tell me what you've discovered, and I shall tell you my news."

George was unsure how to begin. "It was a strange affair. I almost laughed a few times at the oddity of it. First of all, you speak German?"

Anna laughed nervously, feeling shy at the display of her ability, but pleased to hear the impressed tone in George's voice.

"Ah, yes. Perhaps I should have mentioned it before if it could have been useful to us. My father provided me with many different tutors. He is a good man, and he wanted me to be all that I could be."

"Would it bother you greatly if I told you I already knew you could speak German and other languages besides?"

"Did you?" Anna's voice was high with surprise.

"My fiancée, or shall I say former fiancée, knew that you're Ophelia's cousin. When we were discussing the case a few days ago, she told me of some of your language skills, among other things."

Anna was solemn. "Former fiancée? George, I'm sorry."

She didn't know what else to say, especially since the fact that it was the word 'former' that made her feel a slight tingle of relief and delight. She hadn't known his situation with women, but now that she knew, she was happy that he was unattached.

But why? What should it matter?

George shrugged. "It was for the best. However, *your* Mr. Mason appears to be the owner."

"Yes. How strange." She pulled the man's coat tighter and shivered as they braced themselves against the onslaught of the cold night wind. It was as if winter had never left.

"Just so you know, the man in the doorway is named Darren, and that's what the owner called him, not D," George told her.

"I see. Well, I didn't assume that man in the doorway was related to my cousin romantically at all, but it is good to rule his name out."

George hesitated, "So you think that man in the den was your Mr. Mason, Frederick Mason, right?"

"Yes, even though he looked a bit different than he did the night I met him or the afternoon he visited me."

"Well," George pushed his hands deep into his pockets. "Your Mr. Mason looks a lot like my former fiancée's Mr. Mason, the man who I saw her with and who she believes will soon make her an offer of marriage."

CHAPTER

21

"Pardon?" Anna said, feeling suddenly breathless. "You recognized him as well?"

George nodded, feeling gratified that they had made a slight break in their investigation, even though he wasn't sure yet what to do with the information.

"Yes, dark hair, sideburns, the whole lot. His face is etched into my memory. When I was interrogating victims' families with Officer Barnum, I saw him and my old fiancée, Jenny, on King Street, laughing arm in arm."

Anna's eyes turned to her feet as they walked. "I see. He did look different to me, but also the same. The teeth, the eyes. They were so similar. My Mr. Mason does not have sideburns, has brown hair, and has a mustache. He could be wearing a disguise? But why?"

"To keep his identity as owner of an opium den a secret? It's easy enough to dye one's hair and add fake sideburns and a mustache."

"I suppose, but you said he showed that opium den 'disguise' to your fiancée."

"Right. He did change his name though. This man tonight claimed to be David F., the owner of the establishment, but Jenny told me that her new man's name was David Mason."

"What a puzzle! Then, George, it must be him! Simply using another name but close to his own. He didn't seem to disguise that very much. And he answered all your questions?"

"Yes, that was the strange thing." George also wanted to make sure they fleshed out all the possibilities. "Just listen to this." They were nearing her home, and he was disappointed, tremendously enjoying this time with her. He couldn't remember the last time he'd had as much fun. "You know a Frederick Mason, businessman who has a mustache, and who has come calling. Jenny knows a David Mason who has begun to call upon her, and Ophelia knows and is supposedly in relationship with a D who owns an opium den, who is also calling himself David F."

George took a breath after his long speech, and Anna nodded.

She replied, "I know it sounds mad. It's quite the conundrum, but I think it's all the same man. It has to be. He looked too similar not to be, unless they're twins."

George lifted his eyebrows in surprise. "It's possible, certainly, but I see only one problem."

"What?"

They slowed as they passed the St. James cemetery, for Anna's home was only a few steps beyond. He did not want to chance them being seen together for Anna's own sake, especially not dressed as they both were.

"If they're all the same man, then why didn't your cousin recognize him at the ball when he danced with you? His disguises are not all that different, and if she was so in love with him, then she would have known who he was right then."

"I had thought of this, but I don't think she got a good look at him that night. If her lover is the same Frederick Mason, I would've been able to tell from her face that she recognized him. Besides, we were talking of him extensively, and I know that she would've made a comment on his appearance if she'd seen him."

George didn't like the sound of the word 'extensively'.

"There's no chance she could have spied him before she left to meet him in the cemetery? It might not be the same man."

"No, no. That doesn't feel right. It has to be. It could simply be that he had used a third disguise when meeting with Ophelia. Remember that Darren had said they would have days that they would meet. He could have changed into his disguise before he was to meet her."

George was impressed. None of the other men he worked with before would ever think so intently about a case. They were only happy the *faster* the investigation would go, and then they could return to the pub or head home to sleep off the hangover they already had.

"It's a good thought. Very possible, but then his coworkers might have noticed it."

"Not that they would have said anything to him about it. He was the boss after all."

George nodded. "So, we're working on the assumption that either it is the same man, or they're twins, or it's a completely different man who just happens to look the same."

Anna waved a hand dismissively in the air. She seemed to be brimming with excitement. "Yes, yes. Now, I must tell you my news. I heard from my witness that she had seen Ophelia there a few times, meeting with our Mr. Mystery Mason, and the woman said she saw them kiss once. So, perhaps even if he's using a third disguise, it is not all that good if a woman under the influence of opium can recognize him as well as my cousin."

At the mention of the kiss, George's mind transported him back to the moment they'd shared in the alcove, his eyes hazy with sweet smoke, his hands were around Anna's waist, and his mouth on hers. It sent a flush of heat through his veins, and he could see Anna's cheeks redden in the moonlight. He cleared his throat, desperate to move beyond his own dangerous path of thoughts.

What's the point of following that path anyway? It's not as if I can do anything about it.

George answered hastily, "Ah well, that ruins the third disguise theory. If both the patron smoking opium recognized David F. while he was with Ophelia, then he must have been wearing the same thing, and Ophelia must not have seen him at the ball until they met in the cemetery."

Anna snapped her fingers. "I forgot! There is something we have not considered. My dear cousin is troubled with rather poor eyesight. However, her vanity prevents her from wearing her spectacles when in the public eye. I totally forgot because it is so unbelievably rare that I see her wearing them." Anna smiled. "It's possible that she could have only seen a room of blurry faces at the ball. And since her D was dressed in a way slightly different than was his usual disguise with her, she would not have immediately recognized him."

George lifted his brows. "Very good thought indeed, Anna. That will help us tremendously. Unfortunately, if the killer is not this David, then she may not be able to describe the man very well who is holding her, especially without her glasses, if we are able to find her again."

"That's true." Anna sighed, and he could tell that her mind was flitting back to her cousin's potential death and current discomfort.

George was reluctant to let her go, but they would both need time to think.

"Well, it's time you go home, I think. I wouldn't want to be the cause of home unrest if someone finds out you're gone and spending time with a homeless man like me."

Anna smiled. "Of course. Is there anything else you were able to glean from David F.?"

He nodded. "One more thing. When I told him about Ophelia, he seemed sad. Then, when I mentioned what you'd told me, that she was in love with this D, he looked deliriously happy and surprised to find out that she was in love with the man. If you want my opinion, he didn't look like a killer or a kidnapper to me, certainly not one that takes the hearts of their victims. He looked genuinely besotted as well as upset by her disappearance."

"Well, I hope you are right. But the other thing I don't understand is if he was so in love with Ophelia, then why is he paying court to me and to Jenny? It's not the kind of thing a man does when he's truly in love."

"I agree," George replied, afraid to look her in the eye as they discussed the inner workings of love. "Go now, Anna. We're here. Uh...thank you for your help tonight. The trip was a lot more--"

"Interesting? Fruitful? Useful?"

He laughed. "Definitely, with your help."

She grinned triumphantly. "Good, I'm glad to hear you say it, although I'm a little surprised to hear words of gratitude coming from your lips."

"Ah, see it's beyond your bedtime, Lady Anna. Hurry off now."

Anna laughed quietly. Remembering the kiss as she turned away, George felt like something had to be said about it or else they would go on never acknowledging it, and that didn't seem right, not when it was still pulsating through him as if it had just happened. He also knew he'd never be able to forget it. He wanted to say something, but he wasn't sure what.

Anna, to his surprise, was the first to say something. "I wanted to apologize about my unladylike behavior at the den. I hope you--"

George held his hand up. "Nothing to apologize for, Anna. All in the spirit of solving a mystery, right?"

Anna blushed a little. "Oh. Yes, you're right. We needed a good way to make sure that David didn't know it was me. All in the spirit. Goodnight, George. Thank you."

She turned towards her house. Her lonely footsteps echoed on the quiet street.

"Goodnight," he called out in response, but she didn't hear him mutter, "All in the spirit of solving a mystery. I'm a complete idiot."

He rolled his eyes and walked away in the opposite direction, hating himself with a passion.

"Anna Lovelace has been a very naughty girl," I tell Ophelia this morning before I leave for the factory. A naughty girl, yes, yes.

"She is not solving this puzzle the way I'd hoped." I heard who visited the den last night. The news has left me fuming.

I do not want the police involved, Anna, but perhaps it is my fault, for I was not entirely clear, my dear heart.

What a lioness you are, for D did not mention you by name, but I know it was you. I know you were there, flouting your German skills while your officer friend asked all the questions. D looked upset too when he told me. The memory of his poor Ophelia being taken. He does not understand what I do! These women are nothing. Women are nothing, except when they can amuse and entertain. D merely fell into one of their traps, but I will help him out of it.

You must be careful, Anna, or else you will cease to entertain me, thus becoming useless. When you have ceased to do so, it will be my job to cease your breath and take that which keeps your earthly time and place it into my jars. That will stop your naughty ways. Tsk, tsk, tsk.

Perhaps I was foolish to bring this girl into the works. I was so intrigued by her at the ball and her desire to break free without my help.

I will have to send her a warning, to let her know that I do not approve of the steps she is taking. She must take other steps, or there will be the consequences she so fears, and more than that. So much more than that. My patience goes only so far, my dear. You should know that. You who have followed me for so long in the newspaper.

Perhaps I will need to take greater measures to scare the police? I thought that the removal of that officer's fiancée from his life would be enough, but it seemed that it only spurred the man to break it off with her. I must do more. But what?

First, I shall write a new letter.

Anna sat at the breakfast table with her parents the next morning, waiting for pieces of the newspaper as her father finished them. Her mother was drinking her tea quietly and looked tired, most likely from staying up late comforting her sister. According to that morning's newspaper, nothing that exciting had been happening. There was a small article about the missing Marshall society girl, but other than that it was the same hum-drum news. Work riots were still going on, and it appeared the bosses were not doing what their employees asked of them.

"Father, may I ask you something?"

"Of course, my dear," he mumbled from behind what was left of his paper.

"Do you have riots at your company, Father? I often see that it's the cigar factory that has them, but I wonder what you would do if your employees made such demands?"

Sighing, he folded the paper down in front of him on the table. He glanced at his wife for a moment before smiling a little sadly at Anna.

"I am afraid they have begun to make demands, Anna, but that is more for your Uncle Jack to decide. I am merely a silent partner, and I do what work I am given. I have been reduced to merely following orders."

Anna was surprised her mother hadn't stopped her inappropriate questioning.

She must be very tired, indeed.

"What kinds of demands, Father?"

"Well, they are asking for an increase of pay, less hours, and they want better working conditions. I had never realized it before, but the conditions of a working cotton mill are not very good. The air is heavy and filled with flying bits of material. Fans are employed, but it only reduces the problems somewhat. It can get into the workers' lungs and make them very sick, even kill them."

Anna was horrified. Her father had never told her anything of the sort, but it was also true that she'd never asked.

"What will you do, Father? Surely these kinds of things would be important to Uncle Jack and to you."

"My Anna, champion of the lower classes. You are right. It does not sit very well with either of us, but our hands are tied in many ways. We cannot simply submit to their demands at first. When would their demands end? Along with the other factory owners of the town, we must show a united front on this matter, and unfortunately, I do not believe any others wish to do anything about it."

Anna nodded, not totally approving, but when her father mentioned other factories, she knew she had to ask.

"Is Frederick Mason one of the owners? He owns the cigar factory, right?"

"Ah, yes, your current suitor." He winked. "He is a fellow businessman, yes, but I'm afraid he does not own the company. He is in business with his cousin, and his cousin owns the cigar factory. He only inherited a small part of it from his uncle, or so I am told, but there were some problems, and

I believe he lost his share. He is a very pleasant man, as you and your mother can attest to."

It is possible for cousins to look very much alike, she mused. *And what problems, I wonder?*

Her father continued, "We are the two largest companies in the city, and the smaller ones do not have the rioting problems that we do. Or at least not the same ones. They would not be able to afford any pay raises. They would have to cut their employee number down to nearly half in order to do so. And their conditions are just as bad."

Anna could feel her heart thundering away in her chest excitedly. It felt like she was edging close to something.

"Do you know his cousin's name?"

Her father frowned in thought. Anna was amazed her mother still had not spoken the whole time but could be heard taking quiet sips from her cup.

"A Richard Mason, I believe, but I have heard his cousin call him Dick." Anna's whole body tensed at this new turn of events.

Another Mason, another D.

All she would have to know is if they looked similar. One of them was connected to Ophelia's disappearance, she was certain of it. These mysterious Masons were looking ever more suspicious in their attachment to Ophelia, especially considering the opium den owner's seemingly emotional attachment to learning that she loved him. Perhaps that was another reason why Ophelia was not found dead yet.

"What does Dick Mason look like?"

"A little like Frederick, but he has the darker hair of the two."

Anna chewed on her lip. Would an owner of a cigar factory have the time to also run an opium den? She wasn't certain. The David F. and Frederick were beginning to sound again like one and the same person. Her head began to ache a little. She could feel time ticking and sliding away. She had to solve this and quickly, but it still felt so out of reach.

"Why do you ask, Anna?"

Her mother broke into the conversation at long last. "Yes, why do you ask? Surely, the next ball is the only thing that should be on your mind, excepting Ophelia."

Her mother had returned to life and was back to scolding.

"I was just curious about the happenings of the city. One more thing, Father. Do *you* have any ideas about who Ophelia's captor might be?"

He coughed, glancing up at her mother, evidently fearful he might say the wrong thing. "I think that it's very possible it could be this D, the one you said she was going to meet. That usually happens, does it not? Kidnappings, murders, and the like, the victims usually know them. I heard there has been some progress made with the Ophelia case. Your Uncle Jack told me about his meeting with the police officer."

Anna colored. She hoped that her uncle had said nothing about her appearance at the office. It would have been somewhat fine if he'd only told her father, but not her mother.

"So I've heard from Uncle Jack."

Anna's mother stood up. "Anna, I need to go and lie down for a few moments. We shall discuss your next dress for the upcoming ball in a little while. I advise you to cease questioning your father about things that are no business of yours. You are giving me a headache." She left the room with a sour expression, but Anna was relieved. Now she could speak to her father without her mother's chastisements getting in the way.

As soon as her mother had shut the door, her father said warily, "Anna, Jack tells me he saw you at the police office at a rather late hour. I thought it best not to tell your mother."

Anna scrambled for an excuse. "Yes, Father. Thank you. I was there at his request. He needed to ask me more questions about what Ophelia divulged to me."

"I see." His tone told her he didn't believe her. "My dear, I know how much you want your cousin to return to us. I want the same. I know how headstrong you are with your desires to be free of the strictures of our lives, and I know that I cannot stop you unless I stationed a guard outside your door, but I plead with you to be careful. Anna, dear, you and your mother are my greatest treasures. It is a dangerous world out there, and it would scare me terribly if I knew that you were off mixed up in some treacherous business."

He patted her hand from across the table. Anna smiled weakly, feeling touched by his love and concern. She had no idea her father had known of her escapades. He certainly would not approve if he knew all.

"I will, Father. I have no intention of getting myself into any danger. Besides, the police do not want a woman snooping about and getting in the way of their investigation."

He laughed. "Well, I suppose they ought to get used to it. I'm certain they have half your intelligence."

He returned to his paper, and Anna felt overwhelmingly grateful to have such a man for a father. He was a man who truly understood her and her all-encompassing desire to be free. Yet, she thought that she was an even luckier woman, for perhaps there was another man who was beginning to understand her just as well.

CHAPTER

22

That afternoon, George sat in his office, writing. At first, he'd begun to write a few notes about what he and Anna had learned the night before, but then he'd been bogged down with his usual work as senior officer. He was only allowed partial time to act as detective. An old woman had come in, claiming she'd been robbed last night of her silver spoons.

Then, a young boy had been brought in, having been accused of stealing from the fruit basket at the marketplace. All events had to be duly recorded in the register and dealt with, but George didn't have the heart for it. He knew the importance of keeping the peace in his town, and he wanted that to happen, but the elusive killer was still on the loose, and his mind was wholly focused by it. He and Anna had made a break in the case the previous evening, and now they seemed so close to finding the man who had taken Ophelia.

He paused and looked down at his notes. There were two questions that were scratching at his mind, and he'd written them down. The bold dark words stared back at him from the page.

> Why do we think that Mason is connected to
> Ophelia's disappearance? What do his multiple persons
> or disguises have to do with it?

Last night they'd been so excited and energized about what they'd found out. They learned that David F. (aka maybe Mason) was the owner of the opium den, that he knew Ophelia, and that he was attached to her in some way. The expression of sadness on the man's face was unmistakable. Plus, one of the patrons had seen them kiss.

He wished he could go back and question the German patron about that again, but he wasn't sure if that was possible or wise. David F. had been understanding and polite, but there was a wariness to his questioning by the end of their discussion. George understood that it most likely appeared odd to David that a man would come to the den to question its owner and not buy anything, but he hoped that his identity was not guessed.

Damn!

Suddenly, he remembered Jenny and her interaction with this David F. She probably had told him of her former engagement with a police officer, and maybe even described his appearance. Even if she did not, his image was strewn all over town in the newspapers whenever he was involved in catching any criminals or in photographs taken for police charities and events.

The man could find out his identity easily if he so wanted to. If this man was the killer or connected with him, then it would be all too simple, considering the killer's wily skills of mystery and lack of detectability. George had been disguised but maybe not well enough.

He needed to speak to Anna again. Why were they so focused on this man? This could cloud their judgment as to the other parts of the case. He reminded himself, though, that the other victims were also linked to a mystery man and to the den in some way. He groaned. There was so much to do.

He had to speak to Anna and to the other victims' families who hadn't been able to see them last time he and Ned were wandering the streets. But this time when he went to question, he would take a drawing of the Mason/David F. character and bring it along with him. He would also show them the photo of Ophelia that he now carried with him in his coat pocket. He also realized with dread that even though they had parted ways, he would need to speak to Jenny. His heart told him what he feared.

She too could be in great danger.

***

Anna needed to talk to George again, but they hadn't discussed when they would meet or even if they would, and she didn't know if she could simply burst into his office again to orchestrate a meeting. She resolved instead to settle for sending him a letter about their next plans.

Unfortunately, even though she was itching to write to George to create their plans and tell him of what she'd learned about the cousin, Anna was currently trapped by her mother who was determined she select a dress for the next ball. This one would take place at the Jordan family's rather large home on Orange Street, and only a select few families had been invited.   Her mother had been thrilled at the invitation, and Anna knew she would be forced to go. She had promised to be kind to her mother and to do what she said, so her fate was sealed. Anna knew that these balls were all her mother had to remind her of her old life back in England. Before everything went sour.

"Anna, this could be your chance to meet with Frederick Mason again!" She frowned. "He had to leave so suddenly the last time he came to call; I hope he was not discouraged in pursuit of you because of it."

Anna smiled. "It was a strange circumstance, Mother. I don't think he will have minded."

She stared into the mirror, watching as her mother moved in a circle about her gown, pulling and pinching in different areas. Anna tried to keep her balance despite the movement. Norma stood close by, waiting to be called into usefulness. Despite Anna's reluctance to go to the ball and to see Mason again, she knew this could be an easy chance to get more information. She could slyly attempt to question him about his cousin or any connection with an opium den.

Perhaps that is not delicate enough dancing conversation. Maybe Mr. Mason's cousin Dick will be at the ball?

The idea both thrilled and terrified her.

"Mother, do you know who else was invited? What about Mr. Mason's cousin?"

Her mother did not look up at her as she continued fussing with the gown, concerned about the folds at the bottom which were not folding to her precise instructions.

"Why do you ask, Anna?"

Anna grit her teeth. She would have to lie to convince her mother to answer her question.

"Well, if I am to get to know Mr. Mason, then it follows that I should get to know his family. It might be the only family he has left, at least in the area. I should like to be sure I am not caught unawares by the man's connection to Mr. Mason when we are introduced."

Her mother brightened. "Yes, of course. That would be most kind of you to be attentive, but I do not know if he will be in attendance. Like your father said, he is a rather shy fellow. At any of the times we were meant to be meeting your father's business associates, it was only Mr. Frederick Mason who was there, and he spoke for his cousin in all matters. Although, I do believe he was at the last ball, the one where Ophelia went missing. But he left early, and I did not speak to him."

Anna suddenly felt a little faint. Had she noticed anyone there who had looked like Frederick?

With as much cheer as she could muster, she said, "I see. Well, I hope that he is there, and that I have a chance to meet him. Now, I like this gown very much. Do you approve, Mother?"

Her mother stood back, clasping her hands in front of her.

"Norma, we shall do her hair up on the evening of the ball, with long curls falling over the shoulder." Norma nodded.

Her mother continued, "Yes, I approve heartily. Louisa gave us this dress with her blessing, but I do hope that Ophelia does not mind very much." Her mother's smile faltered for a moment, and Anna could see her eyes misting.

Anna touched her on the arm. "Mother, she would not mind at all, but don't worry. There is still hope. We can find her. Soon enough she will be back dancing in her own gowns."

"We?" Her mother said, lifting a curious eyebrow.

"'They', I should say, rather. The police."

"Of course." For a moment, her mother eyed her curiously and then said, "Good, well, we have found a suitable dress for you. The ball is tomorrow night. So soon!"

Suddenly, a brilliant idea popped into Anna's mind, and she grabbed her mother's arm.

"Ouch! Anna, do be careful. What is it?"

"Oh, sorry, Mother, but I just had a thought. You remember the police officers who came to ask us about Ophelia when her disappearance was first noticed?"

"Yes, of course."

"It was the same one that Uncle Jack met and questioned for any new information about the case."

"So, what about them?"

"Well, I was thinking that since Ophelia disappeared from a ball, it might behoove us to have the police come to the ball and watch out for any suspicious characters. The killer or kidnapper could be lingering outside or even be inside the ballroom."

"You think it could be one of the gentry? Of the wealthy people of this fine city?"

"I didn't say that, but it could be anyone. A servant, a footman, a driver, anyone. Or it could be someone totally unrelated to those on the inside of the ballroom, but they may come to the outside of the ball to see if they can find any fresh victims."

Anna's mother placed a hand on her chest. "Anna, your speech is becoming practically savage! I confess, I barely recognize you anymore!"

Anna did not respond, but she waited patiently as she saw her mother's mind working, thinking over the possibility of police involvement.

"Even so," her mother replied at long last, "I think it could be a fine idea. I shall mention it to Uncle Jack, and he will send a message to the police officer. Promise me you will not go seeking him out yourself to tell him?"

Anna smiled, trying to contain her excitement.

"Yes, yes, of course, Mother. I shall let the police do their work!"

"Good, now go and change out of your ball gown. It needs to be pressed and made ready for the event."

Nodding at Norma, Anna's mother left her to do her duty. Anna was thrilled, going over in her head just what she would write to George, happy her mother had allowed the police to join them at the ball. It would give her a little comfort to know that he was nearby, watching. For if Frederick or his cousin were the killer, then she wouldn't feel as unsafe or uneasy being so close to them.

Even though the killer had expressed his desire for her to get involved, praising her abilities, he could turn at any moment. He was most certainly not to be trusted, for if she made any wrong moves, it could mean the death of Ophelia or perhaps even herself.

Walking downstairs a half an hour later, she came upon Mrs. Bonds. "Lady Anna. A letter has come for you."

"Thank you, Mrs. Bonds. Would you please have tea brought to the library? I will be there for a few hours."

"Of course, My Lady."

Anna looked at the letter with curiosity, for there was no return address. As she stared at her own name and address written in a familiar scrawl, she gripped onto the banister for support. It was a second letter from the killer.

***

George had a drawing in his hand of David F. His friend had done his best to recreate it from George's description and while not perfect, it would do the job credibly when he was on the beat, asking the victims' families about their knowledge of the man. He was looking forward to getting some satisfaction about their knowledge of Mason, but first, he knew he had to visit Jenny to see if she knew anything more about the man that she was seeing.

He dreaded having to see her again after all that had passed, but at least they'd ended things without malice or embarrassment. They had that to say for themselves, but he didn't like the idea of word getting back to her father about George trying to contact her again. He didn't want to deal with the overly religious, zealous, unyielding man.

George had never subscribed much to any religious path, but he had been willing to put up with its rules and regulations for the sake of Jenny. Now, he wished only to be as far away from her and her family as possible, for each day that he was not embroiled in that relationship, he was a free man. He decided to walk towards the center of town, for on these days, Jenny was usually at the busy Central Market making a few purchases. This could be his chance to speak to her in a public place, without fear of meeting any of her family.

He stood at the town square, waiting to cross the road. Carriages were moving in a thick mass, for it was a busy time of day, and while he waited, he stared at the monument in the center of town. It had served for many years as a reminder of the Revolutionary and Civil Wars with names of heroes etched into it, its stone head pointing towards the Heavens. It was like a beacon, displaying the center of the beautiful city, but now, all that George saw when he looked at it was the body of the killer's latest victim, gingerly laid out for all to see at its unfeeling stone base one moonlit evening many days ago now.

He had not been there, but even the description would forever haunt him, and he wondered why the killer had chosen such hallowed ground for his purpose.

Maybe it was symbolic?

At first, George had assumed he'd done it because it was ostentatious, but now perhaps it was because he respected the land of the heroes commemorated there. He had laid his victim out lovingly and beautifully. The woman was not beaten, nor raped, and the only sign that she was dead was the deep slash by her heart, and the paleness of her skin under the light of the pearly moon.

Finally, a space in the road opened, and George rushed across, his hand gripping the folded picture tightly. As he neared the bustling Central Market, he took off his policeman's cap, hoping to draw less attention that way so that he could pretend he was off duty, simply buying a piece of fruit or a hot cake. He folded the page into his front coat pocket and slipped into the busy crowd, whose occupants were searching for jams, meats, and fresh vegetables to take home that day.

He looked around at the different stalls and heard the cries of the fruit and vegetable sellers filling the market air, attempting to sell their wares.

Where could she be?

He hadn't really expected it to be so busy. He pushed through the throngs of people until he spied Jenny with her light brown hair, basket in hand at one of the egg sellers. Despite the thick crowd, he did his best to move quickly towards her. He was so close; he was amazed she didn't spot him since he looked so different compared to the crowd of civilians which pulsed around him. He was just about to call out her name when seemingly out of nowhere, David F. or whoever he really was, sidled up next to Jenny and smiled.

CHAPTER

23

Anna's hands were trembling as she raced to the library and broke the seal of the letter. She took a deep breath and unfolded the page. The hand was just as beautifully elegant as before. Hoping it was not the prideful announcement of her cousin's death, she read the words, feeling a growing sense of unease with each sentence.

Dearest Anna,

May I call you Anna? For I believe we are beyond titles now. We had an understanding of minds and hearts, or so I thought. Yours is a most beautiful one, and I would treasure it dearly if it were to join my company of jarred treasures.

At the same time, I hope that it does not fulfill that destiny, for the loss of your mind and what you could bring to the world, my world, would be great. You are different, Anna, and I had hoped you might be able to succeed where others could not, especially those foggy-minded policemen.

However, you have disappointed me, my dear. I heard you were there, asking questions with a policeman at D's den. How could you? How could you turn to those idiots when it is you who has the sterling, shining mind? You stand out from the crowd and yet you tarnish yourself by association with that lot?

This letter comes as a warning. I grow impatient, and Ophelia grows weak.

She is tired of waiting for you to do what is right. Leave the police behind, my dear, and search on your own. Do not involve them any longer, or I shall get angry. I do not like to be angry, but I will if I must, to teach you. For you shall be my student, my dear. I can see your unharnessed potential. I feel like I hold it in my hand like a rough diamond, ready to be cut into shape until it sparkles in the light.

Leave the policeman behind, or you will have cause to regret it. To spur you on, I have given you a little present from Ophelia, just to let you know that she is here with me. And waiting.

X

Still trembling, Anna turned the letter over to see if there was anything else written on the back, but there was nothing. However, when she looked inside the envelope, she dropped it to the ground. She sank to her knees, feeling that growing sense of horror that had continued to reside deep inside of her. She opened the envelope again. Inside, like some horribly cruel joke, sat a lock of reddish-blond hair. It was such a unique color, that Anna knew it was Ophelia's. Gripping the piece in her hands, for the first time in a long time, Anna gave up the hardened defenses she had so carefully put into place and began to weep.

Either a few moments or hours had passed, but her tears abated, and she was left with a sodden letter, the ink bleeding across the page, and the hair, still gripped in her fist, now lank from sweat and pressure.

Dear, dear Ophelia, I came so close to ending your life by my poor choices. How could I have made such a foolish mistake? It was because I let feelings get in the way of logic. I wanted to work with George, to prove to him that I could do it. To see his smugness removed.

Another voice popped into her head. *And to spend more time with him.*

Overwhelmed by so many feelings, Anna didn't know whether to feel angry, ashamed, or full of despair. This letter was most likely her final warning from the killer. She had to rid herself of her association with George if she was going to save Ophelia. How on earth could the killer have known about her trip to the den? She had been disguised as a man and had pretended not to speak English!

Apparently, this was a man of connections and skills of detection and invisibility that were unprecedented. How did he know? He was clearly in contact with D, or David F. or whoever the man was. The killer hadn't said anything about her success in following the right clues in the letter, but she had a feeling that she was on the right track, and the only problem was that she had to get rid of George somehow. She didn't want to, but after the killer's warning, it was the only way. A cold fear seized her heart as she remembered.

The ball! If George and the other policemen come to the ball, then all will be lost!

✻✻✻

George pulled back against one of stalls, hoping to hide amongst the crowd and the boxes of fruit that lay nearby. He had to turn his face away somewhat, but he also needed to be able to see their interaction. It was the same man. He had not been wrong when he told Anna that the previous night. It was the same dark hair, the same sideburns, and the same teeth that seemed to strike Anna as so enticing. David was saying something softly to Jenny and she laughed demurely before turning away with her basket of eggs.

Damn! How am I to get to her now?

He had to hear what they were saying if he was going to glean any information and make this trip worth it at all. As they walked away, he kept his policeman's cap tightly against his side as he moved expertly between the people, ducking between vendors, watching the way Jenny flirted copiously and the way David F. treated her with his gentlemanly charms.

This man was a puzzle. Moving like a mist, changing and transforming into a different person or the same person. It was all so confusing.

Just like the killer.

George knew in his gut that this man was related both to the killings and the disappearance. Maybe he was even the killer himself. He was not just a criminal, a man who owned and ran an opium den and flirted with multiple women, making them promises he couldn't keep. George knew he was someone far more sinister, but he just had to prove it. He sidled his way through the rows of market stalls, and then Jenny and David stopped, looking at a different vendor's wares. He crowded himself as near to the table as he could without being seen, his ears straining to focus only on the familiar sound of two specific voices.

"How is your police fellow doing after you ended things?"

Jenny did not end things!

George's pride prickled as he listened to the lie that she had told her new suitor.

"He is a little disappointed, I guess, at the end of our acquaintance, but I'm not worried about him. I worry only about you and us."

She smiled up into David's face, and George felt nauseous at the extent of her flirtations. It was too far and too much. She had never acted that way with him, and he was grateful.

Well, I wouldn't be so disgusted if I really liked the person flirting with me. Someone like Anna.

George rolled his eyes at his own lack of focus and tried to keep his gaze on the couple. David kept the same toothy smile plastered across his face.

"Well, you should not worry about the future, my dear. All will be handled, and in good time. May I ask, have you seen this Officer Ford of yours since the ending of your engagement?"

It almost sounded like the man was jealous, but at least George's listening in had given him the information that David had most likely known it was him who had questioned him at the den, and he may have told the killer, if he was not the killer himself.

Jenny smiled, "No, not since we ended things."

David grinned wider, and the large, shining, white teeth put George on edge. If it was the same exact man who was courting Anna Lovelace, then he didn't quite understand the appeal. In the light of day, he got the full picture of the man, and if he was being honest, the man made a shiver run down his spine. But who knew what women really found attractive? It was a mystery to him. Perhaps only because he suspected this Mason of wrongdoing that he gave George an ill feeling, but George knew there was more than that. There was an air about him that was not to be trusted.

"My dear, I need to return to the factory. There are some important business matters that I must handle."

George could tell in the tone of her voice that Jenny was slightly distressed.

"I understand, but when will we see each other again?"

David looked a little perturbed for a moment, but that expression was gone as quickly as it had come.

"I shall write to you, of course, but at this point, I cannot say. Good day to you, Jenny."

Jenny's shoulders sank, and she said, "Good day," with as cheerful a voice as she could muster. George waited until the man was lost in the sea of people, having taken his sideburns and strange teeth with him, and then George walked up to Jenny, tapping her lightly on the arm.

162

"Jenny. We need to talk."

Jenny jumped, nearly dropping her basket of eggs.

"George Ford, what in the blazes are you doing? You scared me half to death!"

"Sorry, but it's urgent. Do you have a moment? We can meet over there by the apples. It's about the case."

Jenny looked confused, but she agreed. The two of them braved the onslaught of market customers as best they could until they reached the apple stand on the freer, more open outskirts of the market, finally able to breathe a little bit of cool, early afternoon air.

Jenny was impatient. "What is it? I thought we never needed to speak to each other again. If any one of my acquaintances see us together--"

"Yes, I understand," George replied hastily. "But this is important. Tell me, how'd you meet your man, your David Mason? The man that you were just with."

Jenny crossed her arms, suddenly defensive. "Why on earth do you need to know? Here I thought we'd ended things properly, and there had been no malice or shame between us, but this looks different. This looks like the questioning of a jealous man."

George sighed, trying to control his temper. "Jenny, I promise you that it's nothing to do with that. I wouldn't have chanced to speak with you unless I had to, and I have to."

Jenny's eyes widened a little, and she glanced over her shoulder. "What is it, George?"

"It has to do with the case of the Ophelia Marshall kidnapping. I've come across a bit of new information, and I'm afraid it has to do with you."

"With me? What do you mean?"

"I saw your new suitor at a rather less than reputable sort of establishment last night. I found out that he's the owner, and I asked him a few questions about the missing Ophelia, under a disguise, of course. Apparently, he knows her or knew her, and she was seen with him a number of times at this establishment. Now, I need to know how you met David yourself."

Jenny's eyes searched the scene around her, trying to grasp what George was saying.

"David knew Ophelia? And what sort of establishment is this?" She paled slightly but didn't wait for George to answer. "We met normally, I suppose you could say. I was purchasing some cigars for father at the tobacconist on King. David was there, and we got to talking. He asked if

I was often on King Street, and I said yes, I was the one who bought father's cigars, but my friends and I would often go for coffee at the small coffeeshop around the corner."

George nodded, trying to register everything that Jenny was saying. He now felt the loss of his small notebook which he had so carelessly left on his desk.

"Before I knew it, he had begun to flirt with me and to mention that he should meet me there the next time, since he was a frequent customer of the very same coffeeshop. I remember feeling excited to meet him. And he was right. The next time I met a friend there, he was there as well, and we spent a lot of time talking before he decided to meet Father and ask him about courting me."

"So, the courtship is official?"

Jenny shifted on her feet, moving her basket between her hands to hide her discomfort. "Yes, it is official. Father approves wholeheartedly. David is a wealthy and successful businessman."

"I see. Did he ever tell you what business he was in?" George frowned and looked up at Jenny, trying to get across to her the seriousness of the situation.

Jenny frowned. "No, but I didn't see the need to ask so early in the courtship. You can tell the measure of a man by the clothing he wears and the way he treats a lady. It hasn't yet come up. But it appears you know this business and disapprove?"

George could tell Jenny was attempting to punish him for his own lack of ambition in her eyes.

"Jenny, I suggest for a time, that you avoid any more interaction with this David. Perhaps you could go visit your aunt in York for a few weeks. I can't say for certain that there's something suspicious about the man, but I've learned too many things lately not to be cautious. I came here today to warn you. You could be in danger, if my theories are correct."

"And what theories are those?" She said, and despite her narrowed, suspicious eyes, he could see her pulse flutter fearfully at her throat.

He looked around at the throng of customers. "I can't tell you right now. All I can say is that I think you should try to get away. Surely your parents will allow you time to visit with your aunt."

Jenny swallowed. "Of course. I'm certain they would. If you can promise me, George, that this is about my own safety and not about jealousy of my new suitor."

George smiled. "I'm sorry, Jenny, but I can promise you it's about your own safety. I hope that I'm wrong about the man, but I don't want you to take any unnecessary risks, especially since I had the chance to warn you."

Jenny nodded. "Thank you, George. If you're certain, I'll do as you say. Good day to you."

Her formerly angry and stiff demeanor was replaced by one meek as a mouse. He hoped to God that she would take his advice. David F. might do something terrible to Jenny if he had any connection to the killer. Perhaps he was the link who supplied the killer with all his beautiful victims? And it also seemed strange that he had chosen Jenny, since it was well-known about her previous connection with George himself. Perhaps it was the killer's way to get revenge against the man trying to bring the killer to justice?

"Goodbye, Jenny."

George watched the back of his old fiancée as she blended once more into the market throng. He was glad he was moving in the opposite direction, happy for more reasons than one, and to give him encouragement, he felt for the drawing in his pocket. Ned was going to meet him at the pub nearby soon to help him interview the victims' families once again. But this time, they'd show them the picture and hope that each one of them at least recognized the man. It would bring them one step closer to nabbing him. The killer's amorphous features were slowly taking shape.

CHAPTER

24

As soon as Anna had realized her mistake in telling her mother to bring the police to the ball, she ran downstairs, searching for her. She found her reading in her own personal parlor, and to her mother's dismay, Anna had startled her most indecorously.

"Anna Margaret Lovelace, what has gotten into you? You are rushing into my parlor as if you were a wild banshee! Please tell me I raised you better than this!"

In a different situation, Anna might have laughed at her mother's horrified face. Women were bound by so many ridiculous rules; it almost made them inhuman. Besides, it was hard to remember the long list of rules, and ever since Anna was a child, she felt her emotions were her guide to her actions, and she could never quite master the austere, noble look in a way that satisfied her mother.

Anna tried to catch her breath. "Do forgive me, Mother. I was carried away by the impulse of the moment. You did raise me better than to simply run from room to room shouting a person's name. You can depend upon it."

Despite Anna's sarcasm, her mother nodded imperiously at Anna's apology.

"I only came to ask if you had sent that message to Uncle Jack already about the police coming to the ball."

"I did, and I have had a reply. We pay well for good service, my dear. Your uncle loved the idea and wrote that he was just on his way out, but he would stop by the police station on his way to give the message to the very particular policeman that you mentioned."

Anna made a sound that was a cross between a groan and a whimper. *It's too late.*

Her mother said, "Are you all right, dear? Do you not approve of the idea? It was yours to begin with."

She glanced at her mother's worried eyes. It would have been so easy to alert her of the killer's warning, to let her know all that was at stake, but she couldn't risk her mother's emotional welfare. Telling her would be the same as killing her, for she would never be able to forgive Anna for what she'd already done, and she would swear to lock her up until doomsday.

"It's no matter, Mother. I was only curious. I'm glad that Uncle Jack was in favor of the idea."

Her mother again looked wary. "Yes, so was I."

Anna tried a new angle. An idea was forming in her mind, a way to keep the killer unaware of her involvement with the police.

"Mother, did you write in the letter that it was my idea to send for the police to attend the ball?"

Her mother shook her head. "No, I did not, actually. I simply put forth the question to him, wondering how he felt about such a plan. You do not mind, do you?"

Anna smiled with relief, and it felt like a huge weight was lifted off her shoulders. There was now no evidence that she in particular had been involved. The killer could say nothing on that score. It was a feeble hope, but it would have to do.

"No, Mother. That's perfect. I don't mind at all. Well, enjoy your reading. Forgive my disturbance."

She left the room, quietly shutting her mother's door behind her, and she rushed back to the library. It was strange, but she wanted to sit with Ophelia's lock of hair, the one piece of her cousin allowed to be free from the killer's grasp. It made her feel closer to her and that she was closer to seeing her cousin alive and well again.

"Soon, Ophelia," she whispered. "I just know it. I'll get you out soon."

Anna hoped she had found a way around this situation and the killer's warning, and her mother had been the one to help. She smirked.

If only Mother knew how she'd helped.

If the police were there to watch over the ball, then she would feel better, and she could tell the killer that it was her mother and uncle's idea to send for the police, if of course he happened to ask. If only she could write to him to tell him herself. She sighed as she fell into the armchair, her hope slightly precarious, ignoring the pang of guilt she felt about

George.

How on earth was she going to explain any of this to him? She would just have to ignore any communication with him and go about her business on her own. Even at the ball, she would have to do her best to ignore him. The idea hurt her, for she was not the type of woman to do something so rude. She hoped that he would somehow understand, or that she would have the chance to explain it to him one day.

Right at this moment, though, there was nothing that she could do. Her next step was to speak to Mr. Mason at the ball. So, for now, even though it would be agony, all she could do until tomorrow night was wait.

***

"Hi, George. Stay for a drink?" Ned asked, lifting his nearly empty pint into the air when George entered the pub.

"No, not right now. We should go to the interviews right away. The sooner I have the information I want, the better."

"Sounds good." Ned swallowed the rest of his ale in one upturned swig and followed George out of onto the narrow, cobbled street. "Same beat?"

"Yes. Same victims. Won't take long. I don't think we even need to go inside. I just want to go to each doorway and see if they've ever seen this man."

He unfolded the page from his pocket and passed it to Ned as they made their way to King Street. Passing by the theater, Ned scrutinized the drawing.

"Fine. It's a clear enough picture. Good likeness, right?"

"I think so. I saw him again today, you know, at the market. He was with Jenny."

"The market?" Ned took another look at the picture. "Hey, this is the guy we saw with Jenny the other day."

"Your police skills are astounding," George said with a sarcastic drawl, but it was only to quell his own nerves.

He looked forward, and his brows twisted in thought.

Ned didn't seem to notice the jibe. "Wait a minute. You think that Jenny's new man has something to do with the killer?"

George nodded and then turned right, Ned hurrying to catch up with his quickening pace. "What? You serious? You've got to explain everything now. This sounds mad, as if you're jealous and want to get your revenge."

George scowled at Ned. "You know that I'm not jealous. I ended it with Jenny the other day. She's in love with this new man."

"Wow, I'd no idea. Sorry, George. I know you were keen on her."

"Not anymore, Ned. Things have changed a little. I'm happy to be free of the engagement. Like I said, I was the one who ended things."

"This has something to do with that Lovelace girl, doesn't it?" Ned asked with a little humor in his voice.

George paused. "It does, but not in the way you imagine. Listen," He looked around to make sure no one was within earshot. "Anna and I went to the opium den I told you about to ask questions. We found the owner, and it is just as we thought. Ophelia had been there a few times, and she seemed to be in some sort of a romantic relationship with the owner. The owner is that man that you and I both saw with Jenny!"

Ned's mouth opened in shock. "I can't believe it! Incredible! George, you're really making headway! Just like you hoped."

George smirked. "Thanks. Now, come on. If I'm right, then this man is connected to all the victims, and I want to make sure. I think he's somehow the link, somehow luring these women into the killer's sphere, like leading lambs to the slaughter."

Ned shook his head in disbelief. "I don't know that I've ever heard of such a thing. No one claimed that Jack the Ripper had someone else lure his victims. Sure this guy isn't the killer himself?"

"No, but that's what I mean to find out. Let's go."

They rounded a bend and stood in front of the doorway to the latest victim's home, Emily Wilson. When they knocked, George was nervous to see Mrs. Wilson again and the way she carried her grief like a shroud. Everything about the house was filled with it, like a wet, heavy blanket.

She opened the door, that continually strained face looking at them without recognition. "Mrs. Wilson. Senior Officer George Ford and Officer Ned Barnum. We came to speak to you a few days ago." She nodded, but George thought it was more a matter of course, not that she actually remembered.

"This won't take but a moment of your time." He unfolded the drawing and let Mrs. Wilson take a long look at it. "I just wanted to check if you have ever seen this man before. I think this might have been the man that your daughter had been meeting."

Mrs. Wilson frowned, straining her eyes to look at the page. George waited, feeling like he couldn't breathe until she said yes.

"No, I don't recall seeing him before."

George took the drawing back, feeling his shoulders sink. He could have sworn there was a connection.

"I'm sorry for wasting your time."

Ned stepped forward. "Wait, Mrs. Wilson, is your other daughter Sarah at home?"

"Yes, but why do you need to see her?"

George looked at Ned with a frown until he understood the reason.

"Yes, Mrs. Wilson. Please will you let us see her? I'd just like to show her the picture too."

Mrs. Wilson nodded, "But I don't want her mixed up with any of the sad business of Emily. I don't want her to know any of the details."

"Agreed."

He waited, tapping his foot in anticipation while Mrs. Wilson moved back into the dark house again, and they were left standing with a yawning dark doorway in front of them. Partly because he didn't want to look into the gloom, he turned to Ned.

"Brilliant, Ned! I was just about to give up hope. I must be losing my touch. Of course, we should have asked her sister!"

A young woman's face appeared in the doorway, the exact replica of her mother but without the heavy-lines or as much of the sorrow.

"Yes?" She asked hesitantly.

"Sarah Wilson? We're police officers looking into the details of your sister's case. We just have one question for you. Have you seen this man before?"

He showed the paper to the younger Miss Wilson, and she took it in hand, looking at the face deeply. A spark of recognition crossed her face, but she didn't say anything.

"Miss Wilson? Do you recognize him? We think this could be the man your sister was meeting in the weeks or days before her death."

She swallowed and looked up at the two officers. "I don't know, but I think that I do."

George clung onto that hope, and he moved closer to her, trying to keep his excitement at bay.

"You've seen him before?"

"Just once, I think, but he talked more to Emily than to me."

"Where was it?"

"She'd met him once before I met him, but she didn't introduce me. I think she met him out sometime."

Sarah looked back into the darkness, perhaps looking for the form of her mother behind her. When she turned back, she lowered her voice.

"Emily had a place she liked to go. Near S. Shippen. She never told me what it was, and I never went, but that's where she met him, I think.

The first time."

"Black hair? White teeth? Just like the drawing?"

Sarah nodded, and George took the paper from her.

"Thank you, Sarah. That's all."

She gave him a sad smile and disappeared away into the darkness, closing the door behind her.

George turned to Ned, feeling light-headed with his small victory. "On to the next, Ned."

***

"Ophelia, my dear!" I call out my victim's name as I descend into the lair.

Our interactions of late have become part of my daily routine. Never before have I kept a victim for so long, and while my fingers itch to kill, I also enjoy the small intimacy I have with her. Holding bread and tea in hand, I place them on the small table before Ophelia and sit down to watch her sleeping form for a bit. She stirs and wakes, her lovely reddish hair in disarray after too long away from her boudoir and lack of bathing. She glances at me with those sharp eyes of hers, still sharp after all that has happened.

"So, would you like to hear my news?" I say, feeling an energy I haven't felt in a while.

"What is it?"

"It is about your cousin. I think you will be most gratified to learn of what I have done, and what I have planned next."

Ophelia pauses while lifting the bread to her lips. Such sweet lips, but her beautiful form is intriguing me less day after day. I have a new face in mind who I see at the end of my journey, but that must wait.

"What have you done?" she asks, her poor voice trembling.

"Oh, do not concern yourself, my dear. Your cousin is just fine, but I had to write her a letter to let her know what I have thought about her progress thus far. I had to warn her. She was doing something exceedingly dangerous."

"What was she doing?" Dearest Ophelia pales a little.

"She is on the track to solving your little mystery, dear heart. Does that not make you happy?"

For a moment, Ophelia's lovely eyes light up with joy. "Are you serious?"

"As serious as the grave." I laugh at my own little joke. Oh, I can be so humorous.

"Well, what did you need to warn her of? Are you not happy that she has made progress?"

I move to my writing desk, a new idea taking hold. "Of course, but she was being a naughty girl. Instead of working out the facts of the case on her own, she is working with the police to do so, or in fact, one policeman."

"D?" she asked softly, and I chuckle.

"Ophelia, my dear, it is good that it is not you who is in charge of solving your own disappearance. D is not a policeman, you beautiful little fool. It was all a facade. A game of mists and shadows. He could never tell you his real identity."

Her face twists once more into that uncomfortable position as she tries to hold back tears. I am losing patience. Why does she not appreciate my kindness to her? All the others were dead within hours.

"Now, I really am disappointed you are not interested in my news, but I shall tell you anyway. I have written a letter to Anna that she must cease working with the policeman, or your chance and her chance of survival are both in jeopardy. I want to play a game, but if she is not going to play it right, then it is not worth it at all. It is a pointless frivolity and frankly, a waste of my time."

Ophelia pulls the blankets closer around her, seemingly to protect herself. I smile, trying to reassure her.

"Do not worry. I have sent her a little piece of you to remind her of her quest. She will do as I say, do not be alarmed."

"A little piece of me?" Her voice is quiet, like a whisper.

"Yes. You are sleeping so much, that it was as easy as could be. I snipped a little lock of that bright hair of yours and sent it to your cousin. I had to remind her of you and her ultimate goal of saving you."

Ophelia does not respond but continues to look at me with those bright eyes, now wide.

"Now, listen. I have a new idea. I hope she follows my instructions, but I think that it might be best if we meet in person. I have such a longing to see her, to see how her mind whirrs with action. She is a fascinating creature to me. I want to study her."

Ophelia is still silent.

"There is a ball coming up tomorrow. I will be in attendance. When I get the chance, I shall slip a note to Anna asking to meet. She will not be able to refuse me. It is just one meeting. I want to see how close I can come to my ultimate prize, without snapping it up, desiring to preserve it for the rest of time."

I reach forward and let my index finger land on Ophelia's pale cheek, and I wipe away a tear.

"I simply wished to alert you. Your time could be finished soon, Ophelia, one way or another. Or your cousin could be victorious after all. We shall see."

Smiling, I leave her to thoughts of her own morbidity or potential freedom. She must finish her meal after all. I couldn't bear to have a victim that starved to death under my care. What carelessness, and what an ugly, wasteful death that would be!

CHAPTER

25

Anna woke up thinking about the ball that was to come that evening. It had consumed her mind the whole of yesterday. The killer could be there, and she had to make sure her every step was made carefully, backed by thought and logic, or else it could mean her demise.

As Norma helped her dress for the day, Anna watched herself in the mirror with a frown. Never before had she given a ball as much thought as she was that morning.

"My Lady, are you all right?"

Anna broke out of her thoughts and smiled down at Norma.

"Yes, Norma. Oh, I should tell you thank you for your help with the men's clothing. I hope you were not in too much trouble."

Norma grinned. "Oh no, My Lady. Mrs. Bonds did not even notice! I returned the clothing after you'd come back that evening, and then all was well. May I ask how things went?"

She had hesitated in asking, but Anna could understand her curiosity. It was an odd request for a lady to make of a lady's maid.

"Ah yes, everything went according to plan. Thank you for your assistance. It was very much appreciated. Your continued discretion would also be appreciated."

Norma bowed her head. "Of course, My Lady. I shall be as quiet as a mouse on the subject." After a pause she said, "I look forward to dressing you for the ball this evening."

Anna's focus returned to the events that might happen that night. She thought about seeing George again as well as the potential killer and trying to flirt with Mason so that he'd give her the information she needed. Suddenly, her appearance that evening became all the more important.

"Yes, Norma. I am looking forward to it too. I know my mother is basing a lot of her hopes on it."

During the day, Anna's time was spent in unfocused idleness, and her mother was practically unbearable due to her excitement at the prospect of the ball. Anna tried her best to avoid her by stationing herself in the library, hidden behind a volume. The hours ticked by despite her lack of ability to focus on her reading. It was nearly time to dress in her gown, but Anna wasn't quite ready for the evening yet. There was so much at stake, and even if she was a little bit thrilled at the prospect of another potentially dangerous escapade, she had to keep the safety of Ophelia in mind.

There was no way she could speak to George or even acknowledge him tonight. She took a breath, thinking about how he would feel when he realized she wasn't looking his way. Blushing, she let her mind wander to the way George's mouth felt on her own in the alcove of the den. She had never been kissed before, but her body had responded to him like an experienced woman. It had been so easy.

When she'd pulled him to her, she hadn't even worried about what it would be like or the fact that it was her first time. All she'd known in that moment was that she wanted to experience it and experience it with George, a man that wasn't a part of everything that she'd been confined to her whole life. It was almost like she could get away with it because no one would ever know what she had done. He was on the other side of that dangerous border she'd been begging to cross over for so long, and now that she had, she couldn't ever go back. He had been the catalyst.

She knew that now. After all they'd shared in the past few days, Anna was afraid that she might lose whatever she had gained with George Ford when she ignored him tonight. It was kind of like a friendship but something a little bit deeper. A kinship, she supposed. There was more to it, but she couldn't allow silly feelings to get in the way.

"For you, My Lady," a servant said suddenly, and Anna nearly dropped her book in fright.

She looked up to see the servant standing in the doorway. When the servant came closer, they held out a letter. "Ah, thank you." Anna took it, blood thumping through her brain with curiosity and anticipation. She prayed it was not from the killer, but when she saw George's return address, she tore it open with fervor.

Dear Anna,

I wanted to let you know what information I've gleaned. I went to Jenny at the market today, and she was with our man with the black hair once again. When he left, I met with her to tell her it would be wise to leave town until everything is figured out.

He looked the same in daylight. His hair was dark, but it was heavy, like smothered in a tinted pomade. Some men do these kinds of things, but this seemed like a lot to me. It was very clear in the daylight. Just something I thought you should know.

Jenny told me she met the man at a tobacco shop on King Street. Also, I met with each of the victims' families, and almost all of them had at least one member who recognized the man. I took a drawing with me which was a decent enough likeness. What do you say to that? I think we could have our man or at least an accomplice.

I received word from your uncle. I'll be one of a few policemen who will be guarding the ball, searching for any suspicious characters. I assume you'll be there. You know this already but see what you can find out from Mason. Be your naturally charming self, Anna.

Until tonight,

George

Anna groaned and laid her head back against the chair. Here he was, starting contact, letting her in on information he would never have given her before, and she was just about to openly reject him tonight while he guarded the ball! She chewed on her lip with frustration. Perhaps she could slip him a note somehow just like he had done with her? She could keep a note on her, and drop it somewhere for him to notice?

Despite the killer's warning, she knew that it would behoove her to keep the police on her side, and she would have to have a backup situation to keep her and Ophelia safe. If she were to lose George and his trust and openness, then she would be entirely at a loss as to what to do next. He had access to things that she could never have access to. While she knew that wasn't all his connection meant to her, it did mean a lot if she was determined to free Ophelia from her captor.

"Anna? Where are you?" A shrill voice called from the passageway.

Anna groaned again, rising to meet the bright, cheery face of her mother who entered the library.

"Anna, how can you read at a time like this? You are about to go to one of the best balls in town, and you will meet with your lovely suitor again!" She pointed her finger at Anna. "Remember to be kind, charming, and listen to all of the stories he might have to tell you. A man likes to feel important, that his accomplishments are acknowledged, and his stories listened to."

"Yes, Mother. I will be just as you ask."

Anna wondered why her mother had been interested in her father, for he was nearly the complete opposite to the beautiful Regina, wanting to break barriers, and allowing his daughter more freedom than was usual.

"Good. Now come, it is time that you got dressed. We do not want to be late!"

As hurriedly as she came in, her mother fluttered out the door. Anna knew that her mother was also excited about the ball so that she could forget the aching uncertainty of Ophelia's disappearance at least for a time. It felt a bit wrong, but Anna could understand her mother in that regard. Anna followed her out of the library, setting her teeth, determined not to let her fears get the better of her as she spent that night in the company of killers and their accomplices.

***

Ned was smiling gleefully as George smoked a cigarette next to him outside of the huge Jordan mansion on Orange Street.

"This is a good job. My wife hated that I was asked to work an extra shift, but I've always wanted to see one of these big to-dos. The old gentry of London trying to remake whatever they had in England here in Lancaster. Good thing the Sergeant let us go through with it."

Ned's eyes were everywhere as he looked in wonder at the lights and listened to the sounds coming from the mansion. George had to admit it was impressive. They had both seen inside of the Lovelace home, the biggest one they'd both seen before, but it was only the drawing room, and he hadn't seen it decorated for a big event. However, this house and this event was something special, something his class of people would never have a chance to see. Any celebrations with his own kind would have been done in a home or a pub somewhere, with a few candles, drinks, and food. Certainly, there would have been dancing, but not the kind he expected to see in here.

This was the world of Anna Lovelace, and as he smoked, waiting for more guests to arrive, he felt the distance between her and himself keenly. Anna was so high above him and had been given so much more than he. Not only was she an English noblewoman with wealth and a title, but she had been given the chance to be educated even as he had not! And he a man! She could speak many languages, and her sharp intellect was evident in their every interaction.

He felt ashamed now. He had been excited for the ball that night, hoping to catch a glimpse of Anna since they shared their kiss back in the opium den. Even though it shouldn't have, and he had tried his best to keep it quelled, that kiss had given him hope that something was now broken between them. In a good way. A barrier had been shattered, and there was some small part of him that wished there could be something between him and a beautiful, intelligent, vibrant English lady.

But now, with the mansion behind him and Ned's obvious amazement, expressed in his lower class, rougher accent which he shared with George, George felt like he and Anna were a million miles apart. Yet, somehow, he hoped that if they could get one glimpse of each other tonight, he would be able to see in her eyes whether that distance was too insurmountable.

He would find out the truth tonight. That seemed to be a theme of the evening. After today, when most of the victims had claimed knowledge of a black-haired David, he was bolstered with confidence that he was on the right track with this case.

"George? Are you listening? Are you not completely impressed by this place?"

George turned around, sending up a curl of smoke, and he watched it lift over the ornate facade.

"Yes, it's good. Better than I've ever been close enough to. Lucky we got this job. Makes things around the police station a little more interesting, huh?"

Ned snorted. "A killer's not exciting enough for you, George? I'll take a job like this over a multiple murderer any day. I can tell you that right now. So that Anna Lovelace attends this kind of thing."

George nodded, sucking in a new round of smoke, not wanting to be reminded.

"For certain. This is her set of people after all."

Ned whistled. "What a life. Greta would love this. If only she'd married a Duke instead of a police officer."

George laughed, thankful for the company of his friend. At least Ned never made him feel less than he was. There were a few other police officers stationed around the house, but he requested that he and Ned be at the entrance. They would even be allowed brief entry into the ballroom, and that he was really looking forward to.

A few guests began to come up the walkway, and he and George kept silent in the shadows as they entered and were greeted by the Jordans at the grand entrance. Many of them had English accents, but some did not. He knew that there was a lot of new American money in the town, even if they were just visitors for a time, and he sighed, thinking that he would never be one of those people. His mood was souring with each moment as he waited for Anna's arrival. He knew what it would be like. City boy, rough and wild, looking like trash against the backdrop of a noblewoman's elegance and sparkling wealth.

And then he saw her. Anna had just descended from a carriage lingering in the street, and George's cigarette dropped from his mouth when he saw her.

"George, what are you looking at?" Ned was chuckling, and then he turned to the street. "Ah, I see."

Anna was with her parents and uncle, shimmering under the lamplight stationed along the path. Her gown was deep mauve, and it clung to her every curve while falling in rich folds at her feet. Her blond hair was curled up around her head, and he could see little sparkles of light in her hair, looking like trapped stars.

George swallowed. He didn't know what to say. Ned was laughing, louder this time, but George didn't turn to him. He didn't want to miss a moment of looking at her.

"So, I believe you now," Ned said, once he calmed down. "Anna Lovelace has nothing to do with your decisions, then."

George wanted to hit Ned because Anna was getting closer. Instinctively, he moved into the light of the doorway, hoping that they could make some sort of interaction before she would slip inside into that world that was entirely her and nothing of him. Then, he realized that these were the people who had requested his presence, and thus it would be wise for him to speak to them. He cleared his throat, and Anna's father and uncle looked towards him.

"Mr. Marshall," he greeted. "Lord Wincherton, I am Senior Officer George Ford, and this is Officer Ned Barnum. We are here by the request of your family to watch over the ball and its attendants."

Jack, Anna's uncle, moved closer to George. "Excellent, I thought it a novel idea, and am happy you're here to watch. Best of luck to you both."

George nodded. "Thank you, sir."

He could see the similarity between Anna and her father. They shared the same eyes, and the same kindness showed through them.

Anna's father added, "Yes. Stay warm in this cold. I hope you are well-dressed enough, young man."

George searched for Anna's eyes, and when he found them, her look was inscrutable. He frowned when she turned away. It was like she was telling him something, but he couldn't quite make it out. There walked ahead, and there were mumbled greetings to the hosts. Then they were gone, inside and away from him. George was itching to be in there, to see if he could decipher Anna's meaning.

Why had she said nothing? It's not as if she had to hide that she knew me. Her uncle and father both knew that already.

He couldn't focus on his own confusion any longer when he spotted the man he was looking for. Frederick Mason arrived up the walkway in a new, freshly washed carriage, looking as dapper as a rich factory owner ought to look. He had the mustache perfectly in place, with brown, not black hair, with the same face as the man of the opium den. He was just the same, just the same as David F. and just the same as David Mason.

Behind him, with a sourer expression was a dark-haired man, of very similar appearance, but it was not David F.

PART IV

CHAPTER

26

Anna's heart was pounding furiously in her chest as she walked up to the entrance. The Jordan's house was larger than her own, and she had always found it much more beautiful with its old paintings, sculptures, and well-selected furnishings in every room. Miss Jordan, however, was not half as pleasant as her house and continually wore a sour expression, but duty was duty, and Anna wanted to do her best to make her mother happy that evening.

Even though Ophelia's life hung in the balance, Anna's thoughts were on George at that moment. She really didn't want him to think ill of her. The thought made a line of dread pierce her heart. To lose George entirely would be a very great loss indeed. And so, before she'd left for the ball, she had crumpled up a note and kept it clamped in her fist. At the very first opportunity, she would toss it out near George if she saw him, hopeful that he would find it and understand that they must keep their association hidden.

She held tightly to her father's arm as they headed under the lamplight towards the house. Anna was looking one way and then the other, wondering when George would come into her sight. Then, there he was. He'd approached her father and her uncle seemingly out of the shadows, explaining that he was the one chosen to be there. She blinked in surprise at the sight of him. He was not in uniform, nor was he dressed as someone he was not, like the stuffy rich men she would find in the ballroom. Here was the real George in front of her.

He was wearing a dark coat with a gray waistcoat underneath. His collar was bright white, and she could see he was wearing a thin black tie.

His dark hair was slicked back in the way she had seen it so many times. It made her think of the way he'd pull off his cap and push his hands through it in frustration when they would argue. Even in the shadows, she could see that he was freshly shaven, and the line of his strong jaw was even more evident. Anna's breath caught as she realized that George Ford was the most handsome man of her acquaintance, and Frederick Mason with all his charming ways would never compare. Of course, Mr. Mason might also be a murderer, but that was neither here nor there.

Anna loved the way that George didn't dress as the other men of her circle, with such care and an eye for being observed. He was rough, yet elegant in his own way. Now without the bulk of his uniform, she could more see the shape of his body. His shoulders were strong underneath his coat, and his waist was cut thin, not like the many older men here amongst the gentry, overfilled with food and wine. And then there were his lips. She remembered the strong yet gentle feel of them. He looked at her, and she could see a question in his eyes, but she had to tear herself away. She couldn't look at him for it made her dizzy, unfocused. And she had to focus on saving Ophelia. If the killer saw her acknowledge George, then all might be lost.

The conversation with her father was over, and she saw George turn away. She knew that she had hurt him, but there was no helping it. There was nothing she could do. Ophelia's safety was paramount. Glancing quickly around, she threw the crumpled note in her fist to the side into the grassy yard, hoping that somehow, fate would help George find it.

Once her deed was done, she put a smile on her face and greeted the Jordans kindly, her eyes darting about as she entered the ballroom. Miss Jordan, tall, beautiful, and preening, lifted a brow.

"Lady Anna, how lovely to have you grace our ball here this evening. Your dress is quite lovely."

Miss Jordan had the uncanny ability to add slight surprise to her already condescending tone.

Anna curtsied. "Thank you, Miss Jordan. You look lovely as well. We do appreciate the invitation."

"I know that this is a difficult time for you and your family. I hope that all will be well and safe in good time."

Stiffly, Anna thanked her, and once the footmen had taken her father's and uncle's hats and gloves, she floated inside, watching the sway of couples on the dance floor, and listening to the merry music from the musicians in the corner of the room. The ballroom was laid in wood, and artwork in gilded frames lined the walls. A chandelier of bright candles cast a dance of shadows to match the music. As she stared at it, she was reminded of the killer's words: she was a rough diamond, ready to be cut up until it sparkled in the light. She felt queasy as she remembered it. How pointed that he used the word "cut" to describe her transformation.

I need champagne. At least one glass will help to ease my nerves.

A waiter passed by, and she took a thin crystal glass from the tray with her gloved hands. Her mother came to her side motioning to the doorway with her eyes.

"Look, my dear, your Mr. Mason has come, and that man there, I do believe that must be his cousin. We shall wait for your father to come and confirm it."

Anna felt her palms break out into a cold sweat, and she feared she might break her champagne flute as she turned to view the two men. Frederick looked as handsome as ever, returned to his usual brown hair and mustache. Smiling at his hostess, with his bright white teeth, Anna knew. It *was* him at the opium den. She was certain of it now. He must have simply changed his hair color to both run the den and meet with Ophelia. And then, her eyes turned to the cousin. She gripped her glass even tighter, and she paled.

"Anna, what is it? It is not like you to pale so amid so many people. Are you well?"

Her mother began to fan her, and the cool air felt soothing on her flushed cheeks. Anna had recognized the man instantly. How could she have been so silly not to remember? This was one of the other men she had danced with at Lady Croft's ball.

Her mind began to shift and organize, putting pieces together. The cousin, Dick Mason, looked around at the couples on the dance floor with a condescending air. As his eyes moved around, Anna turned her own away, down to her glass. She didn't want to meet his eyes, fearful that he could see what lay behind them, what moved about in her mind. He looked like Frederick, but there was a harshness to him, while Frederick was all smiles and cheerful friendliness.

Unfortunately, Anna and her mother would not be left alone for long. Frederick spotted them as soon as he made his greetings to the Jordans, and her mother smiled widely at his approach.

"Lady Wincherton! Lady Anna! How wonderful to see you again! I had rather hoped you would be at this ball."

He took Anna's hand and kissed it. Anna pulled away as soon as she could, conscious of the trembling in her hands. She was about to speak when her mother cut in.

"Mr. Mason, we have rather missed your visits. I do hope we did nothing to deter you from resuming them."

He laughed, and his large teeth were very visible, spread across his face into a charming, potentially frightening smile.

"You must forgive me, Lady Wincherton. The lack of reoccurrence of my visits is my own fault and nothing to do with you or your enchanting daughter."

He glanced at her with his mesmerizing soft brown eyes, and Anna got caught in them for a moment, fearful he might recognize her from the den, despite her manly appearance at the time.

He continued. "I have been rather occupied with business matters of late. My cousin and I are forever inundated with work matters at the factory. As your father knows, I am sure, we recently have had many riots and pleas for work condition changes."

"Dear cousin, why should you bore these ladies with trivial business matters such as our own?" Dick Mason appeared from behind Frederick, apparently having finished his analyzing perusal of the ballroom.

Frederick stiffened slightly but resumed his smiling expression. "Lady Wincherton and Lady Anna. This is Richard or Dick Mason, both my cousin and my employer. You may have met before."

Dick smiled and bowed as Frederick introduced him. Anna thought it interesting that he did not smile with his teeth. Perhaps he had not been so toothily blessed.

"How lovely to meet you once again. Lady Anna, I remember you from our dance at the Croft's ball."

Anna stood still as Dick took her hand to his lips and lingered there a little before flicking his eyes to hers. They were blue, so different from his cousin. Icy blue. She remembered them even more now. She did not like to look at them, but she curtsied politely.

Frederick cleared his throat. "Dick, I did not wish to bore the ladies, of course. I merely wished to explain my recent absence from their home, as any gentleman would."

Dick closed his eyes and nodded in agreement. Her mother folded her fan and said, "Mr. Dick Mason, do tell us why we have not been graced with your lengthy presence at other functions? I had no idea that you had danced with my daughter, but I did know that you left very early, and we could not speak to you."

Anna watched as a quick glance passed between the cousins before they faced her mother again, all smiles. Dick put his hands behind his back and chuckled. It was a light act with an attempt at merriment and yet seemingly mirthless. She saw Frederick watching her.

Dick said, "Your Ladyship, you must forgive me. My cousin is the one blessed with the happier manners. I fear that I am never quite up for company, and so it is a rare occasion in which I enter into society, and if I do, I find I cannot stay long."

Lady Wincherton opened her fan again. "Ah I see. I am sorry for it, and I hope you know that we are most happy to have been able to speak to you at this ball."

Anna closed her eyes, fearful that her mother was being too obsequious for the sake of Frederick.

Frederick said suddenly, "Lady Anna, will you dance?"

"Thank you, Sir, I would be much obliged."

She hoped he had done so to keep them all from further embarrassment, but she remembered her duty. Now was when she needed to kick into action and find the words to ask Frederick all that she wanted to know. But how? Her mind whirred with possibilities as she was led on his arm out to the ballroom floor.

***

George lit another cigarette, watching the passing figures of Anna and her family. So, it was over now. Whatever spell he had been under, he had to break, for she had made her decision. At the point where their worlds had intersected, George had been left behind, and she sailed away, far away from him.

It's fine. I won't be needing to disillusion myself any longer.

Ned came up to him. "So, there they are, then."

George nodded. "There they are," he breathed out, watching the smoke as it curled away from him.

"She was quick to dismiss, I see. Desperate to get inside."

"So she was. It appears we're not suitable company for a high-class party, Ned. Only here to do the work." Ned chuckled.

"That's no surprise, is it? We're merely policeman, here to service the upper-class and keep them safe."

George shrugged, and Ned's smile grew.

"I see. You were hoping for more of a greeting? Perhaps an invitation to dine with them?"

George pushed away from Ned and wandered along the hedgerow, desperate for another cigarette even though one was already filling his lungs.

Ned clucked his tongue. "Tell me now, George. What is it that ails you? We'll be here awhile. We've got time. You might as well tell me."

George pushed a hand through his hair, remembering that he had used a hair oil and now had to wipe his hands on his coat. "Damn it."

He looked up at Ned, who was waiting for a reply, his arms crossed. Both of them turned at the sight of more guests walking up the pathway. Once they were out of earshot, George sighed. He supposed he could share with his closest friend after all these years.

"I had a foolish hope, I think. But I no longer believe in it. It was ridiculous."

"Foolish hope?" Ned watched him with a slight concern.

"It's too foolish to even put words to it. But it doesn't matter anymore. Forget about it."

Ned patted George on the shoulder. "It's not foolish if it's real, my friend. That I can say for you."

"Thanks, Ned." George walked along the side of the house, wanting to refocus his mind on the matter at hand. "We've got to focus now on watching for a killer. He could be anywhere, and we have to be the ones to find him."

***

Anna's hand shook a little as she allowed Frederick to take hers in their waltz across the floor. He smiled.

"Please do accept my apology for leaving so abruptly the other day and my lack of renewed visits."

"Yes, of course. It is no trouble." She could feel her face flushing, for she knew that if he stared at her overlong, he would be able to find out the truth.

"You are busy of late?"

Her heart fluttered, and she clenched her jaw. "What do you mean?"

"With the matter of your cousin, of course. I assume it has filled your mind and the rest of your family's minds these last days."

"Oh, yes." She smiled. "Unfortunately, it has rather placed a pall upon our existence. With each passing day, we lose hope in finding her."

Anna dared to look at his expression. She was not sure if she searched truthfully or if she merely willed it to be so, but there was a sad look in his eyes. They spun around to the music, and Anna could feel her skirt rustle against his legs.

He leaned close to her ear ever so slightly, and said, "What if I could offer you a way to help your cousin?"

Anna pulled away with a jerk.

Frederick's eyes were serious. "What would you say? Would you agree?"

Anna's tongue felt thick and dry, but she managed to stammer out, "Yes, yes, of course. I would do anything to ensure that my cousin is safe and could be returned to her home and to her family."

"Anything?" Frederick lifted a brow, and then nodded tightly. He looked up, searching the room as well, and Anna wondered what he searched for. His cousin was still in conversation with her mother, and for a moment, she pitied her.

"Meet me. Outside. In the back garden. Do you know where to go?"

Anna blinked, frozen for a moment, until Frederick jerked her hand a little as they turned, begging her to reply.

"Yes. I know. But what of the officers?"

"Officers?"

"Have you not seen them? They are at the front. I assume they are at the back as well."

Her face heated, realizing the mistake she had made. She hoped that Frederick did not notice it in her expression. He paused the dance, looking down at her, his face a mixture of sadness and hopelessness.

"Dear Anna, what have you done?"

CHAPTER

27

Frederick paled. After he asked his question, he began to look frantically about the room, and she had to keep holding tightly onto his shoulders in the dance, to make it seem as if all was well.

"I only meant that there are police. You saw them, surely."

But her tone was not convincing, and she feared that it was to no avail. They knew it was she who had brought them. The killer would see through her feeble rebuttals. But after a pause, she realized that she and Frederick had never spoken of anything relating to the case. It felt that she had known for so long about Frederick, Mason, and David F. and that she and he could speak openly about it, but then she realized that had not occurred.

Anna said, "Wait. What do you mean? Why do you ask me? Why have you grown so pale?"

Frederick flitted his gaze around the room again, still keeping Anna in his arms, moving in time to the music. Anna was on edge as she waited for his reply. This was the moment in which something important might be revealed. So long had things waited under layers, ready to be peeled back, but Anna and George hadn't had all the information they needed to peel back everything effectively.

Anna watched Frederick's throat as he swallowed. He said, "You know exactly to what I refer. You must meet me. That is all. Do you agree?"

His tone was harried, quick, and Anna could no longer see the shadow of a smile on his lips. He was an entirely new person, controlled by fear.

"Yes, I will. When?"

He lowered his voice and moved his lips closer to her. Just a few weeks ago, that would have made her quiver with a sort of feigned desire, but now, she only loathed the weakness he showed, the fear that consumed all his features.

"As soon as the dance is over. I will go first."

When the dance ended, Frederick left her arms with barely a goodbye. Anna moved her hands to her hair for lack of anything better to do, searching the room, hopeful no one had seen his hurried and rude departure. It was not the way of a gentleman.

She waited a few moments, and then slunk away to the side wall to sip at a fresh glass of champagne, watching to make sure that her parents did not see her. After a few moments, she slipped out the garden door, leaving the crystal flute behind.

Walking quickly through the flowered hedgerows, Anna inadvertently startled couples who had wandered out from the ball looking for a place to shield their clandestine rendezvous. She hurried past while averting her eyes, hearing their startled gasps but not registering their faces in an attempt at discretion.

She ended out in the middle of the garden, under the center lamplight. She looked around, her heart thumping in her chest. Where was George? Where were any of the policemen? Hearing a soft whistle, she turned and saw Frederick standing in the shadows. His teeth and white collar stood out in the darkness. As she approached, he pulled on her forearm, to bring her deeper into the bushes.

"Come. There is much to say."

Anna nodded, keeping her breath steady. She crunched along behind him, pulled by him into the darkness. Suddenly, her head was jerked back, a hand covered her mouth and nose with a cloth. Her eyes widened and the last thing she saw was Frederick's worried expression. But then his image went fuzzy, and she felt herself fall back, falling lank into someone's arms.

***

George was completely unfocused. Once all the guests had arrived, Ned and he were simply idling about until a half an hour later when a servant came outside to greet them.

"Senior Officer Ford?"

The man looked about the darkness, and George stepped forward, stubbing out his cigarette in the grass.

"Yes, that's me."

"You're asked to come inside now that all guests have arrived. The Jordans ask that you please keep inconspicuous. You are not to interact with any of the guests."

He nodded, and waving to Ned, the two of them walked inside.

Let them drink their champagne without fear of interaction from the lowly sort, even though a murderer is afoot.

He took off his hat, and he felt like a young boy as his eyes were distracted by the extent of the decor that surrounded them. He glanced back at Ned's surprised face. It was not that they'd never seen the houses of the wealthy elite of Lancaster City, but never had they been allowed to see into one of their exclusive affairs. The house had been completely transformed.

It looked like what George imagined a fairyland would be. It was the world of a storybook, and George was flooded again with the realization of how distant he and Anna's worlds truly were, even if on the streets at night and in disguise, they were on the same level. He felt worthy of her smiles then, but now, he felt like a shabby man come straight from the poorhouse holding out a hand for coins.

As his eyes moved about, they landed on Anna in the middle of the room, dancing in the arms of *her* Mr. Mason. George moved against the wall, keeping close to it to avoid the crush of the crowd. He wanted a drink, and his arm twitched whenever a waiter would walk past with a silver tray, shiny crystal glasses of champagne calling to him.

His eyes did not leave Anna as she swayed delicately in Mason's arms. This was the man that had called upon both Anna and Jenny in recent weeks, and Jenny claimed to be engaged to him, or almost engaged. It was also the man he'd interrogated in an alcove while the scent of opium filled his nostrils. Ned moved to the other side of the ballroom, his eyes looking over the crowd and occasionally glancing at George, but George did not look his way.

George had to clench and unclench his fist to rid his fingers of the automatic temptation to light another cigarette. He had wanted to smoke so often these days; his nerves were at an all-time high, but this was not the place for it. It would make him feel dirty surrounded by the glistening crystal, light music, and the swish of silk. Besides, he was on duty; he was meant to be watchful. High nerves were an asset. But he didn't like the look of Frederick's hand on Anna's back as he smiled down at her.

George's jaw clenched at the sight. He wanted it to be his own hand on her back, holding her while they danced. He tried to look away, to turn his mind to the present, but he found he could not. The realization was too strong. He was in love with Lady Anna Lovelace, and if he had not known before, then he knew now. Even though she had rebuffed him outside, the truth was still there, staring him in the face. The love would be entirely hopeless, and he wondered at the pointlessness of it.

It was also a foolish thing to have fallen in love so quickly. He felt like a total idiot. He tore his eyes away at long last, if nothing else but to give himself some reprieve.

Now is not the time for these things.

George searched the room, wanting to find the man of a similar description he'd seen on the walkway, to see if perhaps there was a set of twins amongst the wealthy elite of Lancaster. That would explain a lot of it.

He saw a man speaking to Anna's mother, and it was the dark-haired man who he had seen earlier. He nodded to Ned and moved to be able to watch him from afar and to get a better look at his face. As he did so, the music ended, and he looked around to see where Anna had gone next. But she was not among the couples departing the dancing area. His heart assumed the worst.

If anything happens to Anna, I will kill whoever did it with my bare hands.

The thought scared him, but he knew deep down that he was capable of such violence. Perhaps they all were, all humans, although he could not imagine cutting up a woman and stealing her heart for his own keeping. He looked around until he saw the glass door shudder on the edge of the ballroom. It might be nothing, but he felt in his gut that this was the way to go. He rushed over to it, but Ned caught his arm.

"What is it?" He said gruffly.

"The man we wanted to see. He's gone."

"Gone? Which way?"

"I didn't see. He vanished into thin air. I only looked away for a moment, I swear."

Ned was holding tightly to George now. He realized his own expression must surely have been quite grim.

"Damn it." George looked around, his eyes narrowing. "Come. Out the garden door. I think we've got to run."

Once they exited the ballroom, they tried to run as quietly as possible into the garden. They interrupted a few surprised couples as they left the balcony and rushed into the open garden beyond, surrounded by tall bushes and shrubs.

"Ned, she could be anywhere." Ned paced around the perimeter and nearly stumbled over an arm.

"George!" George's heart clenched at the nervous tone in Ned's voice. "Come here! It's one of ours!"

George rushed to his side and knelt by an arm splayed out into the cut grass, uniformed in blue. He looked up at Ned, whose face was trembling. They pulled at it, and a body slid out from under the hedgerow.

"Jim!" Ned cried out, touching the man's face. "George, he's just a boy, barely nineteen."

George nodded solemnly. He knew it. Jim had always been so eager to help, to join the team. George thought this a calm enough assignment for a young officer, for he wasn't entirely certain anything would happen tonight. And now, he was stabbed through the heart, lying in a heap in a bush, his eyes sightless to the world forevermore.

George cleared his throat, trying to avoid the pressure of tears.

"Ned, we've got to leave him. We must go and find them! They are on their way now! I shudder to think who else has come between them and their path of terror!"

Both got to their feet and began to rustle through the bushes that surrounded the squared off garden, looking for an opening through which to escape. The lamplight was dim, but it shone off the branches and leaves well enough. In a matter of moments, George called out to his partner. He had found a place where the bushes had been stomped through, and he ran through it, his heart in his throat.

He was able to push out all the way through to the street, but he saw nothing. No carriage, no people running away, nothing. He was too late. He turned around and smashed a fist into his hand.

"Hell! We've lost them. Maybe Anna's still inside, and it's just the Masons who left?"

He saw Ned's face in the light of the lamps, pale and wan.

"What is it, Ned?"

Ned lifted a piece of fabric between his fingers and handed it to George. "This was just on the branch here." His tone was low and soft.

George took the piece of cloth in his hand and felt it. He held it up to the light.

"It's mauve, isn't it, Ned?"

"Yes, it is."

He clamped the cloth in his hand and drew his fist to his mouth, fearful of what he might say or do. He wanted to burst into a thousand pieces. He felt hollowed out. Empty.

"She's gone, then. They've taken her."

***

Oh, what a delight! What adventure and what fun! I have finally found my prize, and she sleeps sweetly upon my lap as we ride to her salvation. My dear sweet cousin is ever fearful.

"What have you done? What will become of her?" he asks.

I simply laugh at his fearful expression. He was always the softer one, the kind one, the one the ladies favored.

"It is for the best," I tell him. "She is wanted. Do not worry. She is safe, for now."

"But her family? What will they think? They will try to search for her, you know. Did you not see the policeman there? They will catch us!"

I laugh again, loudly and heartily. But my pretty diamond does not yet wake up.

"They have not done so, yet. Why should they now? They are a party of fools, and we will not suffer them. We will simply go about our work!"

"Our work?"

My cousin is now spluttering, so full of little rage he is.

"This was never our work, cousin. This was all from you, all stemming from your heart of evil and malice. I wanted no part in this. I wanted...I wanted her. Ophelia."

"Ah, yes. What a name for her. Shakespearean tragically drowned beauty now turned to soon-to-be dead woman upon the streets of our fair city. Her fate will be a good thing, cousin. You will see. She will be redeemed. But if you desire her physically, then perhaps that can be arranged. If dear, dear Anna is willing to help her."

I stroke my Anna's hair, for that is what she is. My Anna. So delicate, so intelligent, so sparkling even under the influence of the drug that has seduced her into sleep.

My cousin says nothing. He looks out of the window. I remind him of everything we desire together.

"You have nothing without me. I am your only family. Your only chance for a life. Perhaps you should think of that and allow me my little," I laugh, "indulgences. I will not let you starve to death or freeze in winter. But you must be kind to me."

"As I have been."

"So you have. Keep it that way, cousin. Your future hangs in the balance as the rest of my pretty little hearts."

"Anna is special, though, cousin. You must remember that before you decide to do...anything. I thought you allowed her the chance to find Ophelia. That you would keep them both alive."

I look down at Anna's fine face. It is too bad her eyes are closed for they are quite mesmerizing.

"She is special. That I will admit, but my dear Anna has been quite the naughty one. I have warned her of her continued connection with police, and now she will pay the price for it. You saw them there tonight. She asked them to come. I know it."

My house looms into view, and I hear the carriage slow.

"Ah, we are here. Help me cousin, or I shall have D whip you for your insolence."

At my cousin's forlorn expression, I want to laugh again. I can be so humorous, and yet still no one seems to appreciate it. Perhaps Anna will, when she wakes?

CHAPTER

28

Anna had the strange feeling of falling into darkness as well as being cocooned in a soft warmth. It was like nothing she had ever felt before, both pleasant and strange at the same time. She heard a voice calling to her in the darkness, or rather cooing to her with kind words. Her eyes blinked open, and she could see a pale light coming from one corner.

It was like waking from the dead as her mind continued to register what it viewed before her. Moving her fingers a little, she could tell she lay on a sort of bed with a thick, cotton blanket wrapped around her, and the air was cool but not too cool. She moved one of her hands to the side and felt the jagged edges of uncut stone, piled one above the other. She was in the basement of a house.

She tried to piece together where she had been and what she'd done, but nothing was coming. There was the swirl of a dance, the clink of a crystal glass, and the touch of fabric upon her cheek, and then that was it.

"Anna," a voice called again, and dreamily, Anna turned to its direction.

She frowned when she saw red hair, lying in a bed also, not an arm's length away from her.

"Is this a dream?" she was able to mumble out.

The voice that replied was filled with tears as it spoke in a hurried whisper, "No, it's not a dream. Anna, you are here, and I am here. It's real, although I fear it's more akin to a nightmare. I can't believe that you came!"

As Anna's vision cleared, she could see the face of her beloved Ophelia come into view.

"Ophelia!" Anna's voice was weak. Her tongue was so dry that it felt like thick, heavy paper.

Ophelia gave her a watery smile. "Yes, cousin. It's me. Here, drink some water." She passed a glass to Anna, but her reach was limited. On her wrist, Anna could see a chain attaching her to the metal bedpost.

Without taking her eyes from it, Anna grabbed the cup and drank the water rapidly, grateful to sate her incredible thirst. When she put the glass down, she didn't know what to say first. Ophelia looked dreadful. The formerly cheery, beautiful cousin of hers was thin and pale with dark circles under her eyes. She had not bathed in days.

"Anna, tell me, what're you doing here?"

Anna smiled weakly, but tears were beginning to run down her cheeks. This time her voice was stronger and clearer.

"It's you. It's really you. You're alive, and I have found you."

Anna, not being tethered, reached out her hand to hold her cousin's warmly. Ophelia began to cry as well, and she smiled but only briefly. Soon her expression was replaced with one of fear.

"We don't have much time, Anna, for now that you're awake, they'll surely hear our talking and come for us."

Ophelia kept glancing towards the base of a stairwell far in the dark corner of the room. "What do you know of how you have come here?"

Anna shook her head, trying to clear her mind of its haze.

"I don't know anything much. Wait." She paused, pressing a finger to her head as she waded through the sea of memories in her brain. "There was a ball, yes. I was at a ball. I wanted to ask questions."

A sharp pain shot across her forehead, and she winced.

"Questions. About me?"

"Yes. We were close to something. We were very close."

"The man. He told me that. He knew you were close." Ophelia's voice took on a new sense of urgency. "Dear Anna, I don't know if your presence here is a good thing. The man told me he would find you and would bring you to heel if you didn't listen."

"I know. He told me so. He wrote it in a letter." Anna sat up, glancing at the stairwell herself, to make sure that no one was coming. "Who is it, Ophelia? Who's taken you?"

"He's somehow connected to D. I don't know how, but I fear for the worst, even though I've been kept alive longer than his other victims, or so he keeps telling me."

"This is the man, the man who has slain the other women."

Ophelia did not speak, but she nodded, and she pointed to where the candle stood. Anna turned there, her eyes still adjusting to the hazy darkness, and she noticed a large, wide, wooden desk. On top of it were large glass jars. Six of them. She couldn't clearly what was inside of them, but a few gray masses were floating in water.

"What is it, Ophelia? What is there?"

Ophelia started to speak, but all that came out at first was a slight squeak. She swallowed slowly and then said, "Those are the hearts. The hearts he keeps. He'll sit and gaze at them sometimes. He talks to me about them every day. He calls them his 'little treasures'."

Anna gasped. She had known about this. The hearts that were taken. The letters he wrote had told her thus, had told the whole of the city thus, and yet to hear them on the lips of the trembling Ophelia who had been his victim now for so long, made the facts all too real.

"I knew this. I knew what he did, and yet," Anna swallowed, trying to keep back the bile, "it is still so shocking, cousin. What a horror. How will we reason with this madman?"

"There will be no reasoning, Anna."

Footsteps were heard overhead, and Ophelia gasped and lay back, shutting her eyes tightly, as if to keep the outside world away.

When she spoke, it was barely above a whisper. "All I know is that something depends on him speaking to you. I'm still alive because of you. You seem to intrigue him in some way."

Anna was going to reply, but then the footsteps got louder, and Dick Mason entered the room still dressed in his ball attire.

"Well, what a lovely party we make!" He said, and he smiled widely. Not like his rather reserved demeanor from the ball room earlier.

His voice was practically shrill with glee, and the forcefulness of it made Anna shrink back a little.

Dick Mason is the killer.

Anna spoke out the words in her mind. "It's you."

Getting them out at long last relieved her but was replaced with a horrible feeling of dread. She had learned the truth but at what cost?

"I shall sit first," Dick said and pulled a chair closer to their beds. "You may be quite right, dearest Anna, but I must know what you accuse me of. What is it?"

He sat down smugly, crossing his arms over his chest. Chains began to rattle, and Anna turned to see a trembling Ophelia, trying to push closer to the wall as if she could not wait to escape. Anna turned back to him, oddly emboldened. She was the last thing between this evil killer and her cousin. Her moment of strength had come. She could not let Ophelia and any other of the female victims down.

"You're the one who has killed the women. It was you, not Frederick, but he has something to do with it. Doesn't he?" She lifted an inquisitive brow, trying to get across just how calm she felt, when indeed, inside she was terrified.

Dick crossed his legs. "I was right to be so interested in you, so intrigued by you. Your intelligence is far superior to any 'copper', as it were. Yes. You are quite right, my dear. It was me. All me. By Frederick, I assume you mean David. Yes, he had something to do with it. And to help you put all the pieces together, he is also our dear Ophelia's D as well as that police officer's fiancé's beau and the owner of the den. He is quite the costume artist."

Ophelia shrieked again and began to cry, her shoulders moving with the vibrations of her despair. Anna wanted nothing more than to reach out to her, to comfort her, but it was not the time. It would have to be later. Everything would have to be later if they were even able to survive this.

"D is Frederick and David both?"

Dick smiled again; an uncomfortable smile that would make any woman feel a discomfiting tingle down her spine. "Correct again. My cousin is David Frederick Mason. He has done work for me for a few years, and he has done the work I see before me. Shall we call him down here, so that you may dissect everything, Anna? And feel some measure of satisfaction in your success?"

***

George and Ned ran around to the front of the Jordan house again, searching for the officers that were sent to surround the place to guard it. All three of them were found in crumpled heaps, all unconscious. It was only Jim who had been stabbed, strangely.

Ned said, "Perhaps Jim was the only one who got in the way of the real murderer. The man does like the heart."

"Yes, yes, I think you may be right. Ned. You've got to tell our hosts what's happened, and then you should go to the police station to tell them to bring more men."

"To where, though, George?"

As he scanned the scene before him, his eyes spotted a crumple of white on the grass. His heart froze as he leaned down to pick it up. "It's a note, Ned!" he called out, and opened the paper up in his palm.

George, I can't speak to you tonight. The killer has written to me that I may not work with police any longer, and if I do, he will find his vengeance somehow. I don't wish to cause any trouble and so must pretend that we are strangers to each other.

Anna

Also, my father says that Frederick Mason's cousin, Dick, looks like Frederick. Seek him out.

George laughed with triumph. "Ned, to the Mason home we go! Do you know where it is?"

"No, but it can be found easily enough by those inside. Shall we go and ask them?"

George nodded. "Yes. I'll ask one of the servants. I cannot tell the parents that Anna is gone. You'll have to do so yourself, for they'll wish to accompany me, and that I can't risk. Not yet. Only tell them when the police are here, ready to follow you. You understand."

Ned nodded, but George could see that his friend's hands were trembling a little.

"I'll ask a maid inside. You go now to the station. First, tell someone inside that we will send more men here." He tried to smile comfortingly.

"Yes, George. Be safe. Take the pistol."

"No, it'll draw too much attention if I use it. The killer may react and kill both women. I can't risk that. Thanks, Ned. Now, go!"

Ned rushed inside, and George walked in after, hoping to find a servant in the hallway, so that he would not have to go into the ballroom and risk seeing Anna's parents. He was to be blessed. A servant walked by, placing coats and hats in the coat room. George ran up to the young woman so abruptly, she jumped back with a scream.

"Forgive me, girl. I have a question, though. I'm a police officer."

"I know it, sir."

"Tell me. Do you know the home of Frederick Mason? Dick Mason?"

The girls' expression darkened. "I do, sir. My brother works for them in their cigar factory, and they never listen to the workers' cry for better pay and better conditions!"

George was growing impatient. "We can't think of that now. Tell me. Where do they live?"

"On Chestnut Street, sir," she said, as if he was to know it. "It's one of the most beautiful homes on the street. Tall white pillars in front. Red door. You can't miss it."

George finally felt vindicated. He had a place to go to. A goal. A destination.

"Thank you!" he said and pushed his hat on his head and left for the streets, hailing for a cab before any of Anna's family came tumbling after him.

Waving his hand at a passing cab, he practically jumped in front of it, so that the horse whinnied, and the driver yelled at him. "Oy! What are you doing there? I could've killed you!"

"I'm a police detective. Take me to Chestnut Street. To the home of the Masons!"

It seemed the whole city knew of the home, for the driver nodded without complaint and they were soon off, rumbling down the cobblestone streets, the wheels loud against the cobbled road. George opened and closed the note from Anna in his hand. The paper was growing weak with his fiddling.

It was them. It had to be them. Either one or the other was the killer, and he was hot on their heels. Finally, this case could be solved. The smoky mist that had so pervaded these streets was about to become a physical being, and George felt a strong satisfaction that he and Anna could be the ones to send the evil man to the noose and be rid of him forever. London was rid of its Ripper, and now Lancaster could be rid of its own.

It was not a far journey to Chestnut from Orange, but even in that short time, George felt his anxiety grow. He was about to enter the home of a killer with nothing to protect him. The man was a wily one and would not show fear. Of that he was certain.

"Here, sir," the driver said.

George pulled out a few coins from his pocket, not even looking at them as he thrust them into the hands of the waiting driver. He could tell he gave the driver more than was normal, as the man thanked him feverishly.

"Will you wait a bit? Once the police cab arrives, you don't need to stay any longer."

The man nodded, still looking at the coins in his hand. George turned his face to the white columned house. It was just as the servant girl described it. It was a magnificent facade, greater even than the Jordan's house, and two lanterns hung alongside the door, casting eerie shadows on its red, blood-like color.

George took a breath and walked up the path to the doorway, wondering what he might find inside. He had to waste time, to keep the killer from his acts until he had enough men to burst through the house. He knocked, and after a few moments, a man opened the door, gruff and angry-looking. It was Darren from the opium den.

George smiled. "Ah, D, is it? From the door of the opium den?"

The bearded man opened his eyes wide in surprise and then tried to slam the door shut.

"No, you don't!" George yelled and thrust his whole weight against the nearly closed door.

Darren squealed against the pressure. George pushed with his shoulder until the door gave way, and Darren was pushed back further into the center of the room, heaving for breath. He then smiled, his yellow teeth looking like little corn kernels as he straightened up. George adjusted his ruffled coat.

"Ye will nae find him, lad." Darren laughed. "The man is a clever one. He knows how tae remain in the shadows. Ye will never find him if he doesnae want tae be found."

Turning to the hearth, Darren pulled out a fire poker and brandished it wildly in front of George. George regretted leaving the pistol behind, but fists would have to do.

George said, "Well, it's clear I found him already. It's only a matter of finding in which room he resides and performs his evil deeds."

George's heart was beating wildly against his chest, but his courage grew. He clenched his fists as he and Darren circled each other like two lions stuck in a cage together. Darren snorted, and then took a step closer, swinging the lethal metal stick in George's direction. George ducked out of the way, and when he rose again, he thumped a fist hard into Darren's jaw. It was one hit, but it was enough. The poker clattered to the floor and Darren fell backward, into a chair and was silent.

"So much for quietly entering," George whispered to himself and then got on his knees to handcuff an unconscious Darren to the arm of the heavy oaken chair nearby. At least he had brought those with him.

"That'll keep you for a little while, I think."

The police had still not yet arrived. George could hear time ticking by. The clock on the mantle did well to assist him in that respect. Each second could bring about Anna's death, and he had to find her now, or else he might never see her alive again.

CHAPTER

29

Ophelia started to whimper softly, and Anna said to Dick, "Yes, I would have you do that. But first, tell me. Why am I here? What's my purpose to you? If we are here to save my cousin, then let us do it, now! I have done my duty."

Dick stood to fetch his cousin. "You will see, Anna, you will see. I am not yet wholly decided."

He left for but a moment, and Anna waited in bed, looking at Ophelia.

"I was a foolish woman, Anna. So very foolish, and now I have paid for it."

There was no time to comfort her. The men returned, and in the candlelight, David looked pale and shaken. When he spotted Ophelia in the corner, he took a step towards her, but Dick placed a hand on his arm and Ophelia placed a hand on her mouth, to stifle the sound of her sharp cry.

"Sit, sit, David. We are here to dissect you." At David's nervous stare, Dick burst into merry laughter. "Oh, you must never worry about me preserving your heart in one of my jars, D. I would never keep a man's heart, you know. Not worth it."

He patted his cousin's shoulder as if it was a common statement, and David sat down slowly, his eyes flicking between Ophelia and Anna.

"Now, Anna," Dick pulled a cigar from his coat pocket and lit it. "Do tell us everything that you know, everything that you have discovered, with the help of the police, of course." His voice was calm, but his look was dark and angry, and Anna nearly lost her nerve.

I must stay strong. For Ophelia's sake.

Anna thought briefly of George and wished for him to come plunging down the basement stairwell, to pluck her and Ophelia from the killer's claws, but that was not to be. She had to solve this on her own.

Was that not what I wanted, all this time? To prove myself in some way?

The first step would be to remain as calm as possible and draw out the conversation until she could think of her next move.

"Well, we went to the address written in Ophelia's address book. You know the place, of course. We were greeted by who we thought was D at first but later realized he was not the D we were in search of. A rather malodorous man if you ask me."

Dick chuckled and took a large puff of his cigar. "Go on, my lovely. You are entertaining me already. I told you, David. I told you that she would be perfect."

David nodded dutifully, and Anna continued, sitting up straighter in her bed, but fearing to fully come out of it lest Dick rush forward in an angry rage.

"D told us nothing, really. Only that there was a sort of establishment run there that people kept coming back to. He knew Ophelia, though, and that gave me a sort of hope."

"And how did this involve the handsome policeman, my dear?"

"Well, I had gone to this establishment on my own at first. It was mere chance that me and the police officer were to meet. He happened to be in the area. Later, after we had discovered that information, and once I received your letter, I went to him. You encouraged me to think, to help, and that was what I dearly wanted as well. I had been following the cases for many weeks in the newspaper."

Dick bowed his head as if he had just completed a performance. "You do me credit, dear girl. Such a thing for a young lady to read. I am justified in my respect of your rather fertile mind."

Anna swallowed, trying to think of enough words to say to draw out her story. She also looked around the room to see if there could be anything she might use as a sort of weapon, in case either of them came any closer.

"We both agreed to go in disguise to the opium den, for that is what the policeman thought the place was."

"Ah, now we get to it. This is where you met dear David under one of his personages."

David bowed his head, casting his eyes away from Anna. He had barely watched her during the entirety of her story. What could possibly have made a seemingly normal man aid and abet a killer? Even if he was the killer's cousin?

"Yes, although I knew him as Frederick. And at the den, I suppose my disguise was not as good as I could've hoped."

Dick chuckled. "You have too pretty of a face, my love. Too distinct. David knew it was you, and he told me what sort of embrace he found you and the policeman in when he entered the alcove. It seems you and the policeman are very close, indeed."

Dick clucked with his tongue. Anna couldn't tell if it was approval or dismay. Ophelia was still watching the two of them with fear in her eyes.

"It matters not," Anna said in slight defense of her actions. "I was attempting to remove suspicion."

"Well, what a plan. Go on, now. Continue your story."

Anna was beginning to grow irritable. "But why should you wish to hear any of this, when you know all of it already from this point? Is it not pointless?"

Dick removed a fleck of cigar from his lip. "Not at all, Anna!" He looked at her and no one else, and since the other two members of their party weren't speaking, it felt like they were the only ones in the room. "I wish to hear how your mind works. You are the first person of which I have wished to hear the state of their thoughts. The first woman, especially."

Anna cleared her throat, the question of why bursting through her brain. Why did he do any of this? But she needed time, and so she bided it.

"After that, we knew that something was going on. I recognized Frederick at the den, but George recognized David, the one who is courting his former fiancée."

Dick tapped his fingertips together. "Ah, yes, I did enjoy that bit of flair. I thought it would get the policeman out of the way, so to speak, if his fiancée was so engaged, but I did not count on them ending their betrothal and her scurrying off somewhere after that."

His expression grew dark again, and Anna knew that she had but little time left.

"George and I simply discussed who the different variations of Frederick, I mean David, could be. There is the man who called upon me, the man who owned the den and was spending time with Ophelia, and the man who was betrothed to Jenny or nearly so. It was tonight that we decided that they were one and the same man, although it is my cousin and Jenny who saw the opium den version. He must have told her that he was undercover, for he had also lied and told her he was involved with the police? And George interviewed the other victims' families and found that most of the family members recognized a drawing of David that George took around with him."

David still said nothing, but he seemed even paler and sicker. Dick clapped.

"Well done, Anna. Well done, indeed. You have found nearly everything out. But why the disguises? What was David Frederick's role in all my work?"

Anna looked between the two of them. She had thought of it so much, but she'd never put it in words.

"I believe he is your 'catcher'. A man who collects the ladies for you but for what reason he agrees to do so, I can't fathom. As you mentioned this evening, David is the one with the happy manners, and I know from first-hand experience that he is quite charming if he wishes to be. I understand very well why each of the women were wont to follow whatever he said. Sometimes he would take them from society but sometimes from the opium den, where the women were all too eager to do as he asked if they could get their hands on the source of their addiction. But Ophelia seemed different somehow. He seemed genuinely sad about the loss of her."

Ophelia made a sort of whimpering sound, and David put a fist to his lips as if to quell some emotion. Dick looked upon him with disgust.

"Yes, my cousin is a weak man no matter all his charms. I believe he fell for the woman he was sent to 'catch', although I could not allow that. I knew of their growing affection, and I knew they would want to meet outside the ball. I intercepted them in the garden." He sighed. "And yet, I do not think that you have fallen for his sort of charm. You did at first, but then, something else happened. No, I do not think your heart was ever entangled in him."

Dick cocked his head to one side as if he was analyzing her, and then he turned to David with the same expression.

Anna was amazed that her and George's thoughts about David were true. He had cared something for Ophelia? In response to Dick, Anna said confidently, "No. I have no interest in marriage. It was never one of my goals, although my mother fervently bemoans that fact."

Anna sat up straight, her convictions keeping her steady. While it was true, she attempted to play it up even further.

Dick stood up, lifting a finger into the air. "Ah. This was your former thought, your former dearly held goal. But something new has entered your heart."

He began to pace, like a doctor watching his patients carefully, attempting to assess what sort of treatment they needed.

"The heart is such an interesting organ, Anna. It fills the body with blood. It gives life, and it pumps endlessly until there is one day when it decides to stop. But besides the physical capabilities, we have given it such emotional power. The thoughts of the heart move us or stay us from action, and it does not always follow the patterns of logic. The heart leads us to things we might never have desired or sought. For example, I think your heart has led you to a certain policeman. This George Ford. And yet you deny it."

Anna could feel sweat coming out on her forehead, and her head began to swim. Dick Mason was an artist. Truly. The way he spoke made it feel like his hands had really come into her chest and fingered her heart, knowing all its rhythms and all the secrets it harbored within its depths.

"Why must I deny it?" It was not a question she had consciously formed, but it fled her lips anyway, and it made Dick smile. She did truly yearn to know the answer.

"Because it would not suit you. It does not suit your highly treasured convictions. It does not suit society either. And so, you push it aside, pretending that such feelings do not exist."

His ability at truth made a person wish to melt into the floor with relief. It was so refreshing to hear the truth spoken out in words, in front of others. While it terrified her and made her feel so exposed, at least it was true and honest. The truth spoken out loud can often be the cause of one's release, and Anna felt released.

"It is true. You are correct. My heart has been taken. But you are correct again. I must deny it for the sake of many reasons."

Anna folded her hands in her lap, staring boldly back at Dick. He was continuing to smile.

"Perhaps I have come to the end of my exploration of you, then, Anna, for you know yourself, and you reveal it so easily. I have read your every thought and every idea."

Anna sighed. The time was finished. There was nothing else to say. It was only the matter at hand.

"And so, what is your decision? Have you made it?"

Here her heart began a dull, thudding beat as she tried to focus her mind on confidence and strength. It would have broken her to look at Ophelia then, for her cousin was cowering even more than she thought possible. This was the dreaded moment. Dick looked at David who watched him with fearful eyes. The man was so weak. Had he nothing to say in defense of his supposed beloved or in defense of his own part in all the crimes?

Dick sighed. "I think that the time has now come."

A fire flashed in his cold blue eyes, making them look even fiercer. Anna had to steel herself not to pull back in fear.

"The truth at the bottom of it all is, Lady Anna, you have betrayed my instruction. You have brought the police and involved them, even after I expressly asked you not to. It was to be yourself alone who was to solve the case."

"But--" Anna tried to retort, but the words died in her throat at the sight of Dick's face.

"Do not try to refute it, Anna, for I know it. I see all and everything. Surely you must know this by now. The police were there to watch the proceedings this evening. Who else but you could have suggested such a thing?"

Anna felt tears pressing at her eyes, waiting to be released, but she swallowed, trying to hold them back as best she could. Tears would only make her appear an even greater fool in front of Dick, and she could not bear that. Not if these were to be her last moments.

Dick watched her with a smile and began to pace again, sharing his insights as if he was a teacher in front of a class.

"Now, it will be the same as any other of the ladies which I have liberated, but I will give you even greater beauty, greater freedom, dear Anna, since you are so deserving of it."

"Why? Why do you do this?" Dick's fiery gaze flared, but Anna kept her eyes on him while Ophelia's shoulders shook as she cried silently. She had still said nothing. "If I am to die, I wish to know why that is. What makes you do what you do? Why do you find it such 'noble' work?"

Dick's smile widened, and his hands clasped in front of him as if he was to begin a monologue.

"Do not think that I take much pleasure in removing you from the earth, Anna, not as much as I might with other ladies, for I do much enjoy speaking with you, and I wish that we could continue. But," he looked down at her sternly. "I must not let bad deeds go unpunished, for if I was to do so, what kind of reputation would I have? And then you will become part of my lovelies. I can look upon your heart for the rest of days and know that I have encapsulated the very dearest and most intelligent of the female species of my acquaintance. What a treasure that would be."

Anna's throat was thick with emotion. So much was undone in her life. She had done her best to free her cousin, and yet she had just embroiled her in further damnation. They were to die, and Anna felt as if it was she who had made the final cut. And there was George. Dear George. She would never see him again because of her stupidity. For some reason that thought hurt her most of all.

"But why? You still have not answered me why? There must be something beyond mere punishment for wrongdoing."

Against her will, one tear had escaped, and it slid quickly down her face before Anna hurriedly brushed it away with the back of her hand.

"Because women have not been given gifts such as us. They have been tainted by something. It controls their minds and their actions. They hurt a man. They abuse; they torture; they use words as weapons in a way a man could never do. The bile spewed forth by a woman is much harsher than a man's ever could be. My mother was just such a woman. And women are trapped in these lives forever. These women. Forced forever in their harshness and evil. It is I who give them beauty and life. I set them free. They are cleansed by my killing, and they are made even more beautiful."

Anna shook her head. "But what made you choose these women? What made you choose Ophelia?"

Dick grinned. "Ophelia. Dear sweet, beautiful Ophelia. The eyes of the city are upon her. She marches through with her vanity and her pride, knowing that she is the fairest in our fair city. And yet, darkness is through her heart. Vanity is a dark sin indeed. And so, she fell for David when her vanity was stroked. It was simple enough, was it not David?"

David still said nothing, but he stared at the crouching, whimpering Ophelia in the corner. Anna could see that his eyes were red, and a tear streamed down his face. She did not feel sorry for him.

Anna replied loudly, "I see. And so, you think that you are the arbiter of justice in this world? That it is up to you to set women free from their bonds of innate evil?"

Even though her voice was dripping with sarcasm, Dick heartily nodded. "I do. For whom else will stop them? There was no one there to stop my mother from her own vanity, her own self-importance, and her own cruelty. She took our lives from us, and I was grateful for her death and sad that it did not come by my hand."

Dick took a breath, and then he continued. "Men are always told that women are such gentle creatures. We hear of their angelic and fairy-like natures, and yet they steal one's heart. They crush it between their hands as if it were nothing but dust. We have suffered aplenty for it, David as well. His own parents died, and he was left to suffer the abuses of his aunt just as I was. We are here today, to keep women at bay, and to set them free to be the delicate beauties they were always meant to be. I have taken their evil hearts from them."

His eyes had grown crazed. Anna knew that this man was nothing more than someone who belonged hidden away in an insane asylum. His mother had created this creature, and now the rest of womankind in her city was suffering for it.

"I see," she said, for what was there to say to such lunacy? To such fallacious arguments?

Dick was satisfied, and he rubbed his hands together. Anna watched them, a sickening feeling filling her stomach. There was nothing else to say now. It would just happen, and all would be over. Hers and Ophelia's lives would be finished.

"Let us begin," he said, his smile growing.

Anna could feel her heart speed up. *For the last time*, she thought morbidly. But then, something that sounded like a thunderclap filled the house. Dick's eyes flicked to the ceiling and then back to Anna.

Her stomach clenched at the sight of his pale anger. "Your policeman?" he said, his words dripping with hatred and fury.

Anna shook her head and stammered, "I do not know who it could be. No one saw me leave the ball for the garden."

Dick calmed a little. "Darren should handle it well enough. But David, go and check for yourself. We do not need any distractions. I shall begin the proceedings."

David stood but was planted in place. He didn't move for a few moments, his worried glance moving between Ophelia and Anna. In that moment, Anna hated him, and she hoped that Ophelia would forget him in her last moments. He was not worth remembrance. He stomped away, his fists at his side, walking resolutely up the steps.

Dick turned back to the two women. His happy demeanor had returned. "Now, I shall first get my tools, and then all will be well. You will be set free, my dears, and then you will rest peacefully for all time."

CHAPTER

30

George walked around the room, searching for anywhere and anyplace that would serve as a good hiding place for victims. But he couldn't find a door that led down. He raced up the steps, searching through the above rooms but found nothing, and he returned dejected back to the main room.

"Damn it," he said to the room, his heart pounding. "I can't lose her simply because I couldn't find the stupid room. I can't lose her. I can't."

He was becoming frantic. He needed to find Anna. He needed to save her to tell her just how he felt, to tell her that he was so in love with her, and he just needed her to know. Even if she didn't love him back. It just mattered that she knew. For the first time in his life, he felt he had to share his heart.

And then, a miracle. Someone pushed open a bookshelf on the wall in the living room, and George felt a sharp, cold breeze. It was David F., his eyes wide with surprise who slammed the door after he left it, concealing how exactly it could be opened again.

David did not look angry. He looked scared.

"You," George breathed, feeling a hatred burning in his heart. "I knew it was you. I knew it was you when I saw you with my old fiancée. When I discovered that you were the man who had also begun to court Anna. How could you do this? Kill women? Bring them to your lair? What's your name, anyway? David? Frederick? D?"

David actually looked in physical pain as George stepped closer and made his accusations. He held up his hands as he and George began to circle each other.

"It wasn't me. I swear it upon my life. It was not I who killed those women!"

"Then who?" George grumbled, not believing David for an instant.

"It was my cousin. He did it all."

David had one thing going for him. He could be earnest when he wanted to be.

"And where is he then? This cousin of yours?"

"Downstairs."

"Then, I--"

"No! You can't go!" David stood in front of the bookshelf, and George's eyes flashed with rage.

"Just try to stop me."

David pushed George hard in the chest. "You must let him do his work. He will kill everyone if something doesn't go the way he wants it. He will ruin everything if he wishes to. You do not understand him." A cold look of fear passed his face. "He can do anything. He is like a mist. He will disappear as soon as you think you have him."

"Just try me."

George's mind was filled with the image of David's cousin stabbing Anna with his knife and then cutting out her heart. He couldn't bear it. He grabbed David by the lapels of his jacket, and as if the man was weightless, he threw him to the ground. David winced in pain, and George jumped on top of him, latching his wrist into a cuff and attaching it to a beam of the fireplace grate.

"Pathetic," he said under his breath before he returned to the bookshelf door and found a hidden latch. He heaved it open and rushed down the dark stairwell. His fists were clenched, and his eyes struggled to adjust to the darkness. A few candles were burning, and he could see shadows on the wall, but despite his heightened awareness, he didn't notice a large heap at the base of the stairs, and he tripped, nearly falling over until a hand grabbed his wrist and steadied him.

He turned, ready to swing, when he saw Anna's triumphant face grinning up at him in the near darkness.

***

Once David had left, Anna glanced Ophelia's way for a moment. Ophelia was clutching to her chained hand uselessly and had succumbed to grief and despair. Her eyes were frantic, and it seemed that she didn't even notice Anna there anymore. Dick had moved to the desk. Now was her chance. David was gone, and it was just she and Dick. She had no notions that she would be able to overpower him, even if he was rather small for a man, but she did believe she could use surprise to her advantage.

She crept ever so slightly. He was humming to himself, fully immersed in his work as he searched the desk for what tools he needed. She tried to keep her courage as she saw him pull out a shining silver dagger from one drawer, and a hairbrush from the next. She crept behind him, searching for something, anything that she could use to knock him out.

She glanced at the blank stone wall, the bed, and then she had it. The chairs. There were the two wooden chairs right next to her that David and Dick had sat upon while Dick prided himself on his cleverness. Sliding her hands quietly over the back of one of them, she lifted it in the air, and brought it down across his back just as Dick attempted to turn around, a surprised look in his eyes.

He fell down on his face by the steps, groaning, but he was not unconscious. As he was moving about, trying to get his hands under him to stand up again, Anna's vision narrowed. She stared at the desk.

Book, dagger, brush, glass. Jars of glass. Heavy jars of glass.

She tried to not look at their contents as she picked one up in both of her hands and let it fall over Dick's head just as he was lifting himself up.

The sound felt deafening after being trapped for so long underneath the city, caught in another world. Anna was breathing heavily as she watched his head. She could see a cut forming, but it was mixed with the strange liquid from the jar. Shattered glass was sprinkled everywhere: through his hair, on his coat, and over the floor. And then she saw it in the corner.

It had rolled there, a gray lump, and she was afraid to turn her eyes to it. The heart. The heart of some poor woman that had fallen for his and David's traps. A woman who was seen to be less than worthy and so was taken from the world. Sent forward, forced into renewal by the hand of Richard Mason, a man who played a god.

Anna stepped back, suddenly feeling a wave of fatigue when she heard someone running down the steps. She knelt down to grip the chair again as a weapon, when the man practically fell over the lump of Dick at the base of the stairs. She grabbed his wrist out of instinct, and then was met with George's surprised eyes.

Anna had never been so happy to see anyone in her whole life. She smiled, laughed, and dropped the chair out of her hand. She pulled him towards her and then wrapped her arms around him tightly. George hadn't said anything yet, but after his moment of stiffened surprise passed, she could feel his arms snake around her back and hold her tight.

"Anna," he said softly, the feel of his breath on her ear sending a shiver down her spine.

"Anna?" A small voice called out, breaking through her consciousness. Anna reluctantly pulled away, feeling the loss of George's arms around her and turned to her cousin. Her fingertips brushed against George's, who responded by clasping tightly to her hand.

"Oh, Ophelia, I was just so happy that he is here. He has come. We are freed."

George moved over to try to remove Ophelia's chains. He pulled and yanked while Anna rummaged in the desk. "Here!" she called. "This seems to be where he keeps everything."

Anna handed him a key, with one eye on Dick's still unconscious body. George looked sheepish as he unlocked Ophelia's shackles.

"I had hoped to save you, Anna, both of you, but it looks as though you've saved yourself." He glanced at the sodden figure on the floor.

Anna smirked at the regretful tone in his voice. Once Ophelia was free, Anna pulled her into a tight embrace, tears falling down her cheeks.

"My dear cousin. I am so sorry."

Ophelia's face was wet as she laughed with relief against her cousin's shoulder.

"What have you to apologize for, Anna? You saved me!" Ophelia pulled back and held Anna's face between her hands. "You saved me. I knew that you could do it! You've saved me from my own foolishness!" Ophelia pulled her into a hug again, and George cleared his throat from behind them.

"I think it best that we go, ladies. I have a few men a bit tied up upstairs. Let's hope they don't come to and ruin our escape."

She wasn't thinking. That's what Anna wanted to tell herself, that all thought had left her mind now that he was there because his presence was so welcome. She felt like fresh air had been pumped through her body, and she was in a state of euphoria.

Turning back towards him, she said, "George, thank you," before putting her hands on his shoulders and pulling his mouth to hers.

It was just like the kiss in the opium den, with the same feeling of floating lightness, the same sensation of hot hands tightly holding her, and a warm mouth kissing her. But there was something else in it this time. There was a confidence, a need. Anna spread her hands around his neck and held them there. George pulled her waist closer to him, and lifted a hand to her cheek, brushing a thumb across it as his lips moved on hers, opening, accepting, savoring.

It was the most beautiful thing she'd ever experienced. He was the most beautiful man she had ever known. The kiss was full of excitement, desire, and dare she say it? Love. Dick was right. She knew that she was in love with George Ford, but after tonight, there was nowhere it could go. Nowhere it could fly off to, and so with regret, she pulled away, her whole body atremble.

She watched him with regret and swallowed, her hands sliding down from his neck back to his strong shoulders.

"Thank you, George. For everything."

The look on his face made her want to weep. It was full of confusion and questions, and if she was being honest, she could see love there as well. Biting back the wave of affection for this man who had done so much and changed her life so entirely, she nodded, surreptitiously flicking away a tear that had fallen loose down her cheek.

"Let's go."

George cleared his throat and moved to help a surprised Ophelia stand.

"Yes. The police will be here soon."

In fact, as they walked up the stairs, they could hear a sound coming from the top. George still didn't look at her. Anna felt the awkwardness keenly but focused on keeping her hand on Ophelia's arm and helping her weak cousin move up the stairs.

"That could be them now," he said.

As George moved to push his shoulder against the hidden wall, light poured in from the main room. They stepped forward and out of nowhere, she turned to see a crazed David coming towards George, a brass candlestick in hand.

"George!" She called, and in a flash, he turned and dodged out of the way. David nearly toppled to the ground, but he held his balance and turned back, his teeth bared.

"I will not die for my cousin's evil. The evil that has attempted to pervade even me. It is not my doing!"

He swung the candlestick and George dodged again, biding his time before he could swing his fist.

"Damn it. How did you get out of your chains?"

"Not quite the strongest handcuffs, Mr. Ford."

David grinned, and Anna could see that he looked nearly maniacal as he moved and swung.

George stiffened. "You don't think you were guilty? How can you consider yourself blameless? It was you who lured them! You who found their weaknesses! You brought many to the den and attempted to seduce Jenny as well! Hoping to bring her to your cousin's lair. And Ophelia…"

"Ophelia was never about seduction for his sake. I tried to keep her from him!"

To his side, George heard a small croak as Ophelia stuttered out, "D. How could you?"

The sound alone could have broken any heart, and it did so for the man who truly loved her. David looked stunned as he turned to the voice, strangely only noticing the women's presence for the first time.

"You are free," he said and took a step towards her.

Ophelia pulled back, gripping tightly to Anna's arms. "You're horrible. A monster. You'll suffer for what you've done!"

George saw his moment. David had let his guard down, his candlestick lowered, and his eyes were turned to Ophelia, full of sadness and longing.

He clenched his fist and swung it hard at David's jaw until David fell backward, hitting his head hard on the floor. George rushed over to him, grabbed him by the shirt collar and seeing that he was unconscious, laid him back down.

"Where in the hell are the police?" He roared.

At that moment, Ned burst in, pistol held high, his eyes searching from person to person before he put the gun down with a smirk. Two more men burst in behind him, nearly tripping over the stationary Ned.

"Well, it appears we've a hero on our hands," Ned said, turning to the other men. "George Ford. Victory over the murderer?"

George winced. "Not quite. It was ---" He felt a soft hand touch his arm and he turned to see Anna's green eyes watching him, attempting to tell him something. She shook her head and turned to Ned with a smile.

"You're quite correct, sir. Senior Officer George Ford has been our hero. You'll find the murderer downstairs, unconscious."

"Excellent!"

Ned kept grinning as he and his men moved down past the open bookshelf door and into the basement.

George turned to Anna, "What're you doing? Don't you want credit for everything that you've done? You guessed it before I did. And you actually suffered at the hands of the murderer!"

Anna smiled, her hands on her hips.

"You want the detective position, George. I know it. What have I to gain from any credit relating to the case? It will not bring me my wildest dreams. Not yet at least. All I have is the satisfaction that Ophelia is free and well again and safe from anyone who wishes to hurt her. And I have the satisfaction that I have proved you wrong. A woman really can do things."

George blushed.

Good lord, the man actually blushed!

What a far cry from the man she had first met in her drawing room.

"Anna, you're right. I was wrong. I know it now. I think I might've always known it, ever since the first moment you yelled at me in your foyer. But I can't keep all the credit to myself. It isn't right. And what about that kiss?"

He was rubbing the back of his neck, his forehead wrinkled with concern. It seemed his mind was a jumble, and he couldn't quite get the exact words out that he wanted to say. Anna tried to smile as she leaned in to kiss his cheek.

"You are the best man I know, George Ford."

Her heart screamed for her to say more, to ask for more, but she couldn't. She couldn't take his life of peace from him. Nor could she be the wife that she was sure he really wanted. The domesticated homemaker who spent her days washing and ironing and bearing children. It could never be. They both needed to be free.

George swallowed and stepped closer to her. She sucked in a breath. She looked up into his eyes and felt everything. She let it all tingle over her in a flash.

"Anna," he said, and she thought she would have given him everything in that moment, even weakened enough to hear his argument, but Ned came back through the door, clearing his throat to alert them as he approached.

Anna and George stepped apart, and the moment was gone. The two officers came behind him, heaving the body of Dick Mason between them. Ned coughed again.

"I saw the hearts." Ned shuddered. "Well, he's not dead, but I think he might be on the brink of it. Good thinking, George, using the glass to hit him."

Ned looked between George and herself, and she nodded with a smile while George said stiffly, "Ah, thanks, Ned."

"Well, the sergeant will want to speak to you. You may even get a promotion." Ned clapped his hand on George's shoulder and moved out of the house with Dick, calling for more officers to take Darren and David with them.

George stood awkwardly before her as if torn between staying or going. Anna clung to Ophelia's arm and heard the cry of her aunt as Aunt Louisa, Uncle Jack, and her mother and father ran through the door.

"Ophelia!" Louisa cried, clutching her daughter to her. Uncle Jack embraced them both.

Anna moved away, relieved. Satisfied. She allowed herself to sink into her father and mother's embrace. Suddenly, she was exhausted. All had been completed at long last. But when she looked up, George was gone. Smiling politely up at her parents, she let them help her out the door into the waiting carriage, wanting nothing more for the moment than to sleep.

CHAPTER

31

"You did well last night, Ford. Very well." George shifted uncomfortably on his feet as he stood in the office of Sergeant Donaldson, his hands behind his back. His stiff boots felt even stiffer that day, as he let the praise of a job well done fall over him, even though he didn't feel as though he entirely deserved it.

Donaldson smoothed his hand over his chin. "I confess to you that I never expected it, but I'm happy to say I was wrong."

George wondered for a moment if he should be offended, but he had had those very same fears himself. If it wasn't for Anna.

Anna.

The memory of the previous evening came back like a tidal wave through his mind, and he felt nearly dizzy with the sensation. What had it all meant? Now that the killer was taken away, would he ever even see her again?

"Welcome to the world of detection. A position is yours if you want it."

George could see the sergeant's lips moving, but he had been so lost in thoughts of Anna's embrace that the words didn't register. He cocked his head to the side and crinkled his forehead. Donaldson laughed heartily, his belly bobbing up and down as he did so.

"Surprised, are you? Don't know what to say yet? I told you that the job is yours if you want it. You've proven yourself tenfold. Detective Barclay has moved on. Better position in New York and all that."

George merely blinked for a moment before the words clicked in his brain. "A detective position. It's mine?"

"Yes, yes," Donaldson nodded. "I think you must be exhausted from the case; your mind seems to be a little worse for wear."

"Ah, yes, Sergeant. Forgive me. I think I'm just pretty addled."

"Certainly, after taking down the most fearsome murderer we've had in Lancaster. Why, even London itself cannot boast for having captured Jack the Ripper. If only one could brag to the policemen over in Whitechapel, I would. Hmm…I have a mind to send a telegram over there."

He grinned, and George felt queasy. He knew that Anna wanted him to take all the credit. But why? Why should she not wish the world to know just how talented, intelligent, and incredible she really was? Would it harm her reputation that much?

"Now, Ford, it's possible I could take such a position away, if the person did not want it or was not grateful for it." Donaldson still looked merry, but there was a note of irritation in his voice.

"Not at all, sir," George said hurriedly. He bowed his head. "You have my deepest thanks, and I accept heartily."

"Excellent. Now, going forward, I'll share the duties between you and the other detective, Detective Swanson, evenly, but you understand Swanson already has current cases under his belt. At the moment, there is nothing for you, but do not think this sea of calm will remain flat forever. Something will come your way soon enough. I suggest you go home and get some more rest. Return fresh tomorrow with an ability to respond more quickly to your superiors."

Donaldson gave a dismissive nod, meaning the conversation was now at its end.

"Thank you again, sir. I won't disappoint."

"Let's hope not," the older man said and turned his eyes to the array of documents on his large desk. "Good day to you."

"Good day," George said softly before he left the office and walked back to his own desk. He sat down in a daze, when Ned walked in cheerily, flopping himself in the chair opposite.

"So? What happened? What did he say?"

George glanced at Ned's cheerful face and was comforted, if only just a little.

"He promoted me. I am now Detective Ford."

Ned's eyes opened wide. "Why, that's excellent! Great news, my friend!" George's expression didn't change, and Ned added, "Aren't you glad?"

George sighed and put his feet up on his desk. He supposed that now, the action would not be so scandalous for he was at one of the highest positions of the office. He pushed a hand roughly through his hair, feeling suddenly antsy.

"I don't feel like I can take it, not when Anna wasn't credited for what she did. It feels like I didn't earn it myself. I don't know. I don't know what I think," he groaned.

Ned crossed his arms. "But you told me what she said. She asked you to keep it to yourself, to take it all so that her name wouldn't appear anywhere. She doesn't want the credit, and I agree with her. What would this town do if they found out that a woman was involved? Her reputation would be in tatters."

"While I get rewarded with a position I've wanted for as long as I can remember. It doesn't seem right."

"Regardless, it's the way of the world, and Anna knows that. Why not respect her wishes?"

George looked out of the window, seeing the activities of the street below, wondering idly what Anna was doing right at that moment.

Helping her cousin recover, no doubt.

Ned said warily, a joking tone in his voice, "Unless there is something more you haven't told me? I saw how close the two of you were last night." Ned leaned back and removed his hat, settling comfortably into his chair.

George turned to him, annoyed that his friend could spot the issue so easily. He suddenly stood up and grabbed his coat from the back of the chair. "Come, then," George said, and Ned stood up, surprised.

"Where are we going?"

"Well, seeing as I have the day off, I want to go home, but you want your explanation first, and I'll give it to you. But let's get coffee. It's too early for a lager."

Ned grinned, rubbing his hands together. "Ah yes, the moment of truth, but what will the sergeant say about my absence?"

"Nothing," George said, shaking his head. "For we're discussing a few matters of the case, aren't we? There'll be useful lessons we've learned and can use for the future." Before he moved to the door, George grabbed his notebook and pencil from the desk, showing them to Ned with his eyebrows raised.

"Why yes, there most certainly will be." Ned followed George out of the room with a grin.

***

Even though her fatigue was seemingly endless the evening before, Anna had insisted that she be allowed to sleep with her cousin through the night, to make sure that all was well. No one argued with her, and so Anna woke up to the bright sunshine in Ophelia's large house and heard her cousin breathing contentedly beside her.

Anna laid back on her pillow turning her eyes to look at her dear cousin's face. Ophelia had been through so much, and it showed. She looked slightly gaunt, and dark circles were under her eyes, creating a stark contrast against the white pallor of her skin. But now she was free. Anna hoped that in a few short weeks, Ophelia would feel much better again and would return to her old, joyous self. She also hoped that Ophelia would be able to forget David and forgive herself for what happened.

Ophelia stirred and blinked up at Anna. She jumped back for a moment, but then stilled when Anna laid a soft hand on her shoulder. "Everything's all right, Ophelia," Anna whispered with a smile. "You're safe now."

Ophelia looked around her, trying to register her surroundings, and soon Anna could feel her cousin's muscles relax under her hand. "I'm home?"

"Yes," Anna said lightly, tears filling her eyes. "You're back. You're safe." Ophelia slid over to Anna's side, and Anna put her arms around her.

"Anna, you really are a miracle." Suddenly, Ophelia burst into tears against Anna's chest, wetting her nightgown, but Anna merely kissed her on the top of the head and shushed her gently.

"No, you are. For you've survived an incredible ordeal."

Ophelia pulled away from her and looked up, shaking her head.

"No. I was a fool. An utter fool. I thought that he was different from the rest, and that he loved me. I let my heart get in the way of sense."

Anna felt her words keenly, for they were truer than even Ophelia realized. "Now who could not be guilty of that, dear cousin? You were simply a victim to an evil man. It was not your folly that brought him to you. Don't distress yourself on that account."

Ophelia sighed and closed her eyes again. "What will happen to him now? To D or David? I know I shouldn't care, but I just have to know."

Anna sat up and leaned against the headboard, folding her hands over her stomach. She knew but was afraid to say.

"I fear, Ophelia, that he will receive the same punishment as his cousin, for as you know now and heard, it was he who brought the victims to his cousin. And he owns the opium den. He's also a criminal."

Ophelia nodded wordlessly, and Anna saw a glistening tear slide down her cousin's pale cheek.

"Come," Anna said with a smile. "Why don't we go to breakfast?"

Ophelia groaned. "Oh, you know there will be such a hubbub about my return." She put a pillow over her head and groaned.

"As well there should be." Anna's tone grew serious. "Your mother has barely slept nor eaten since you were taken. Give her the chance to spend time with you now that you're back. She was in a right state."

Ophelia nodded. "But only for you, Anna. My cousin, friend, and rescuer." They both slid out of bed at the same time, and when they turned to each other, they laughed at the way their hair was looking more unkempt than they had ever seen before. Anna had not even changed out of her gown before she'd slipped into her bed, and her corset was beginning to cut into her hipbones.

"I suggest we both bathe before we go down to breakfast," Anna said, the tail end of a laugh still in her voice. She looked down at the grime on her skin. "And to think that I—" she thought of George, his mouth hot on hers in the basement room of Dick's house, clutching to her as if she was the very reason for life itself.

"What?" Ophelia asked, watching Anna with narrowed eyes.

"Nothing," Anna dissembled.

Ophelia smirked. "I saw what happened, you know. I didn't have my spectacles on, but I could tell what was happening." She turned to the looking glass, took up a brush and started combing through her hair. "You kissed that man, that police officer."

Anna blushed, remembering how she had thrown all caution to the wind. "Yes, I suppose I did. I'm rather glad you didn't have your spectacles on for that. Although you should wear them more in future." She tried to scold her cousin to draw the focus away from her, but it was not successful.

"Why did you kiss him?" Ophelia grinned, and it made a smile flicker across Anna's face as well, seeing a part of her old cousin return.

"Do you really want to know? It seems so frivolous after what you've been through."

"Tell me," Ophelia said, her eyes intense. "I will not spend the rest of my life having people tiptoe around me because of what happened. Besides, I could use a bit of entertainment, and this sounds very entertaining indeed." She smiled, waiting for Anna to begin.

"Fair enough." Anna sighed, tugging at the ends of her long hair which tumbled over her shoulder. "I care for him." She couldn't look directly at Ophelia. "I think I love him in fact. He's a good man. He has done so much for me and for you. He believed in me when no one else would. And yet—" she hesitated.

"And yet? Why, he sounds wonderful. I must thank him, of course. Why hesitate to tell him you love him?"

"I can't be what he wants."

"What does that mean?" Ophelia kept her eyes on Anna as she sat down on a cushioned chair near to the looking glass.

"I know he may think that he cares for me, that he wants a woman like me, but he doesn't. He wants a wife to stay at home and to do as he asks, to bear children and to prepare his meals. I could never be that person. I want a different life. One of excitement and intrigue. One where I could be more than what my gender tells me I must do."

Ophelia nodded and sighed. "You've always been this way, Anna. I understand you wholeheartedly. It appears we both don't wish to conform to the rules. What our parents must think of us." They both laughed lightly, but Anna pushed a tear away, her heart aching for George. "But why not speak to him, give him a chance? Perhaps he really has changed?" Ophelia was looking at her earnestly and with hope.

Anna swallowed and shook her head. "I don't think so. I don't think he could let go of what he used to be."

"Well," Ophelia stood. "If he could kiss you looking as you are, then I know that the man loves you in return, and he would likely do anything you asked."

Even though sadness threatened to swallow her up, Anna laughed. "Well, I am off to bathe then. Do so yourself, and I shall see you in the breakfast room. It will be like the old days."

Anna moved to the doorway, putting her robe around her. "I will never forget, you know," Ophelia said from behind her. Anna turned to see her cousin watching her. "What you did. You saved my life. Anything I achieve now after this, anything that I can do, it's all due to you. You're an incredible woman, Anna. What would I have done without you?"

Anna cried in earnest now, the tears spilling down her cheeks. "It is I that wouldn't have survived without you, Ophelia. You are the breath of fresh air in a rather stale existence. Let's pursue our dreams now, with no thought to the past."

Ophelia smiled, and Anna left to dress in the guest room, her heart a little lighter. An hour later, down in the breakfast room, the parents were all in a tizzy, each of them desperate to hear how Ophelia fared after a good night's sleep. Every so often, Ophelia would turn her eyes to Anna and give her an exasperated look, especially when Ophelia's mother held her daughter's cheeks in her hands, asking her question after question, but Anna simply smiled. This is what it was to be loved.

Ophelia was lucky. While both of their mothers were equally desperate for their daughters to behave as they ought, there was real love there. Anna felt her own hand squeezed under the table by her mother.

When she looked up, her mother had tears in her eyes, and she whispered, "You are a brave woman, Anna. My Anna. You are far better than I could ever be."

"Mother," she said, feeling her heart well up with emotion. "You are proud of me, then?"

Her mother nodded her head. "As much as you have infuriated me over the years, I must concede. You have made us both proud. Your bravery and your thoughtfulness for Ophelia. You suffered alongside her in the end."

She nodded her head to Anna's father, and he beamed back at her. Could she ever tell them both the truth of just how much she was involved in the process?

The focus turned back to Ophelia when she said, "Now, enough of these tears. I have come back, haven't I, and in no small part to my dear cousin. Just think, if she had not been kidnapped herself, I might not be here!"

Ophelia winked in Anna's direction, and Anna was grateful. Ophelia knew she could never reveal the entire truth. Not yet at least. The family began to eat their breakfast, slowly relaxing into their old ways, and Anna kept glancing towards Ophelia's seat, trying to tell herself that it really was real and that she was really there in the flesh.

Suddenly, there was a knock at the door. A servant entered the room a short while later, and said, "Mr. and Mrs. Marshall, Detective Ford here to see you." Anna's heart flipped at the mention of his name, and her fork fell from her hand and clanged against the plate.

"Detective?" she asked, confused as the maid trailed away, having been given permission to send him in.

And there he was, entering the room in plainclothes. He pulled his hat from his head.

"Do forgive me for the intrusion Mr. and Mrs. Marshall, but I thought I might provide my services for you this morning or at any other time you might have need of me."

Anna's heart clenched at the sight of his handsome face. He looked well after a night of good sleep and the fact that the killer had been apprehended.

Mr. Marshall stood up and shook his hand warmly. "Detective Ford. I see your title has now changed."

"Yes, sir."

"You are most deserving of it, young man." Anna's uncle gestured to the table behind him. "You have given us our family back."

Aunt Louisa beamed from her seat. "Thank you, Detective. We shall always be grateful to you."

Anna blushed for George under their heavy praise. His eyes had not yet met hers, and she wondered if he was angry or too hurt to look at her.

"And Miss Ophelia? How are you?" George asked, his kind eyes looking towards a surprised Ophelia.

"I am quite well, Detective. It is no small thanks to you. And my cousin, Anna, has also recovered nicely."

Ophelia pointed to Anna who blushed a little deeper when George's gaze wandered to her. It had been difficult enough to see him in the evening light, under duress, when he had just done his part in rescuing them. But now in the morning, in sight of her relatives, his heated gaze was unbearable.

He nodded. "I'm very happy indeed, Lady Anna. Your family must think you very brave for what you've been through."

"We certainly do, Detective," Anna's mother said proudly.

Her father suddenly piped up. "Oh, what will happen to the men you apprehended?"

George cleared his throat and tore his eyes from Anna. Anna exhaled with what she feared was resignation. It was the last time she would see him, surely.

"Richard Mason will be tried for multiple murders. His cousin, David Mason will also be tried as an accessory. Darren the carriage driver will also be tried but may serve a lesser sentence. All evidence has been gathered from the site. Lancaster City is now free of its bloodiest murderer."

"You've done excellent work, Detective Ford." Anna's remark pulled George's eyes back to her. She was too greedy to go forever without one more look from him. She could see his jaw clench, and she guessed at what was in his mind.

"Thank you, Lady Anna," he answered in reply.

Folding his hands in front of him, he added, "I simply wanted to come by to say that there will be journalists coming to your establishment, and you may speak to them or not speak to them; it is entirely up to you. But I wanted to let you know that the police force can assist you, if needs arise."

Aunt Louisa said, "Thank you, Detective. We will let you know if we need your assistance."

"Good day, then." He nodded and turned away to leave the room. After a few moments and without quite thinking straight, Anna jumped out of her seat and rushed after him, catching him in the open doorway, just as he was donning his hat again.

"George," she said, and she saw his back stiffen.

He turned around. "Anna." The look in his eyes was inscrutable.

Just then, a well-dressed man with a pince-nez began to walk up the steps to the house. In a rather nasally voice, the man asked, "Excuse me, sir, but is this the Marshall resident? If so, what can you tell me about the case?"

"Nothing," George grumbled and moved down the steps, pushing past the tiny man. Anna spotted Ned standing nearby, looking between George and the journalist with wariness.

Anna walked down the steps, her shoulders straight. "That man, sir, is the one who solved everything. He's a brilliant detective, and anyone in this city could trust him with anything. Write that in your paper."

The journalist brightened and began to scribble a few notes in his notebook. "Thank you, Miss—"

"My name doesn't matter, but I am cousin to the victim."

"Cousin," the journalist said, writing more notes down. George turned to look at her from the base of the stairs, the collar of his dark coat up, and Anna stared back. She could see the hurt in his eyes, but she hoped this would be enough to assuage it. He had become a detective after all. He had fulfilled his dream.

Then, even though her heart aching, he walked away, and Ned fell into step beside him. Anna watched George for a few moments longer, that dark blue coat and hat so familiar to her now. The trailing smoke of his cigarette wafted towards her, and as the journalist continued to climb the steps to the house, his eyes eager and hungry, she shut the door in his face.

EPILOGUE

One week later

I t is a sad thing, you know, to be caught in one's endeavors and made to feel as if those endeavors are wrong. Everyone is a fool, I have decided. Even my darling Anna was a fool for not letting me fulfill my mission for her. What a trophy she would have been. What heights of beauty she could have reached!

The prison makes my skin crawl. Instead of sitting, I pace. I dare not touch the soiled mattress they've provided for me. Me! A wealthy businessman and esteemed citizen of this fair city. But my time on earth has come to an end.

David was a blubbering fool, Darren a face of stone until they could find a way to break him. I have no use for them any longer. What care have I for their miseries or their fates? I do not even know in what cell they lie in wait for their punishment as I wait in mine.

I sigh. There is a desk here at least, and they have afforded me pen and ink and paper for any final messages I wish to send. The desk chair, having no soiled cushion, I will sit upon. The lice and other vermin cannot bite me there.

To whom shall I write? The newspaper? One final message, chastising them for their small minds and inability to understand the magnitude of what I have done. What astonishing and beautiful work I have wrought in the world that no one has appreciated. Not one. Except the ones I have taken. They know their worth now.

Leaning back, I smile. No, the newspaper and the fools who read could do without me. It is to Lady Anna that I write. For a message beyond the grave will be enough to tell her what she ought to know.

Chuckling to myself at my cleverness, I write: Dear Anna…

***

George was in his office, the paint on his glass door still fresh, now reading: DETECTIVE GEORGE FORD. He stared at the words, which read backwards from his view from the desk and felt somehow that something was not quite right.

His dream had finally come true. He had accomplished what he'd set out to do and yet, he was unsettled. It had been a few weeks since Mason was caught. The trial was brief and a mad affair. The newspapers sold like hotcakes, for every title was more captivating than the last:

EVIL KILLER CAUGHT; HEARTS FOUND IN BASEMENT

SOCIETY WOMAN MISS MARSHALL FAINTS INTO THE
ARMS OF OFFICERS AS THEY CARRY HER OUT

OFFICER GEORGE FORD WRANGLES KILLER TO JUSTICE

He could barely look at a newspaper anymore. He hoped that it would die down soon enough, and there would be another case to solve. That's what he needed. A new case. Something fresh to sink his teeth into so that he could forget everything that went along with the last case.

He pulled out his pocket watch. It seemed the thing to know to carry a watch, since he was a detective, allowed to not wear a uniform.

12:01. Dick and David Mason were to be hanged at approximately 12:05. Together. He had not even dreamed of attending the private hanging. He had not the stomach for that sort of thing.

He shuddered to think of what the face of a killer might look like experiencing its own brand of pain. The door to his office flew open and shut hurriedly, and a flash of purple lace was in his vision until the figure sat down in front of his desk.

Anna.

For a moment, George was stunned, but he found his words eventually, and they came out angrier than he'd expected.

"Anna, what in the hell are you doing here?"

"George," she said breathlessly. Her cheeks were pink, and her golden hair was a little frazzled. "I needed to speak to you. I wanted to speak to you."

"What about?" He felt his pride bristle.

She had rejected him already. Why did she need to come around and remind him of his loss? His very great loss. The days seemed to yawn before him darkly without her bright presence.

"First, I never got to say congratulations on the detective position." She smiled, and despite his best efforts, George felt his heart soften. "You deserve it."

"Do I? It feels like there's something missing in the approbation I've received. Your credit." His tone was clipped.

Anna winced. "Never mind that. I've had a letter, and I thought you might like to see it. It's from him."

"Him," he said in a low voice, knowing perfectly well who she meant. She slid a folded white note across the desk with a gloved hand.

"It's most distressing."

George picked it up and scanned the words. His heart began to pound, as he registered the information. He glanced up at Anna's worried face. Just then, Ned burst into the room.

"Oh, forgive me, My Lady, but George, there's big news. A new case!" George stood up, paling a little, his heart rushing into a flurry of excitement.

"What is it?"

"Get this. A man and woman have been murdered in their home, but all the doors and windows were locked from the inside! We had to break in when the bodies were seen from a window after the neighbors called us. The press is going crazy!"

Ned's cheeriness about a murder was not lost on George, and Ned then said a little quieter, "I've got tell Sarge the news. Meet you out front in two minutes. As you're the only detective now, you've got to be there."

Ned left, reserving a small smile for Anna and closed the door gently behind him. The click of the door made George jump. To be left alone with Anna. Really, what good could it do?

Anna stood up, the sound of swishing silk filling the silent room. "Well, I see you have a new case on your hands. Dick is now gone to his death; Ophelia is well, and everything is as it ought to be."

"Yes, I suppose, since you've deemed it so." He knew he was being bitter and childish, but he couldn't help it. "I've got to go. You'll need to see yourself out, My Lady," he said stiffly, copying Ned's reverential tone.

Anna ignored the use of her title. George walked towards the door to open it for her, and she reached out to grab him by the wrist. He turned around slowly, hating the way his body had not yet realized that Anna didn't love him back. It still thrilled at her touch and craved it.

"If you need my help, will you call upon me?" Anna's tone was earnest, and her eyes wide as she waited for his reply.

George frowned. "You want to join in on a murder investigation that's got nothing to do with you?" Inside, he cringed. He was really being too much.

"Yes," she said equally stiffly. "You know how I wish to be and what I wish to busy myself with. Please say you'll call upon me."

George searched her eyes, while he inwardly wondered why she had pushed him away. Why did she not want what he wanted? She had never really said, but he had felt it in the way she moved and in her gaze at the Mason house that night.

"If I need you, My Lady, yes. I'll call upon you."

"Good. I will depend upon it. And we need to discuss the letter very soon. Another time."

"Another time," he repeated hollowly.

Anna stood next to him, and he opened the door, hoping she would go out before him. Instead, in the open doorway, to the tune of typewriters and busy workers outside in the central section of the office, Anna stood on her tiptoes and kissed George on the cheek.

"I look forward to it." She gave him a small smile and then left, the scent of roses trailing behind her.

He stood stock still for a moment, allowing the heat of her gesture to subside. Then, he remembered. There was a case to solve. A murdered man and woman awaited justice. He put on his hat and coat and shut his office door behind him. As he walked downstairs to the waiting carriage, he pulled out his pocket watch. 12:10. Just as Anna had said, Dick was gone from this life. It was finally done. Over.

One killer was gone, and a new one emerged. That was the way of things. George still held Dick's final haunting words folded in his hand, and he pushed the letter into his coat pocket.

Another time, Anna had said. Despite everything, hope welled up inside him.

THE END

ABOUT THE AUTHOR

K. N. Brown

K. N. Brown has written many historical fiction romance novels, but this is the first one under her very own pen name, not ghostwritten for a company. She hails from Lancaster County, Pennsylvania, but she currently lives overseas.

Printed in Great Britain
by Amazon

84002326R00140